THE HUMPHREY BOGART MURDER CASE

THE HUMPHREY BOGART MURDER CASE

BY GEORGE BAXT

George Baxt

ST. MARTIN'S PRESS
NEW YORK

Production Editor: David Stanford Burr

Design: Basha Zapatka

Library of Congress Cataloging-in-Publication Data

Baxt, George.
    The Humphrey Bogart murder case / George Baxt.
        p.   cm.
    ISBN 0-312-11828-7
    1. Bogart, Humphrey, 1899–1957—Fiction.   I. Title.
PS3552.A8478H86   1995
813'.54—dc20   94-45769
                                                 CIP

First Edition: April 1995

10 9 8 7 6 5 4 3 2 1

THE HUMPHREY BOGART MURDER CASE

ONE

Evelyn Wood, a handsome woman in her mid-sixties, was furious. Not because she was a woman scorned, but because her apartment had been ransacked. She was a successful, highly respected freelance newspaperwoman here in her hometown of Portland, Oregon. She dwelled fondly on the memory of her late husband, Jack Methot. He had been a sea captain on the Orient run, away for months at a time, which didn't seem to bother Evelyn. She never referred to herself as Mrs. Methot. Evelyn Wood had a certain celebrity. Evelyn Methot was nobody. They did manage to produce an only child, a daughter who was christened Mayo, presumably after the county in Ireland where Jack Methot was born.

Mayo was a precocious child and while still in her teens, announced to her mother she was off to New York to become an actress. Evelyn wished her Godspeed and good luck, and saw her off at the train station, after which she ate lunch in a coffee shop where she flirted with an army officer. Usually petite, smartly dressed and coiffured, now, thirty-five years later, she was still smartly dressed and coiffured, but in a rage. The two detectives, Marley and Gross, sympathized with her but were surprised when she told them nothing was stolen. They were not too concerned with Evelyn's break-in. Within the past two weeks both had received greetings from their Uncle Sam and knew they'd soon be inducted into the army. There was a glorious Second World War raging in Europe and they knew it was only a matter of time before the United States would be involved. 1941 would hold little promise for either one of them.

Evelyn led them from the living room to her bedroom and then to what had been Mayo's bedroom where, now that Mayo was long departed, there was precious little to ransack.

She then led them to the den which also served as her office where havoc had truly been created.

"This is a disgrace!" said Evelyn.

"Yeah," agreed Gross, "a real disgrace." Eyes narrowed, Marley shot his partner a look. Gross caught it but ignored it.

"You must do something! I have been vandalised! I feel as though I've been raped!" Now both detectives shot her a look. "Well?" Her hands were on her hips and her eyes were ablaze. Gross thought she looked kind of sexy for an old broad. "What are you going to do about this?"

"Well, Miss Wood," said Gross, "if you say nothing was stolen, then that leaves us with the crime of breaking and entering. You're sure nothing was stolen?"

She was breathing heavily, her bosom rising and falling like a small craft in a troubled sea. "There's really nothing much to steal. I own very little jewelry, but it's been undisturbed. I showed you my bedroom. Nothing's missing. The radio is still here. My silverware was handed down from several generations back but has only sentimental value." Gross found it difficult to think of waxing sentimental over some knives and forks. She indicated the desk at which she worked. "They left my typewriter. You might have thought they would have stolen that." Now she sounded indignant. The fact that the thieves thought she possessed nothing of value to steal was beginning to pain her.

"This looks to me like a case of mischief," said Marley.

Evelyn stared at him. "Mischief? What do you mean by mischief?"

"A practical joke in very bad taste," he replied.

"Nonsense! Look at the drawers spilled open. My papers scattered all over the place. Whoever it was was looking for something. Isn't that obvious?"

Marley asked, "Can you think of something you own that somebody might be looking for?" He waited. The look on her face discomforted him. He knew she was thinking they were morons. That was certainly what she was thinking. Throughout her career she'd had occasion to deal with the police, and they were rarely satisfactory. Marley decided Evelyn needed some prompting. "Stocks? Bonds? Bank certificates?"

"They're in a safety-deposit box."

Gross had a thought and expressed it. "Love letters?"

"Who from?" she snapped.

"Miss Wood," asked Marley, "does anyone else have a key to your apartment?"

"My daughter. She's in Los Angeles."

Marley continued, "No special person?"

Evelyn Wood permitted a trace of a smile. "I don't indulge in special persons. There's a woman who comes in to tidy up twice a week but she doesn't have a key. I'm usually in when she arrives. If I'm to be out, I leave the key for her at the desk."

"The door hasn't been forced," said Marley.

"And the window opening on the fire escape," said Gross.

"Oh this is hopeless!" cried Evelyn. "I shall speak to the chief about this."

"Miss Wood, I doubt if there's much he can do under the circumstances. We can arrange to have your place dusted for fingerprints. But I doubt if there'll be much of a yield other than yours and the cleaning woman's."

Gross said, "Perhaps your daughter can think of something. Why don't you tell her about the break-in?"

"My daughter hasn't lived here in over twelve years. She hasn't visited in over five. She's in the movies."

Marley's eyes lit up. "Oh yeah? Maybe I seen her in something."

"Her name is Mayo Methot." Her face hardened. "She's married to a bum named Humphrey Bogart."

Gross's eyebrows went up. "Miss Wood, by you he may be a bum, but by me, he's one hell of a good actor. He was sure swell in *High Sierra*. Didn't you think he was terrific in that one?"

"I never see Mr. Bogart's films. He's my daughter's concern, not mine." The ice in her voice might have given them frostbite.

Marley handed her a card. "If you think of something, Miss Wood, you can reach us at this number. We'll file our report and confer with the chief. There's little else we can do."

"Don't you realize had I been home when the break-in occurred, I might have been injured? I might have been killed?"

"Miss Wood," Marley said her name with exaggerated patience, "criminals who break into homes usually know when the victim will be away from home. Or make sure the victim will be out of the way."

"Oh."

"Yes?" asked Marley.

"I was tricked into leaving the house this morning. A man phoned. Said he was Salvador Dali." She was sure they'd never heard the name before. "The Spanish surrealist. The artist."

"We recognize the name, Miss Wood," said Marley, now with added exaggerated patience. He wished he could contact Humphrey Bogart to tell him what an overbearing bitch his mother-in-law was, though it immediately occurred to him that Bogart was probably well aware of it.

"A few years ago I interviewed Pablo Picasso and this man who said he was Dali said he'd be pleased to be interviewed by me. Well, he's such a notorious publicity hound that I was delighted to make a date to meet him." She mentioned one of Portland's better restaurants. "It was to be an early lunch. I waited almost an hour. He didn't show up. I realize now, of course, I was duped." She made a small, futile gesture. "He did have an accent." She sat. "What the hell could he have been after? I own a few good antique pieces but they're at a shop being cleaned. They're not very valuable so I discount them. This is so frustrating! So maddening!" She arose. "I apologize, gentlemen. I realize there's nothing you can do. It's all so baffling." She added, "And I'm frightened."

"Miss Wood," said Marley, "whoever it was won't be returning. I'd suggest you change the lock on your door except this professional is an exceptional professional. His skeleton key could probably get him into Fort Knox. You should speak to the management about the security in this building."

"I shall." The face was hard again. "I most certainly shall."

A few minutes later after the detectives had gone, Evelyn Wood poured herself some scotch whiskey, lit a cigarette and sat on the sofa. She plagued herself with questions. What was he or they after? It couldn't be anything of Mayo's because all her possessions were in the house in Beverly Hills. She thought of something else. She thought of Jack Methot, her late husband. He had plied the seas of the Orient, a fit setting for all manner of intrigues. But after his death, she had disposed of everything. His clothes went to the Salvation Army. Mayo collected his papers in a large carton and they were now stored in the basement of the Beverly Hills house. There had been some discussion three years earlier, when Mayo entered into her unholy alliance with Bogart, of the possibility of Evelyn relocating to Los Angeles, but Evelyn preferred to remain a big fish in a little pond.

Mayo Methot, the third Mrs. Humphrey Bogart. Bogie, Spencer Tracy dubbed him that when both made their feature-length film debuts back in 1930 in John Ford's prison comedy, *Up the River*. Tracy did well after it, Bogie didn't. He floundered around in small parts, mostly as gangsters until the opportunity to portray Duke Mantee on Broadway in *The Petrified Forest*, a thinly disguised character inspired by 1934's public enemy number one, John Dillinger. Leslie Howard starred in the play and when Jack Warner asked him to re-create the role on film refused to do so unless Bogart was signed for Mantee. Bogart stole the film from its costars, Howard and the volatile Bette Davis. Bogie didn't look back after that though he often wanted to. Warner's kept him in supporting roles with an occasional lead in a B low-budget film. Bogart with his complaints for better treatment joined Miss Davis and Jimmy Cagney as major thorns in Jack Warner's side. Bogart soon graduated to accepting other stars' rejects. When Paul Muni and George Raft refused

High Sierra, Bogart inherited it. It was a surprise success. Only a few days ago Mayo had told Evelyn that Bogie was rehearsing another George Raft reject, *The Maltese Falcon*. Bogie. Heavy drinker. Wife beater, though Mayo assured her mother she gave as good as she got. This had to be true. Bogie called her Slugger, a tribute to her left uppercut.

Evelyn was back pouring herself another drink. To hell with Bogie. Who was the Dali impersonator? What did he want? Why hadn't he thought of phoning and saying something to the effect that he thought she might have something belonging to him and might he drop by to discuss it? She snorted. That would be damned stupid of him. Whatever he was after, she did not know she had it. It had to be something connected to Jack Methot. Jack Methot. Why ever had she married him? That's unfair. He was handsome and dashing and romantic. A sea captain. A girl didn't get many opportunities to land one of those back in 1902. Bogie. Why did Mayo marry Bogie? His first marriage to actress Helen Menken had lasted less than a year. Then another actress, Mary Phillips. How many years did that one last? Not many. And now Mayo. Christ, shouldn't he have built up an immunity to actresses by now?

And who the hell was this smoothie who passed himself off as Salvador Dali?

His name was Marcelo Amati. He was Italian. In international circles he was a notorious playboy supported on various occasions by wealthy women and wealthier women attached to royal houses. He was, when it suited him, which was fairly frequently, a cheat and a swindler. He blackmailed and was twice suspected of murdering or attempting to murder lovers, but not his. He claimed to be descended from the Amati violin family but that was because he had difficulty spelling *Stradivarius*. He was, of course, breathtakingly handsome with a slim and muscular body. He spoke many languages and lied in all of them. He now sat in the drawing room of a train making its way from Portland, Oregon, south to Los Angeles, California. He was not alone. His companions were two women.

La Contessa di Marcopolo was a large woman who carried a great deal of weight. She had remarkably beautiful skin and her last encounter with plastic surgery at a clinic in Switzerland had successfully eliminated her latest cache of facial wrinkles, so that one would never guess her age was closer to sixty than to forty. The outbreak of war had forced her to flee Italy after being warned her estates were to be confiscated and she faced imprisonment having been suspected of secreting some Jewish blood in her veins. She had no idea what brand of blood Marcelo had in his veins; she knew only that it was hot when passionate and cold when homicidal. But Marcelo was quite affably agreeable about fleeing with her and her secretary, Violetta Cenci, who was the other woman in the compartment. La Contessa had rescued her jewelry, and it was several of these valuable pieces that had paid for their flight to freedom. How long the money would last was a matter of conjecture. La Contessa stayed in the best hotels and in the best accommodations befitting a contessa. She traveled first-class and ate first-class. She amused Marcelo and browbeat Violetta who saw herself as Cinderella though minus either housekeeping assignments or a prince toting a glass slipper. Violetta, although well into her thirties, looked much younger and knew in her heart that as the train drew closer to Los Angeles so would her ambition to be a movie star ripen and blossom. She would marry a rich producer, lord it over many servants in a mansion in Bel Air, and give lavish and much-talked about dinner parties to which she would never invite la Contessa. She loathed the fat one, but disguised it brilliantly. Violetta lowered the copy of *Screen Romances* she had bought at the railroad station in Portland. La Contessa, after a long silence, was speaking, and when la Contessa spoke, she demanded undivided attention, or else.

"Portland was a great disappointment." Little did she know there were others who shared the sentiment.

7

"My darling, I thoroughly ransacked the place. Why must I repeat myself? I left no drawer unturned. I even ransacked her refrigerator." He added with a smile, "I helped myself to a cold chicken leg. Quite tasty."

"You're laughing at me," said la Contessa.

"I never laugh at you, Contessa." Only on occasion when I'm soaking in a hot tub and think of you huffing and puffing in bed and making those obscene noises that are supposed to be synonymous with passion.

"Are you mocking me?" She was jamming a cigarette into another one of her hockables, a cigarette holder studded with ruby and emerald chips.

He imitated her voice mercilessly. " 'You're laughing at me. You're mocking me.' I'm beginning to wonder if you're not paranoid."

"Violetta!"

Violetta looked up. "Yes, Contessa?"

"My cigarette!" Violetta reached down the seat for her handbag from which she produced a cigarette lighter and a flame. La Contessa inhaled, followed by the usual fit of coughing, while Marcelo stared out the window and Violetta returned to her fantasies. The coughing abated; la Contessa was exhausted.

"How many times do I have to beg you to give up smoking?"

She ignored the question. She always did. "If the mother didn't have the letter, then the daughter has to have it."

"Perhaps there was no letter," suggested Marcelo.

"My father wrote me from Hong Kong that he would entrust a letter with Captain Methot to be delivered to me. He had a premonition he was dying, I'm sure of that. Premonitions are the family curse. One day I'll have a premonition and then I'll be gone."

"Without having sent a letter."

"You're mocking me again!"

"Cara mia, what has happened to you? You've become so grim and somber. You used to laugh and be gay, you bubbled like vintage champagne. But since you've become obsessed with the letter . . ."

She leaned forward. "The letter will lead us to the cornucopia, my father's cornucopia. His precious horn of plenty. He always told me about it. I grew up on the legend. Marco Polo's cornucopia! A valued gift from the emperor of China. Handed down for six centuries. How often it was stolen and recovered."

Marcelo stifled a yawn. How often had he heard the story. She even repeated it in her sleep. The Baron di Marcopolo's cornucopia. Stuffed to the brim with precious jewels worth millions of dollars. Millions that could keep them in a bountiful existence in Hollywood where the film population were suckers for royalty and foreign accents. How often she reminded him that silent stars Gloria Swanson, Pola Negri, and Mae Murray had purchased royalty as husbands. Constance Bennett bought herself a marquis. They were all penniless but titled. Royal titles! Worth a fortune. Horns of plenty. He realized the countess had ceased her droning.

Her head drooped. She was dozing. Marcelo nudged Violetta with a foot. He indicated the cigarette in the old lady's hand. Violetta removed it to an ashtray and then blew Marcelo a kiss. Violetta settled back on the comfortable seat and stared out the window. She believed la Contessa. There was a cornucopia stuffed with jewels. There was a letter entrusted by the Baron di Marcopolo to Jack Methot, the sea captain. It was romantic and intriguing. She gazed at Marcelo as he looked out the window, admiring again his magnificent profile. He should have been an actor. A swashbuckler, a brilliant swordsman. Zorro. D'Artagnan. Captain Blood. Marcelo yawned, closed his eyes, and settled back for a nap. Violetta's thoughts turned to Mayo Methot. Mrs. Humphrey Bogart. How she longed to meet the movie star. How she longed to meet all movie stars. How wonderful it must be to be Mrs. Humphrey Bogart.

* * *

While Violetta fantasized on the bliss of being Mrs. Humphrey Bogart, Mrs. Humphrey Bogart was in the middle of her living room in Beverly Hills exercising her pitching arm. Her target, her husband the movie star, was too quick for her. He had successfully dodged a number of wedding gifts he loathed. There was a vase that he thought had been a gift from actor Barton MacLaine. It was painted with little bare-assed cherubs connected by a daisy chain. There was a candelabra he recalled came from Mr. and Mrs. Jack Warner. Then there was an oversize ashtray, the selection of comedian Frank McHugh and his wife. The vase had shattered against a wall. The candelabra tore a hole in a Renoir print that he loathed. The ashtray came perilously close to concussing him and Bogie shouted, "Close but no cigar, Slugger. But you're improving!"

"You coldhearted brute! You miserable son of a bitch! Mother might have been murdered!"

"I'm not interested in what might have been!"

She sent a metal pitcher that she picked off the sideboard hurtling toward him. He leaped out of its path shouting, "No wonder I keep losing weight!" The pitcher shattered a window pane. "I thought we agreed no more breaking windows! You gave me your word!"

"She said the police were of no damned use either." Her hands dropped to her side, then she sagged into an easy chair. "What the hell could they have been after?"

Bogie leaned against a wall, eyeing his wife with suspicion. This suddenly sinking into an easy chair could be the warning of a sneak attack. Not too long ago she'd stabbed him in the shoulder with a steak knife and he was now reluctantly entertaining the notion that she might have recently bought a snub-nosed automatic, having heard her admiring one that Joan Crawford kept on her bedside table.

"It might have been the work of some neighborhood kids. What did the cops call it?"

"Mischief. They called it mischief." She thought for a moment as she applied a lighter to a cigarette. "Neighborhood kids don't lay their hands on skeleton keys. There's something very nasty about that break-in."

"Say listen, Slugger," said Bogart warily, ready to duck and dodge if she made a false move. "Your mother being all this frightened and upset, maybe you ought to go up there and spend a few days with her."

Her eyes were narrowed into slits. "You'd love to be rid of me, wouldn't you." Very prescient, thought Bogart. "You'd love me out of the way while you're having your affair with Mary Astor."

He exploded. "I am not having an affair with Mary Astor! She's fully booked!"

Mayo rubbed the cigarette out in an ashtray and then jumped to her feet, fists clenched. "Don't you think I know what this whole *Maltese Falcon* movie is all about?"

"Sure you do. You read the script."

"*I* should be playing Astor's part!"

"Now come on, Slugger. Let's not go through that routine again. It's getting pretty tired. I suggested you to Jack Warner . . ."

"Halfheartedly!"

"Goddamn you, I'm always sticking my neck out for you and what do I get for it? Do I get any gratitude? All I get is the chop! I got you into *Marked Woman*, didn't I?"

"Four years ago! And playing an over-the-hill whore!"

"Typecasting," he said without thinking and to his immediate regret. Between her hands over her head she held a flowerpot, and sent it flying like a basketball player targeting a hoop. Bogart ducked behind a couch. The flowerpot crashed into a mirror hanging on the wall, a wedding gift from the Pat O'Briens. "Ha!" yelled Bogart triumphantly. "Seven years bad luck!"

In the kitchen, Hannah Darrow, their housekeeper and cook, leaned against the sink, arms folded, clucking her tongue. Hannah was a tongue clucker of the old school. Her tongue didn't make little clicking noises; it rose and fell against her hard palate with all the vigor and force of a suction pump. The Battling Bogarts, as they were affectionately known in the movie colony, had earned their reputation. They had neither shame nor discretion. Their battles were not confined to the domicile. They had ferocious scrapes in restaurants, movie theaters, department stores, bowling alleys, and were especially adept at maneuvers in parking lots. Once Mayo had tried to run Bogart down, but he somehow managed to outrun her. Their sadomasochistic union was a joy to the gossip columnists. Why they continued to remain chained in wedlock was a puzzle their friends had long ago ceased trying to solve. Most of the sympathy was on Bogart's side. He was a charmer with a good nature and an affable disposition. He did frequent battle with Jack Warner over better parts and better money because he felt he owed it to himself. He certainly couldn't depend on his agent, who was one of Warner's cronies. This had been a good year for him. After the surprise success of *High Sierra* he went into a circus movie, *The Wagons Roll at Night*, with Sylvia Sidney starting a screen comeback after several years away in the theater. Bogie had balked at doing this one, not because of the actress, whom he had supported in *Dead End* four years earlier, but because *Wagons* was a remake of the Edward G. Robinson and Bette Davis melodrama of four years earlier, *Kid Galahad*, in which Bogart had been the villain. Now he was playing Robinson's role. Bogart thought there was something incestuous about it. But the film did well, and now he was rehearsing *The Maltese Falcon*, the third version of Dashiell Hammett's successful novel. True, he was second or maybe third or even fourth choice for the part, and it would be the directorial debut of John Huston, who had also written the script. And a new director and an old story could be a fatal combination. Bogart didn't care. Bogart believed in Huston, who was a friend, a poker-playing buddy, and a fellow skirt-chaser.

Mary Astor was something else. She had survived an ugly scandal in 1936 when she had divorced Dr. Franklin Thorpe and fought for the custody of her daughter Marilyn. Thorpe's attorney produced her private diary in which she discussed playwright George S. Kaufman's privates most indiscreetly, striking envy in the hearts of millions of readers around the world and sending Kaufman into temporary seclusion. Mary Astor was a fighter. She fought for her daughter and won her and she fought to retain her status as a star. Fortunately, she was extremely well liked in the industry and had powerful allies in most movie moguls. Now she was under contract to Warner Brothers for three features, and John Huston wanted her for *Falcon*. Bogart's pitch for Mayo was made in a whisper that could barely be heard. Mayo was not a star. She would never be a star. She had no charisma whatsoever.

Hannah Darrow hadn't been told yet if the Bogarts were dining in or out or at all. She was doing an inventory of what was stocked in the refrigerator when she realized a rare silence had settled in the house.

In the living room, Bogie had made a flying leap at Mayo and wrestled her to the floor. She was struggling ferociously, face down with Bogart holding her hands behind her in a tight grip. "You give up?" he shouted, knowing full well not to trust her if she did. She peppered the room with a series of expletives that both dazed and dazzled Bogart. Finally, she was exhausted. She was staring at Hannah Darrow who had entered the room with two raw filet mignons on a plate.

"Excuse me," she asked sweetly, "are these steaks for dinner or for your eyes?"

TWO

Hazel Dickson steered her five-year-old Studebaker with her usual panache and joie de vivre toward the very swank Hotel Ambassador in the downtown area of Wilshire Boulevard. Her dented fenders and shattered left headlight were a testimony to her indifference to the safety of either herself or other drivers. Behind the wheel of her car as in life, Hazel's philosophy was every man for himself and the devil take the hindmost. She was in her twelfth year of waiting for Detective Herbert Villon of the Los Angeles police force to declare himself and make her an honest woman. On the other hand, if he ever got around to popping the question, she was terrified she might say "Yes" and give up her long fought for and treasured independence. She recognized Herb as a satisfactory boyfriend and lover, but saw a grim prognostication for his qualifications as a husband.

Hazel was one of those rare creatures indigenous to the film industry. She gathered gossip and news items about celebrities and peddled them at fancy prices to gossip columnists and the Hollywood correspondents from all over the world assigned to the glamour capitol. More people swore by her than swore at her, which was a rare accomplishment in this treacherous town. She had friends in high places and very important contacts in low places. There wasn't an unlisted number she didn't know and she had a legion of faithful spies who supplied her with invaluable tips. One of the desk clerks at the Ambassador Hotel tipped her of the arrival of la Contessa di Marcopolo, a direct descendant of the famed Italian explorer, or so emphasized la Contessa tirelessly and tiresomely. Hazel knew better than to ignore the arrival of a fresh title in town. And the contessa and her entourage of two had commandeered one of the most expensive suites at the Ambassador. Hazel lost no time phoning la Contessa, explaining she had access to such powerful columnists as Louella Parsons, Hedda Hopper, Sidney Skolsky, Jimmy Fidler, and Harrison Carroll to drop the names of the five leading dispensers of gossip, mostly vicious. She also promised invitations to private screenings and world premieres. La Contessa was interested indeed in meeting some famous movie stars, to be invited to their homes and their parties. La Contessa did not express over the phone an ardent desire to meet Mayo Methot, Mrs. Humphrey Bogart. Subtlety was in order here, and if Hazel Dickson was to prove a powerful friend and ally, la Contessa must move carefully into her good graces. If necessary, she'd lend her Marcelo Amati. And if her pendulum swung in the opposite direction, Violetta Cenci was hers.

At the Ambassador, Hazel turned her miserable Studebaker over to a parking attendant she'd known and liked for years. He asked her his usual question about the auto, "When are you going to shoot this thing and put it out of its misery?" and was rewarded with her usual reply, "I'd sooner shoot you. Don't park it next to any limousines. It has enough of an inferiority complex."

In la Contessa's suite, her highness was prepared to enchant and captivate Hazel Dickson. She wore her most alluring Coco Chanel hostess gown despite the fact it was three years old (how would the Dickson woman know?), and had room service stock the suite with liquors and liqeurs and a tray groaning under the weight of some beautifully arranged hors d'oeuvres. (Easy on the anchovies, she cautioned; la Contessa had a sodium problem.) Violetta was smartly dressed in the one suit she owned and Marcelo Amati had positioned himself against a French window leading to an American balcony, the sunlight behind him giving him a radiant halo that proclaimed here indeed sits a golden boy.

The desk announced Hazel Dickson, and Violetta told the clerk to send her right up. La Contessa settled onto the couch, cigarette smoldering in its holder. She instructed Marcelo, "You'll see to the drinks, mi amore. Violetta, you'll pass the refreshments. They do them much more creatively at the Hotel Flora in Rome." She sighed. "How I wish I was having an aperitif at the Flora right now with Edda Ciano." Marcelo advised her not to name-drop Mussolini's daughter in the United States, and la Contessa said, "Oh dear, you're right. One has to make so many adjustments."

The doorbell buzzed and Violetta counted ten and then crossed to the door and opened it, favoring Hazel Dickson with what she hoped was an enchanting smile despite one discolored front tooth. "Miss Dickson?"

"Yes, I'm Hazel Dickson," said Hazel briskly, with her own brand of enchanting smile.

Violetta closed the door and led Hazel across the foyer and into the sitting room where la Contessa sat in all her Coco Chanel glory, aided by strings of pearls around her neck and across her bosom. She lifted her right hand, a ring on every finger except the thumb, and around her wrist a display of bracelets that almost blinded a very impressed Hazel Dickson. Hazel held la Contessa's hand as they exchanged greetings and then was introduced to Violetta and Marcelo Amati.

Hazel smiled at Amati while thinking, movie-star material. He's gorgeous. I could eat him with a spoon. She and Marcelo shook hands and he offered her a drink. Hazel asked for a ginger ale, knowing if she started the gin martinis they'd be hauling her out of the suite on a stretcher.

Once all were seated and settled with drinks and hors d'oeuvres, Hazel said smartly, "So I'm the first to welcome you. I indeed feel privileged. Tell me, Contessa, are you just visiting or perhaps planning on settling here? We have so many refugees from the horrors in Europe." She rattled off the names of directors, writers, and actors, and la Contessa acted suitably impressed. When Hazel paused to take a much-needed breath, la Contessa spoke, Hazel finding her accent more thick than charming. "I have always wanted to visit this famous city. And when circumstances made it necessary to flee my beloved homeland, we were most fortunate to receive visas and passage here." She refrained from mentioning Edda Ciano's assistance in securing the necessities.

"Have you seen much of America?" asked Hazel while sneaking looks at Marcelo Amati, who seemed to be wearing a permanent smile. His teeth were porcelain white and Hazel wondered if she was too old for him. Then in a flash she realized she wasn't, not if he was la Contessa's lover. God, she thought. Not really. But what the hell.

"Just a week in New York City and then directly here by train. That was a nightmare. So much shunting onto sidings to let troop and supply trains through. One would think this country was also at war."

"We will be," said Hazel matter-of-factly, "it's unavoidable."

"Oh, really?" said Marcelo. "What about your isolationists?"

"A minority. There'll be a war. War means big bucks and we're struggling out of the Depression and we need big bucks. Tell me, Marcelo, are you an actor?" La Contessa smiled a very small smile. The fish had taken the bait.

"Interesting you should ask. I have at times in the past given it some thought. You have heard of the actress Isa Miranda?"

Hazel acted startled. "Heard of her? Why she was a buddy of mine when she was at Paramount a couple of years ago making a pair of stinkeroos. Forgive me. I mean failures."

"Isa was also a friend of mine," said Marcelo warmly while la Contessa's eyes were veiled with jealousy at the mention of Miranda's name. "She made with me . . . oh how do you call it . . ."

I'd call it "whoopee," thought Hazel.

"Ah yes . . . a screen test."

"How'd it come out?"

"I never found out. With the confusing first days of the outbreak of war, I lost all contact with Isa. Anyway, I don't think the time was appropriate to inquire as to the outcome of a screen test."

Hazel gushed, "I'll bet you photograph divinely. Now, I must interview la Contessa. Tell me, Contessa, are you truly descended from Marco Polo?"

"Indeed I am."

"But you spell the name as one word."

"It saves time."

Marcelo explained, "The names were joined over a century ago by la Contessa's grandfather."

"Did you see Sam Goldwyn's movie about Marco Polo? It came out three years ago."

La Contessa said with distaste, "I saw it out of curiosity. Absolute nonsense."

"But he did go to China, didn't he?"

"Oh that's quite true. And he brought back the first samples of what the Chinese called Spa Get Ti. And now it is spaghetti!"

"Well, how about that! And I suppose he brought back all sorts of treasures. Jewels, tapestries, and all that jazz."

"Oh, yes," said la Contessa. "He returned to Venice with great wealth. Over the years, much of it was stolen, and equally, much of it was recovered. There are still certain items we are trying to trace."

"Oh, really. Say, you're not here on a treasure hunt, are you? This town goes looney over treasure hunts."

"Does it really?" La Contessa and Marcelo exchanged looks. Violetta passed around the hors d'oeuvres tray. "Actually, there is one interesting object I would love to recover for my family."

Hazel crossed her legs and leaned forward with interest. Marcelo wondered why she wasn't taking notes. He didn't know Hazel had a memory like a steel trap.

La Contessa continued. "It's a cornucopia."

"A what?"

"A cornucopia. It is shaped like a conical horn. Not too large, but big enough to hold a wealth of valuable jewels." Hazel whistled. "Cornucopias are also known as The Horn of Plenty."

"That's a horn I wouldn't mind blowing," said Hazel. "What's become of it?"

"It has disappeared. It was a gift to Marco from the emperor of China. It was stolen shortly after Marco's death. Later it was recovered and the thief's hands were severed at the wrists and his eyes burnt out with hot pokers. Then he was tortured. For centuries there has been a game of cat and mouse thievery until it finally was recovered by my father, the Baron di Marcopolo."

"And where's your father?"

"He's dead. He died on a ship making its way to China where my father rather generously was preparing to return the cornucopia to the Chinese government."

Hazel looked and sounded perplexed. "Wasn't that a bit rash of him?"

"We thought so. It killed my mother. She had a heart attack. When my father's ship docked, there was no sign of the cornucopia. My father was supposed to entrust a letter with the ship's captain explaining the cornucopia's fate. The captain was to have then delivered the letter to me. I never received the letter."

"I see," said Hazel. "Dirty work at the crossroads."

Marcelo spoke. "Of course, there is the possibility there was no such letter. That it didn't exist. And perhaps the cornucopia was not on board the ship."

"Don't be such a fool, Marcelo. My father was seen carrying the cornucopia on board. His intention was to entrust it to the captain for safekeeping in the ship's vault."

Hazel asked, "Are you suggesting the captain might have made off with this treasure?"

La Contessa said, "The ship's personnel, you understand, also had access to the vault. The purser, for example. I never met the captain but my father considered him a very honorable man. My father took many voyages with Captain Methot. One of his hobbies was collecting Oriental art."

Hazel's face was slightly screwed. "Captain who?"

"Methot. Captain Methot."

"Really! I wonder if he's any relation of Mayo Methot. It's a most unusual name." She explained, "Mayo Methot is the wife of the movie star Humphrey Bogart. Surely you've heard of him in Italy."

"Indeed I have."

Violetta found her tongue and gushed, "I adore Humphrey Bogart. He is one of my favorites."

"This is really such a coincidence. If Mrs. Bogart is related in some way to Captain Methot, I'd be most interested in meeting her."

Hazel stood up. "I'll phone her right now. She just might be at home." She dug into her handbag for her address book. "Here it is. The Bogarts." She crossed to a desk on which rested a phone and dialed.

In the Bogart living room, Hannah kept a tight grip on the plate holding the steaks while making an assessment of the damage wrought by her employers. Mrs. Bogart was so charming when she interviewed Hannah, and then her Mrs. Hyde personality slowly emerged. It was Hannah's personal opinion that Bogart was too good for her. She'd read somewhere he came from a very upper-class New York family. Real high society. Not as high as it could get but impressively high enough.

Mayo said to the housekeeper, "We're dining out." She directed her mouth at Bogart, "Dinner at seven at the Brown Derby with Dash and Lily."

"I haven't forgotten," said Bogart. He was fond of Dashiell Hammett and Hammett's lover, the playwright Lillian Hellman who had scored a huge Broadway success in 1934 with her play, *The Children's Hour*.

"I'll save the steaks for tomorrow," said Hannah. And that was when the phone rang. Hannah answered. "Bogart residence."

"Hannah?" chirruped Hazel Dickson at the other end. "It's Hazel Dickson. Is Mrs. Bogart in?"

"I'll see, Miss Dickson." Bogart groaned on hearing the name. He pantomimed to Hannah that he wasn't in but Hannah squelched the movement with "It's for Mrs. Bogart."

Mayo snapped, "You keep forgetting there's another star in the house." Bogart said nothing. Mayo took the phone. "How are you, Hazel?"

"I'm just dandy. Mayo, I'm at the Ambassador in the suite of la Contessa di Marcopolo."

"Sounds real grand."

"Mayo sweetie, was your father a sea captain?"

"It's no secret. It's in my bio on file with my agent."

"Oh how marvelous! Hold on, Mayo." She said to the fat woman on the couch, "It's her father!"

La Contessa was delighted. "We must get together!"

"Mayo, you'll never believe this. But La Contessa's father, the Baron di Marcopolo was a friend of your father's. In fact, he died on one of your father's voyages in the Orient!"

Mayo commented wryly, "I'd say that's carrying friendship a bit far, even for my father." She thought for a moment. "The Baron di Marcopolo. Come to think of it, Jack mentioned him a couple of times. As I recall, there was something about a cornucopia filled with jewels. One of them stories out of the *Arabian Nights*."

Bogart chuckled. "I remember that one. It took your father about half a dozen Boilermakers to tell it all."

Hazel persisted. "It's not a fairy tale. It's the truth. I think it's a great story. Won't you come and meet la Contessa?"

Mayo would have preferred to wipe the smirk off her husband's face. Bogart and her parents didn't like each other. Bogart referred to Evelyn as the Empress and to the captain as Captain Bligh. Jack Methot was dead of a heart attack shortly after the Bogarts married and Evelyn rarely visited them. It was the way Bogart liked it. He heard Mayo say, "Sure I'd like to meet her. Then I can drop in at Magnin's and run up some bills." Bogart winced. Hannah had departed for the kitchen after handing the phone to Mayo. In the kitchen she gently lifted the phone extension and heard the rest of the conversation between Mayo and Hazel. Hannah and the other housekeepers in the neighborhood met daily for coffee, cake, and gossip in somebody's kitchen while their employers were engaged at their studios. This was how, as Hannah put it, they remained au courant. She'd learned the expression from Charles Boyer's housekeeper.

Bogart said to Mayo as he straightened his tie without needing a mirror, "Go easy at Magnin's."

"Why? Are we poverty-stricken?"

"Let's not get into another battle. As far as I'm concerned we've had ours for today. We're not poverty-stricken but you're going a little too heavy on the shopping sprees."

"I'm Mrs. Humphrey Bogart!"

"Well, *I* ain't!" snapped Bogart.

"I have to keep up appearances. If we're so hard up for money why don't you help me get some jobs!"

"Why doesn't your agent get off his ass and get you some jobs?" He raised his hands defensively. "Don't you throw that book!"

She slammed the book back on the table. "You know, with a little more practice, I could really loathe you."

"Naw, Slugger. You could never loathe me. Like I could never loathe you. Be patient, babe, one of these days you might meet Mister Right."

"Go to hell."

"I'm going to rehearsal. I don't know how long it'll be, so let's meet at the Brown Derby at seven. And when you get there, try to be on your best behavior. No pushing your food on the fork with your fingers." The book flew past his head and landed in the foyer. Laughing, he left the house and went to the driveway where his car was parked. He reflected upon his wife as he started the ignition, put the car into gear, and set off to the Warner Studio in the valley.

Mayo.

When did he fall in love with her and why? It was when he saw her on Broadway in *Torch Song*. She'd gotten great reviews and everybody was talking about this exciting new actress so he decided to check her out. She'd gotten the reviews but the play hadn't, so it was playing to half houses, forcing the management to paper performances with free passes. Bogie got himself one for a matinee. It was Saturday, and Bogart recognized and acknowledged many of his fellow actors who were also unemployed and seeing a show for free. Mayo was no great beauty but she could act. Her technique was good and the way she underplayed the rest of the cast was something she might have learned from his second wife, Mary Phillips. Mary was no great beauty either, but she was a superb actress. She was memorable in Kaufman and Hart's *Merrily We Roll Along* in a part based on Dorothy Parker, the Algonquin wit and character assassin. Bogart's first wife, Helen Menken, was a true star given to frequent bouts of indigestion from chewing so much scenery, though she held her own opposite Helen Hayes in *Mary of Scotland.*

Mayo was something else. But her features were mismatched. She had the body of a star but the face of a character actress. It didn't matter in the theater but was a detriment on screen, where the face was magnified over a hundred times. Still, Harry Cohen brought Mayo to Hollywood when her play folded and gave her the lead at Columbia in *The Murder of the Night Club Lady* with Adolphe Menjou as Detective Thatcher Colt. Unfortunately, Mayo didn't have enough footage in which to make much of an impression because as the nightclub lady in question, she was dispatched in reel one which gave audiences plenty of time to forget her.

When the Bogarts met, they had heavy drinking as well as acting in common. They laughed a lot together and were incredibly lonely. So booze, laughter, and loneliness led to marriage, and the marriage soon evolved into disillusions and recriminations. As Bogart became more successful, Mayo felt herself slowly but surely shunted to the background. As Bette Davis had told her when they were filming *Marked Woman,* "There's nothing more unnecessary than a Hollywood wife."

Mayo had repeated the line to Bogart after they were married. Bogart remembered his response, "A Hollywood wife carries more weight than a Hollywood mistress"—this at a time when Mayo was dieting strenuously, which won him his first bruised chin and a begrudging respect for his wife's right uppercut.

At Warners, he found Mary Astor reading the script of *The Maltese Falcon* aloud to herself in one of the conference rooms occasionally used for rehearsals. Most directors rehearsed on the set and then ordered a take, but John Huston was taking no chances with his first film. The script was an ensemble piece, and he had pleaded with Jack Warner for extended rehearsal time. Warner gave it to him because the film's budget was half that of other "A" features. Warner referred to this one as a nervous "A". Almost everyone in the cast was under contract and those who were not contracted were hired on daily rates that were usually cheap. There was a comparatively short shooting schedule; Bogart knew Huston was planning to shoot at a fast clip to give the picture the kind of pacing the previous versions lacked.

"Hello, beautiful, where's the rest of the company?"

"I think they're out scrounging cocaine for Peter Lorre. The war seems to have played havoc with his European connections. How'd you bruise your eye?"

He sank into a chair. "Need you ask? Another scuffle with my bitter half."

She liked and admired Bogart and was sympathetic to his domestic difficulties, having suffered a plethora of her own. "Bogie, sometimes I think there's a touch of madness in you."

"If there is," he said while lighting a cigarette, "there's Methot to my madness."

She smiled. "This is a terrific script. There isn't a poor line of dialogue or a superfluous one. John's done a terrific job with it."

"Let me let you in on a little secret. He stuck to the book."

"I know. I read the book. Hammett is brilliant." She crossed her legs. "He hasn't written anything in a long time. I wonder why."

"I'll ask him tonight. We're having dinner with him and Lily Hellman at the Brown Derby. I'd ask you to join us except I'm hoping Mayo will be on her best behavior and she's already accused me of having an affair with you."

"Christ. About the only actor I haven't been suspected of

having an affair with is Alfalfa Switzer and I'm wondering if he's terribly hurt about that. I read that article on you in this month's *Photoplay* magazine. I'm terribly impressed."

"Oh, yeah? What does it say? I never read that crap."

"I'm really impressed your mother was Maude Bogart, the famous illustrator."

"Well, how about that? Yeah, when I was an infant, I was her favorite model. Mostly because she didn't have to pay me anything." Mary smiled. "I was the Mellon's Baby Food baby. Is that in the article?"

"Yes, and that you were Baby Dimple in *Sleepytime Stories*."

"Christ, I forgot about that one. Yeah, Maude was pretty good with illustrations. She was pretty lousy with her husband and her kids. I had two sisters. Kay died young. Pat had a mental breakdown so maybe there's something to your madness theory."

"Oh, please, come on," she demurred as a blush came to her cheeks.

"My mother could make an iceberg seem like an oasis. What a cold and unfeeling bitch."

"And yet she gave birth to three children?"

"Mary, I get the feeling all three times she wasn't looking. You should have met my father. Doctor Belmont DeForest Bogart. How's that for a fancy mouthful? Mary, I don't know how I got to be a product of that union. I was a real mean kid."

"Stop being so hard on yourself."

"I was! I was a real mean kid." He was warming up to himself, usually his least favorite subject. "I went to this very exclusive private school. Trinity. It was so exclusive, I think it didn't have an address. The kids used to beat me up." He laughed. "I suppose I wasn't exactly a charmer, what with my kind of parents and my poor sisters terrified of both of them. Poor Pat. How she suffered. I think her breakdown was a blessing."

Mary shook her head from side to side. "Isn't there anyone in this town who loves their mother?"

"Yeah. Ginger Rogers." He was on his feet with impatience. "Say, where the hell are the rest of them? We're supposed to be rehearsing. Otherwise I might have gone with Mayo to meet this Contessa di Marcopolo."

"A contessa, no less. Mayo's moving up in the world. Sounds like one of Hazel Dickson's trophies."

"Right on the nose. Sayyy . . ."

"What?"

He snapped his fingers. "I thought that cornucopia sounded familiar. First cousin to *The Maltese Falcon*."

"Come off the wall, Bogie. What cornucopia?"

"Listen to this." He sat down again. He told her what little he knew of the Baron di Marcopolo's cornucopia and the involvement of Mayo's father. He knew he'd get the rest from Mayo, but what he told Mary she found fascinating.

At the conclusion, she said, "Say, that *is* the Maltese Falcon's twin brother. Bogie, do you suppose Hammett knew the cornucopia story and refashioned the cornucopia into the statuette of the falcon?"

"It's a possibility. Aren't writers supposed to write what they know about?"

"They're supposed to, but they don't always."

Bogart was chain-smoking. "You know, I'm going to spring this on Hammett at dinner. If Lily Hellman lets me get a word in edgewise." He lowered his voice. "Who's the fat guy? Is he playing Casper Guttman?"

Mary smiled at the huge, white-haired man in his sixties who approached them with a delightful smile. "Sidney, come meet Bogie."

"Ah, Bogie. At last!" He and Bogart shook hands. "I'm Sidney Greenstreet, the villain of the piece. I believe in a previous incarnation the part was written for a woman. Perhaps I'll use a subtle touch of effeminacy."

Mary Astor said, "You'll have a hard time getting that past the censors."

Said Bogart, "Sure, it'll pass. It's already in the script. Huston's used it the way Hammett wrote it in the book. The kid traveling with Greenstreet and Joel Cairo, Lorre's part. He's obviously Guttman's lover."

"But he's a killer!" exclaimed Mary.

"But aren't most lovers?" asked Greenstreet.

"Sidney," said Mary, "you are a card."

"Oh, my dear," said Greenstreet aware of the actress's scandalous past and possibly a scandalous future, "no offense intended, I assure you."

"No offense taken," she said with a laugh. "Bogie, tell Sidney about the cornucopia. I'm sure he'll be fascinated."

"Cornucopia? A horn of plenty?" He had sat on a hard-backed chair after testing two canvas director's chairs which seemed too risky for his tremendous weight. "Am I about to be regaled with a tale of adventure and intrigue?"

"Well, frankly, Sidney, it depends on how you swallow it. Now then . . ."

THREE

For her meeting with la Contessa, Mayo changed into a diaphanous dress with a flowery print and wore a Lily Dache hat that would have been more appropriate to a garden party. Hazel Dickson thought she should have carried a tasseled parasol in her left hand, and her right hand holding two leashes at the end of which were a pair of borzois. Mayo and la Contessa didn't quite outdo each other in the gushing department though each gave it her best effort. Marcelo almost succeeded in drowning her in Mediterranean charm and sexy innuendo while Mayo accepted Violetta's excessive admiration of Bogart's persona with a polite smile and a suppressed sneeze.

"So our fathers were friends," said Mayo as she refused an hors d'oeuvre and accepted a gin and grapefruit juice. After some chitchat which was the usual time waster and made Mayo wonder if she should consult a psychiatrist (as Bogie so frequently urged her), la Contessa with exquisite timing said, "There is the letter my father entrusted to yours shortly before he died."

"What letter?" asked Mayo with sincere innocence.

"The letter that tells who was in possession of the cornucopia," insisted the Contessa while dabbing at beads of perspiration on her upper lip.

"Search me," said Mayo with an expressive shrug, little knowing la Contessa wished they could. "Why was a letter necessary if the cornucopia was nowhere to be found when the ship docked?"

"My theory is that my father assigned someone to smuggle the cornucopia ashore."

"Why would he have done that?"

"Perhaps it was a matter of distrust."

Mayo's voice hardened. "You mean for some reason he'd grown to distrust my father."

"Oh no no no," said la Contessa so musically Hazel Dickson feared she was about to break into song. "But you see, my dear Miss Methot, in the past people have been killed for this treasure."

"Do you think your father was murdered?"

"I'll never know. He was buried at sea."

Mayo said, "Well, that's what's usually done when someone dies aboard ship in midocean."

"It wasn't in midocean. It was a little over a day away from port."

"Have you any idea how intense the heat is on the Orient run?" Mayo sipped her drink. "My father's ship wasn't equipped with the proper refrigeration for a corpse. So your father presumably wrote a letter to you identifying the possessor of the cornucopia and entrusted the letter to my father whom he no longer trusted." She said to Hazel Dickson, "This one should star Laurel and Hardy."

Marcelo interjected. "I still don't think there was a letter."

"You hush!" said the countess sharply. She told Mayo, "I received a phone call from someone who said he had been on board the ship and my father confided in him the letter existed and to call me to make sure I got the letter from Captain Methot."

"How long ago was this?" asked Mayo.

"Five years ago."

"My father's been dead for three years or thereabouts. My mother and I went through his effects before disposing of most of them. I assure you there was no such letter. Contessa, do you know the name of this mysterious person who phoned you?"

"I shall never forget. His name was George Spelvin."

Mayo's eyes widened and then she exploded with laughter. La Contessa was bewildered. She looked at Hazel who was equally mystified by the eruption and Marcelo and Violetta exchanged shrugs.

Mayo put her drink on a table, opened her handbag, extracted a tissue and dabbed at her eyes. "Contessa," she said after a few more moments, "I am very well acquainted with George Spelvin."

"Aha!" shouted la Contessa. "Where is he? Where can I find him?"

"Where is he? Find him? Oh Contessa, he is up there in the heavens . . ."

La Contessa was aghast. "He is dead?"

Mayo was laughing again. "He is out there somewhere in New York, or Detroit, or possibly Philadelphia and St. Louis, anywhere there's a play to be seen." She sipped her drink again. "Contessa, you've been had."

"I beg your pardon?"

"George Spelvin is a theatrical tradition. It is a name cloaked in anonymity. It is a name used by actors who don't want their own names printed in the playbill or the program, as you better know it. Usually it's an actor down on his luck, once well known, now relegated to playing a bit or a walk-on. You'd be surprised how often in a theatrical season George Spelvin trods the boards."

"You are saying I was duped."

"Very. Boy, wait till I tell Bogie about this one."

The countess barked at Violetta to fling open the French windows, which the young woman did with alacrity. The welcome breeze upset Marcelo's immaculately coiffured hair and he sought refuge in a chair next to Mayo. La Contessa said, "You and your husband will laugh at me."

"Not at all. We will laugh at George Spelvin. You see, in a way he's such an old friend. Bogie was George Spelvin a few times early in his career. It's nostalgic."

La Contessa was playing with her pearls, staring at Mayo with hooded eyelids. "Has your husband ever sailed with your father?"

Mayo smiled. "No, Contessa. My husband has never been to the Far East. Not even on location."

Hazel informed la Contessa brightly, "But they do own a boat. The *Slugger*. Named for Mayo who . . ."

Mayo interrupted her. "Hazel, a most unnecessary non

sequitur. Contessa, my husband and I are dining with a famous mystery writer, Dashiell Hammett."

"What's up?" asked Hazel.

"Oh, can it, Hazel. It's just your ordinary run-of-the-mill non-gourmet dinner at the Brown Derby. As I was saying, Contessa, Mr. Hammett has written a book whose story is similar to that of the cornucopia."

"The cornucopia is not a story. It is a fact. It is the truth."

"Don't fret needlessly, Contessa, I see now you were anxious to meet me hoping I had your father's letter in my possession. And," she added, subtly suspicious, "neither does my mother. At least not to my knowledge. Funny, her apartment in Portland . . . that's up north in Oregon . . . was ransacked this morning. Nothing was stolen. You people haven't been in Portland lately, by any chance?"

"How dare you!" bristled la Contessa.

"How dare I what?"

"Insinuate we were in Portland and ransacked your mother's apartment!"

"Now really, Mayo," said Hazel.

Mayo had risen. "The party's turning sour and I have a date with some sales people at Magnin's. Don't see me to the door, Marcelo. I know how to make an exit." Within moments, she was gone.

In the hallway, Mayo paused to repair her face. She examined herself in the compact mirror and decided all she needed was some lipstick. She applied the special brand prepared for her by makeup expert Perc Westmore who with his brothers catered exclusively to the Hollywood elite. Moments later, waiting for an elevator, she thought about her father. She'd always suspected there was some larceny in her father's soul. It went with the territory, the Oriental route. Drug smuggling. Gun smuggling. Developed by some more unscrupulous seafarers into a sophisticated high art. He had entertained and sometimes frightened her with tales of piracy in the Oriental waters. Had he stolen the cornucopia? Was he capable of such treachery?

George Spelvin.

Her father knew the origin of George Spelvin. He'd heard it from Mayo and Bogie. He could have used the letter and George Spelvin to mislead la Contessa. And taken the cornucopia for himself. She was now descending in the elevator. He'd suddenly been talking about retirement those months before his death. Her mother hated the word. Retirement. Jack at home, underfoot, his constant presence annoying her while she tried to entertain her muse. Leaving the elevator, she entered the hotel bar, sat at an isolated table, and ordered a gin martini. She knew she shouldn't, but she did. There was plenty of time before she was due to meet the others at the Brown Derby. Plenty of time to tank up on gin martinis. She'd better not. She'd better have just this one and get on to I. Magnin's. She could use another pair of shoes. She always needed another pair of shoes. She had almost as many pairs of shoes as Joan Crawford. The martini arrived and Mayo stared at it as though it might have been an ocean in the Far East. She had never seen her father's ship, but it didn't matter. She had a vivid imagination. His ship was right here in front of her eyes. It was circumnavigating the martini, her father leaning over the rail and plotting the future of the cornucopia. It was warm but she felt a sudden chill. Had the Baron di Marcopolo been murdered? By her father?

"What's wrong, sweetie?"

Mayo's head turned to the sound of the voice on her right. She had neither heard nor seen Hazel Dickson sitting opposite her. "Oh. Hazel. You startled me."

"Didn't mean to. I'm glad I found you. I'd like to discuss the cast of characters upstairs. Is that a gin martini I see? It's inspirational. I think I'll have one."

"Take mine. I shouldn't have ordered it. Go ahead, Hazel. Take it. I don't want to show at dinner a bit squiffed. Bogie wouldn't like that."

"If you insist," said Hazel as she moved the gin martini in front of her. "Twist of lemon. Just how I like it. I loved the George Spelvin bit. You had la Contessa going around in circles."

"She's awful fat. Is Marcelo her lover?"

Hazel made a face. "What a repulsive thought. He probably is because he's probably penniless and any port in a storm. And she's quite a port."

"Are you going to peddle the cornucopia story?"

Hazel airily flipped a wrist. "Isn't it a hoot? I think it's a damned good story."

"You know the plot of *The Maltese Falcon.*"

"Sure."

"It's a cousin of the cornucopia."

"Say! You're right! Sidney Skolsky will love it!"

"Why not shoot for the big time? Louella."

"I suppose I should, but I owe Sidney." She downed a healthy swig of martini, and commented, "Could be colder. Mayo, aren't you feeling well?"

"Do I look ill?"

"You have this strange look. Something's bothering you."

"George Spelvin is bothering me."

"Now that was an inspiration, Mayo. You sure knocked la Contessa on her backside." She thought for a moment. "I'm not so sure I like her very much. I could go for the boyfriend though. Couldn't you?"

"I'm a married woman."

"So?" Hazel downed the rest of the drink.

I'm a married woman. So? That's Hollywood.

At Warner Brothers, the rehearsal had still not gotten underway. Bogie, Mary Astor, and Sidney Greenstreet were joined by director John Huston, son of actor Walter Huston and three other important cast members, Peter Lorre, Gladys George, and Elisha Cook Jr. Miss George was looking painfully thin, and Bogie wondered if she was hooked on drugs as the rumor had it. In 1935, she'd been brought from Broadway to Paramount Pictures for the starring role in *Valiant Is the Word for Carrie* and was then signed by M-G-M, who soon had her playing supporting roles because no magic of a makeup man or a special camera lens could hide the fact that she was middle-aged. They'd found cocaine for Lorre in the Mexican barrio in downtown L.A. He was now as dapper and jovial as always. Gladys George kept dabbing at her nose with a handkerchief, a sure sign she was hooked on the funny powder, too.

Mary Astor urged Bogart to tell the late arrivals the story of the cornucopia. "Sure," agreed Bogie, "I especially want John to hear it."

Huston's curiosity was piqued. "Is it dirty? Does it have a great punch line?"

"It's dirty, but not in the way you'd prefer it. As for the punch line, it's waiting to be written." Bogart told the story straightforwardly with Mary occasionally prompting him when she thought he was leaving out an important fact. He didn't, at the time, have all that much story to tell, but what he did tell he told provocatively and colorfully and had everyone's undivided attention. He signaled he was finished when he lit a cigarette.

Huston slapped his knee and roared with laughter. "Why, you slimy son of a bitch, that's a variation on the *Falcon!*"

"I'm glad you noticed," said Bogart, sending a smoke ring past Peter Lorre's left ear.

"Is it supposed to be true?" Huston was openly skeptical.

"Mayo's over at the Ambassador having tea, I hope, with the lady who claims the thing belongs to her if it's ever found. La Contessa di Marcopolo."

"Oh sure," said Gladys George and all eyes centered on her.

"You know her?" asked Bogart.

"Indirectly. I met her father years ago in London when I was an ingenue and looked it. The Baron di Marcopolo. Very rich and very much taken with himself." She closed her eyes. "Let me think if I still remember." Her eyes flew open. "Oh yeah. I remember." Now she was smiling. "He had so many lovers, he was known as the Machiavelli of Mistresses. Quite a horseman, if you know what I mean." She winked at Mary Astor who blushed. She knew what Gladys meant and would never regret that she did.

Peter Lorre had a wicked look on his face. "Gladys, did you ever come down the home stretch with him?"

"He didn't interest me that way," she said coolly. "But I could appreciate what the ladies saw in him. So he died on an ocean liner captained by Mayo's father."

"They were good friends," said Bogart, "or that's what la Contessa says."

Huston said, "I don't buy the letter. That one needs a rewrite."

"You're probably right," said Bogart. "And I find myself not buying the cornucopia when I give it some sensible thought. After all, the *Falcon* never materializes. What we do find is a fake."

" 'Such stuff as dreams are made on,' " said Greenstreet solemnly.

"Sidney, you're stealing my line," admonished Bogart.

"It's such a lovely line. I find it irresistible." He sat with his hands folded across his formidable stomach. "Mr. Hammett, bless him, is no slouch at good lines of dialogue."

Huston wondered aloud, "Do you suppose Hammett at some point was privy to the cornucopia story?"

"Seems to me, John," said Bogart, "there have been all sorts of stories handed down through the ages about priceless articles that have gone lost and are still being sought. The silver chalice of the Crusades, Christ's cloak when he was crucified, the lost city of Atlantis . . ."

"My option at renewal time," said Lorre wistfully.

Bogart told Huston and the others that he and Mayo had a dinner date with Hammett and Lillian Hellman and he had every intention of questioning the author on the subject.

"Okay. Let's get back to our own legend, Bogie, I'd like to start with your first meeting, when Mary comes to your office with a trumped up story about a missing sister . . ."

While a troubled Mayo Methot drove several sales clerks at I. Magnin's to the brink of insanity, Hazel Dickson steered her sad excuse of a car downtown to Detective Herbert Villon's precinct. She wanted to see what he made of the cornucopia story. Darling Herb, longtime detective, longtime lover, longtime name-dropper known as The Detective of the Stars. Hazel looked in the rearview mirror, not to see if she was being followed but to check her face, which was still a rather attractive one.

She drove into the precinct's parking lot, which she wasn't supposed to do. But there'd be no squawk. Everybody in the precinct recognized Hazel's Studebaker with its dents and bruises and gallant defiance of any form of destruction. She turned off the motor while wondering if Hitler had invaded another country this morning. The son of a bitch was gobbling countries as fast as la Contessa gobbled hors d'oeuvres. She locked the car despite its being on a police lot. Hazel Dickson trusted nobody. Had she been a man, she would have sported both belt and suspenders. She breezed into the precinct with a proprietary air, greeted the desk sergeant like a long lost brother, and without bothering to have herself announced marched down the long corridor to Herb Villon's untidy office.

She opened the door briskly and saw Villon and his young partner, Jim Mallory, shuffling photographs. They didn't look up. She hadn't disturbed them. They were too engrossed in the photographs.

"Dirty pictures?" asked Hazel.

"Filthy," said Villon without bothering to look up. Hazel crossed to the desk, looked over Jim Mallory's shoulder, and let out a yelp.

"You son of a bitch, I feel like throwing up!"

"You know where the toilet is," said Villon. Then he sighed with defeat, "Jim, we still have a leg left over."

Mallory straightened up and with hands on hips said, "This isn't a dismembered body; it's a jigsaw puzzle."

"Who is it?" asked Hazel in a small voice.

"We're assuming she was a prostitute. We were able to fingerprint her and we are waiting for the answers, but we couldn't find her head."

"Oh God!" wailed Hazel. "What sort of maniac would do such a thing to a person!"

Villon finally looked up. "Someone, I should think, who

has gone to pieces." He added glumly, "You're wearing that hat."

Her eyes narrowed. "*I* happen to like this hat. It was a gift from an old admirer. My grandmother."

"Tell your grandmother to wear it. It would suit the old bat. She still cheating at pinochle?"

"Of course. It's all she lives for. Listen, Herb, I just spent some time with la Contessa di Marcopolo at the Ambassador and . . ."

"Oh, for crying out loud! Not more of those phony European titles of yours!"

"She's not phony, she's authentic and she's got the royal rocks to prove it. Will you *please* pay attention? She's here on some kind of a treasure hunt."

Villon sank into his swivel chair. Jim Mallory folded his arms and leaned against a wall. He thought of lighting his pipe but remembered his dentist's warning his teeth were eroding from biting down on the stem. Hazel sat in a chair opposite them and placed her handbag on the desk, crossed her legs, and warned them, "Now no interruptions. I'm giving this one to Sidney Skolsky." She told the cornucopia story without embellishments but with a kind of intensity that had them more or less believing it. "Well? Do you think la Contessa has something or she belongs in a loony bin?"

"I've heard crazier ones. In fact I've read one similar to it."

"*The Maltese Falcon*," said Hazel.

"Right on the nose. You think Mayo Methot's father pulled a fast one?"

"I prefer to think not. I'm very fond of Mayo despite that time at Mocambo she threw a highball at Bogie, who ducked and it hit me."

Jim Mallory said, "I like that bit about George Spelvin. I wonder who invented George Spelvin?"

"Don't open that can of peas," cautioned Hazel. "But if the story is at all true, then I think Captain Methot took off with the thing and then pulled the Spelvin thing to mislead the contessa, who, as you gather, is not easily misled."

"Tell me, Hazel," asked Villon, "if you were a stuffed cornucopia, where would you be hidden?"

"How the hell should I know? I've never been a stuffed cornucopia."

Mallory asked, "The baron was buried at sea?"

"Yes, that's part of the plot."

"And the captain remained on board for the return voyage?"

"Isn't that what captains are supposed to do?"

"Not necessarily," said Villon. "He could have arranged for someone else to supervise the return voyage. They sometimes do that."

Mallory said, "I don't think the thing left the ship. I think Methot ran the return voyage and from wherever it docked, he brought the cornucopia back with him. It's more logical."

Villon threw up his hands. "Who needs logic in this illogical world! Anyway, how do we know there really was a cornucopia?"

"Because my woman's intuition, my gut instinct, tells me there is a cornucopia lurking in some dark, sequestered corner."

Villon asked, "You leaving town, Hazel?"

"What the hell for?"

"To hunt for the cornucopia."

"Why would I leave town? If la Contessa is here, then she thinks it's here. And what about that ransacked apartment of Mayo's mother? Mayo practically accused them of doing the job though she'd have a hard time proving they were in Portland."

Said Villon, "The countess sounds too fat to do any ransacking."

"If they were in Portland and did the ransacking, then my finger would point at Marcelo."

Villon asked, "What about this Marcelo?"

"He's her lapdog."

"Oh. One of those."

"Very sexy."

"How would you know?" asked Villon as he applied a match to a cigarette.

"I'm not blind and you know my vivid imagination."

Villon said to Mallory, "I wonder what Bogie makes of all this?"

"Don't ask him, ask me," insisted Hazel. She told him about the dinner date at the Brown Derby. "Maybe you feel like taking me to dinner at the Brown Derby?"

FOUR

A financier named Herbert Sonnenberg conceived
the idea of the Brown Derby restaurant, on Vine Street just
off Hollywood Boulevard. It was a restaurant built and
shaped like a Brown Derby. In no time at all, it was one of
Hollywood's favorite playrooms, the food of secondary im-
portance and rightly so. Sonnenberg had been silent screen
queen Gloria Swanson's second husband and thanks to her
had instant access to all Hollywood. The walls were decorated with caricatures of Hollywood celebrities, an inspiration borrowed from the famed Sardi's restaurant in New
York whose walls were adorned with caricatures of leading
Broadway lights. The restaurant consisted mainly of booths
so situated that they afforded a certain amount of unwanted
privacy to their occupants. Actors ate in public not merely
to satisfy their appetites but to be seen and recognized and
adored. Upon entering the place one had to make one's way
through a sea of gaping tourists and an army of autograph
hounds who through some strange and mystical grapevine
seemed to know which celebrities were in temporary residence. The bar was a magnet for Hollywood's drinkers and
they were legion. If there was a stray husband or lover or
boyfriend on the loose, a call to the Derby usually found him
and sent him on his way.

On this particular night that the Bogarts were dining with
Dashiell Hammett and Lillian Hellman, the place was hop-
ping, an autograph seeker's dream or nightmare, depending
on how they were treated by the celebrated. Everyone remembered with relish when silent star Norma Talmadge, a
very wealthy woman who had failed to make it in talkies,
shouted at an autograph seeker, "Get the hell away from me!
I don't need you anymore!" Hollywood's frequent cruelty

was also remembered, especially the time when silent-screen comic Roscoe "Fatty" Arbuckle, having won a justly deserved acquittal after three trials for murder, nevertheless sat alone in a booth, chagrined at being unacknowledged, ostracized forever.

Dashiell Hammett and Lillian Hellman were the first to arrive and ordered scotch highballs. They both drank too much and swore too much and were presumably the models for Nick and Nora Charles in Hammett's brilliant novel, *The Thin Man*, immortalized on the screen by William Powell and Myrna Loy. Hammett was tall and urbane and cadaverously thin and it was his portrait that graced the jacket of the book when it was published in 1932. Lillian Hellman was urbane, too, and a very gifted playwright. She was also very mean and very rude and did not suffer fools gladly. She was incredibly homely. She had a nose that only Jimmy Durante and W. C. Fields could appreciate. Hellman's very good friend, Dorothy Parker, usually explained it was her intellect that had captured the much pursued (by women) Hammett. There had been a husband in her life, a playwright named Arthur Kober who'd written a Broadway success several years earlier, *Having Wonderful Time*, and contributed humorous pieces frequently to *The New Yorker*. It was said that Hammett had his undying gratitude after Miss Hellman bounced Kober for the novelist.

"I hate this town," said Hellman.

"You just said that," said Hammett nibbling a peanut.

"I can't say it often enough."

"Don't knock it too loudly," cautioned Hammett, "or they might stop paying you all that money you demand and get."

"I'm worth every nickel." She looked at her wristwatch. "What the hell's keeping the Bogarts?"

"The Brothers Warner. Bogie told me they pay him one hundred and fourteen thousand dollars a year."

"Peanuts. Bette Davis gets over two hundred and fifty thousand dollars."

Hammett winked. "He knows that. It's eating away at him like a cancer."

Hellman sat up. "Here comes Mayo. Christ, that getup. You'd think she's planning to be entertained by Queen Mary."

"Keep a civil tongue in your mouth. You know she packs a hefty wallop. Hello Mayo, darling. Where's Bogie?"

"Hello dear. Hello Lily. Waiter, a very dry gin martini with a lemon twist." She moved into the booth next to Hellman, leaving room for Bogart.

"Where's Bogie?" asked Hellman.

"Huston was holding a rehearsal of *Falcon*. Shouldn't you have been there, Dash?"

"What for? I only wrote the book. You know that means less than nothing in this town."

"Come off it, Dash," said Hellman, "they did a great job on *The Thin Man*."

"What about those awful sequels?"

"Oh, come on," said Mayo, "I thought *After the Thin Man* was just plain darling."

"That's just what it was," said Hammett glumly, "just plain darling."

Mayo asked Hellman, "What are you working on now?"

"More money."

"Lily never gets paid enough money," said Hammett. "Ever since Sam Goldwyn filmed her *Children's Hour*, she's been one of his favorite scripters. And he pays her plenty."

"What's wrong with that?" asked Mayo as the waiter served her martini.

"Goldwyn."

Bogart had arrived and was greeting friends at the bar. He waved at the booth indicating he'd be joining them momentarily. For the first time in a long time, Mayo couldn't wait to tell him something.

She raised her glass to propose a toast. "To absent friends."

"Which ones?" asked Hellman.

"Don't be surly, Lily," cautioned Hammett. "The night is young."

"We're not and I'm hungry." She said to Mayo, "Do you think your husband will ever tear himself away from the bar?"

"He just did. Here he comes."

Bogart arrived at the table and demanded of Mayo, "Where's my drink?" He sat next to her and shook hands with Hammett and Hellman.

"I wasn't sure what you might have wanted. I'm not a mind reader."

Bogart signaled a waiter and ordered a gin martini. Hellman added, "And menus and bread and butter. How I miss Sardi's. The service is impeccable."

Bogie wondered why Mayo was dressed like a bridesmaid, but said nothing. "How'd you make out with the countess?"

"It was very very interesting. She's a rather large woman who favors rather large jewelry and worth plenty."

"They could be paste," said Hellman.

"They could be, but they aren't. I know the real thing when I see it. I once had a boyfriend who worked at Tiffany's. He taught me plenty until they sent him up the river for stealing some diamond rings. Anyway, the contessa has a playmate. One hell of a good looker named Marcelo Amati. And there's a pretty secretary, Violetta Cenci. And almost from the minute I got there, the countess began carrying on about the cornucopia."

Bogart interrupted. "Dash?" Hammett turned to him. "You ever hear a story about a lost cornucopia, a horn of plenty stuffed with a fortune in jewels? I thought maybe you did because it's so much like *The Maltese Falcon*."

"The *Falcon* is an absolute fabrication, so help me God. What about this cornucopia?"

"It belonged to the countess's father, Baron di Marcopolo, a descendant of the original Marco Polo."

"Oh, go away," said Hellman as the waiter arrived with a tray that held Bogart's martini, a basket of bread, and a dish of butter. A second waiter accompanied him and distributed the menus. Hellman began reading hers immediately.

Hammett said to her, "You're being rude, Lily."

"No, I'm not," she contradicted, "I'm being hungry. I've had no lunch."

"Bogie is telling us a story."

"Well, you listen and I'll read."

Bogart had always wondered what had attracted Hammett to Hellman. She was homely and disagreeable. A brilliant mind but so what? The story was bruited about that he edited her plays for her yet had never written one of his own. Bogart expressed no opinion of his own about the woman. He liked Hammett and wanted to continue their friendship. He knew Mayo wasn't crazy about her but then, Mayo was crazy about very few people of either sex. Hellman looked up from the menu.

"It's gotten awful quiet around here," she said.

"We're waiting for you to join us," said Hammett in a tone of voice that could easily be taken as a threat. She flashed him a look and Bogart waited to see if she would challenge Hammett. She put the menu down and lit a cigarette. There would be no challenge.

Bogart continued. "Mayo spent some time with the countess this afternoon."

"With Hazel Dickson, who's sitting in a booth over there with Herb Villon and trying to attract our attention," said Mayo.

Hellman said, "Miss Dickson's hands are rather frantic. Why doesn't she throw bread?"

Bogart and Mayo waved back at Hazel who was telling Villon, "Maybe we can have a nightcap with them later."

Villon didn't like Lillian Hellman. He wished hers was the dismembered body that he and Jim Mallory were trying to piece together.

Hammett asked, "What about the countess?"

"Tell us, Slugger. Let's hear it all."

It wasn't often that Mayo Methot was given the opportunity to glow in a spotlight and she took every advantage of

44

the chance. She had their undivided attention, even Hellman's. She left nothing out, even the hint of suspicion that her father might have helped the baron along the trail to his final reward in order to appropriate the cornucopia for himself.

"You ever notice one around the house, Slugger?" asked Bogart.

"I was long gone and in New York. As a matter of fact, I was long gone and right here in Hollywood." She then launched into the George Spelvin incident which delighted Bogart and the others. All agreed there was the probability that la Contessa's George Spelvin was Jack Methot leading her astray.

"Why bother leading her astray at all?" asked Hellman with her usual probing mind.

"Simple," said Hammett. "She knew the thing existed and so where had it disappeared to? Thanks to Spelvin it's disappeared into thin air and we know how thin thin air can be. There never was a letter, there was only the baron entrusting the thing into the care of his good and trusted friend Captain Methot who may not have been very good and probably shouldn't have been trusted with anything. I hope I haven't hurt your feelings, Mayo."

"Not at all. I liked my father. I had no reason to dislike him. He was rarely in residence. I think my mother suspected he was a bit of a scoundrel, though she always spoke well of him. Mother was and still is a newspaperwoman and the profession meant more to her than he or I did."

Hammett smiled and said, "The victim of another miserable childhood."

"Who said I had a miserable childhood?" as Bogart signalled for a fresh round of drinks.

Bogart told them Gladys George had known the baron, who was famed as a bedroom swordsman, in London a couple of decades earlier.

"That's heartening," said Hellman. "So where is all this getting us?"

"Into a very interesting puzzle involving a cornucopia,"

said Hammett. He added as an afterthought, "Say Bogie, this isn't a press agent's nightmare to spark interest in the *Falcon?*"

"No way. Scout's honor."

"Scouts have no honor," growled Hellman. "It's all a myth perpetuated by den mothers. When I was a kid, a Boy Scout tried to rape me."

"Did you help?" asked Hammett.

"Now that's not funny," raged Hellman, "and I'm going to order my dinner. Waiter!" she shouted, attracting the attention of everybody on her side of the room except a waiter.

Hammett said to Bogart, "Too bad we don't have a bullhorn." He caught a waiter's eye. The waiter hurried to the table with pad and pencil at the ready and took their orders. They all wanted steak, fries, and salad, and the waiter, a recent arrival from war-torn Paris, felt they were barbarians. Had no one in Hollywood a sophisticated palate?

The fresh round of drinks was served as Hammett stroked his chin and asked, "Do you think the cornucopia exists?"

Bogart shrugged. "God knows, antique shops are up to their belly buttons in them. I've seen some at the Old Curiosity Shop."

Hellman squinted at him. "The Old Curiosity Shop? You mean as in Charles Dickens's *The Old Curiosity Shop?*"

Bogart laughed. "It's out in Venice. Slugger and I check it out every so often. Especially when she gets this yen to get to the pier for a ride on the carousel."

Hellman stared at Mayo and said, "He's kidding, right?"

"Not at all," said Mayo, chewing on her martini's lemon peel, "I adore carousels. It's a late in life fetish. I never saw one as a child."

"Amazing," murmured Hellman and sipped her drink.

Hammett's words prodded Bogart. "Well, Bogie, do you think the cornucopia's a phantom? Like the baron's letter?"

"I'm a sucker for stories like this. I really am. Yes, I do believe there's a cornucopia because of la Contessa."

"Meaning?" asked Hammett.

"That broad hasn't traveled halfway around the world in pursuit of some ephemera."

Hellman said, "She traveled halfway around the world to seek refuge."

Bogart countered, "She could have settled into Switzerland. It's neutral and just across the border from Italy."

"It is also a very dull country," said Hellman. "All it's got is cheese, chocolate, and cuckoo clocks. And consider the boyfriend. I'm sure he's one of those gigolo types that gets bored easily."

Mayo said with a wicked glance at Bogart, "He's an outrageous flirt."

Bogart grinned. "Oh yeah? How'd you make out?"

Mayo said coldly, "I wasn't looking to make out."

Bogart shook his head from side to side. "Can you beat this broad?"

"I hear you do," said Hellman sweetly followed by "Ow!" as Hammett kicked her under the table.

Bogart rode past her ill-natured statement while Mayo stared across the room at Hazel Dickson and Herb Villon who were absorbed in conversation the way she and Bogart rarely were. Bogart said, "I give her every opportunity to cheat on me but she remains ever faithful."

Hellman was about to say, "Maybe she gets no offers" but thought better of it, reminding herself she was damned lucky there was Dashiell Hammett in her life.

Hammett steered the conversation back to the cornucopia. "I think it exists. And I think the countess might have been behind the raid at Mrs. Methot's apartment."

"That's what I thought after I left her suite," said Mayo.

"Over a dry gin martini in the bar downstairs," said Bogart, grinning again.

"Well, actually, beloved, I did order one but Hazel Dickson drank it. She joined me in the bar and I decided I needed a clear head when I tried on shoes at Magnin's." The grin disappeared from Bogart's face. Mayo said to Hellman, "I never seem to have enough shoes. Are you as crazy about shoes as I am?"

"I am crazy about money and Clark Gable in no particular order," replied Hellman.

"Gable has false teeth," said Mayo.

"So did George Washington," said Hellman.

"Ladies, please," said Hammett, "our salads have arrived and the trip from the kitchen seems to have exhausted them."

"Well, I'm putting mine out of its misery," said Hellman as she doomed a piece of tomato to her yawning mouth.

Hammett got back on track. "If the countess and her gang were in Portland this morning, they made good time getting here."

"They had plenty of time," explained Mayo. "My mother was lured out of the apartment for a seven-thirty breakfast with a man who claimed to be Salvador Dali."

"For crying out loud! What the hell would Salvador Dali be doing in Portland, Oregon?" asked Hellman.

Mayo replied haughtily. "Pablo Picasso was once in Portland and my mother interviewed him. He was there for an exhibition of his work at the art museum. And it so happens a Dali exhibit opened this week so Mother had every reason to believe it was the actual artist. Anyway, it wasn't, probably Marcelo Amati imitating him."

"Makes sense," said Bogart, "good thinking, Slugger. Am I the only one who thinks this salad dressing is rancid?"

"Mine's fine," said Hellman.

"Yours is all gone," said Hammett.

"Well, I'm hungry, for crying out loud!"

Mayo resumed her timetable. "There's the Portland express to L.A. with just a brief stop in Frisco. It gets in at one-thirty. It's the one I take after I visit my mother. They're at the hotel within half an hour to forty-five minutes depending on downtown traffic and then Hazel contacts them, having been tipped by one of her many spies that they're in residence, and then I'm brought in to meet them because if

Mother hasn't got that nonexistent letter then it stands to reason the daughter might have."

"Sure," said Bogart, "there's that carton with his papers in the basement." He said to Hammett, "We've been through them. Nothing." He pushed his salad aside, and lit a cigarette.

Hammett asked, "What about this Old Curiosity Shop?"

"It's run by this eccentric and his daughter."

"He's not eccentric, he's nuts," said Mayo, passing sentence with alacrity.

"I like old Edgar, he's got a great sense of humor. It's his daughter Nell I wouldn't turn my back on. Edgar and Nell Dickens."

"Oh come on!" said Hellman. "Dickens! Old Curiosity Shop! Little Nell!"

"She's not so little." He winked at Hammett. "She's how do we say in the old country, very zoftig."

"Which old country is that?" asked Hellman.

Bogart ignored the statement. "There's also a clerk named Sidney Heep."

"Ha!" said Hammett as a busboy cleared the salad plates and a waiter served the steak and french fries.

"The steaks look great," said Mayo.

"I think mine just moved," said Hellman.

"Lily," asked Hammett, "why don't you ever enjoy yourself?"

"Who says I'm not enjoying myself," fork and knife poised for a fatal attack.

"Lily," said Bogart, "if it moved, kill it."

"Sidney Heep!" exclaimed Hammett as he trimmed his steak of its fat. "Except in *David Copperfield* it's Uriah Heep. The shop is a setup, right?"

"Of course," said Bogart as he chewed with contentment. "It's Hollywood. It's the pier at Venice. It's all for the tourists."

"We go there and we're not tourists," said Mayo defensively.

"I don't care who it's for," said Bogart, "I like the place. It's great for Christmas presents."

"And the prices are reasonable," added Mayo, "and for Bogie, therein lies its charm."

"You insinuating I'm a cheapskate?" He said this with rare warmth. Hellman looked at him and then at Mayo. The Battling Bogarts? It's got to be a sham. He loves her, for crying out loud, and she'd kill for him. I think they beat up on each other because it's their perverted way of expressing love. She looked at Hammett. If he ever laid a finger on her other than erotically she'd cut off his essentials.

"What are you thinking, Lily," asked Hammett.

"Better you shouldn't know."

"You know, the funny thing about Dickens and his daughter is there's absolutely no resemblance."

"Come to think of it, you're right," agreed Mayo.

Bogart continued, "Maybe Edgar's a stepfather, or maybe she's adopted."

"Or maybe she's not a daughter," suggested Hellman.

Hammett said, "There you go, Lily. Always looking for the seamy side of things."

"They're the most fun and the most interesting. What makes my *Little Foxes* so fascinating to audiences, thank God. Most of my characters are rats."

Bogart couldn't resist. "Didn't I read somewhere they were based on your own family?"

"That's right. They were. Thought you'd upset me, Bogie?"

"No, I was just looking for confirmation. That's your best play, Lily."

"How nice of you, Bogie, how very nice."

"And that's all the nice you're going to get out of me tonight. You know, Mayo. We might take a drive out to Venice Beach tomorrow. See what's with the Dickens and cornucopias. There's no rehearsal tomorrow, Mary's doing a radio show and that ties her up all day. Dash? Lily? You want to join us?"

"Do I have to ride the carousel?" asked Hellman.

Bogart said, "Hazel Dickson's been abandoned. Her boyfriend's deserted her."

"No, he hasn't," said Mayo. "A waiter called him to the phone."

"Terrific guy, Herb Villon. And a damned good detective," said Bogart.

"We've met him," said Hellman. "Sam Spade he isn't."

"Sam Spade's fiction," said Bogart. "Herb's for real. He's headed this way. I don't like the look on his face. Something's wrong."

Hazel left her table and hurried after Villon. She could sense something was up that could prove profitable for her.

Villon said to Bogart and Mayo, "Sorry to break up the party, folks, but I just spoke to my partner, Jim Mallory. Bogie, Mayo, your house was broken into. Your neighbor out walking his dog saw the front door open. He investigated. The place has been ransacked."

"Our housekeeper! Hannah! What about Hannah!"

"Now take it easy, Slugger," said Bogart. He asked Villon, "She's okay, isn't she?"

Villon would always remember this moment and the pain it caused the Bogarts. "She's been murdered. A knife in her chest."

"Oh my God!" cried Mayo, "Oh my God!"

And at the next table somebody said, "The Battling Bogarts are at it again!"

FIVE

Hannah Darrow lay on her back on the foyer floor, the subject of the police photographer's camera. She had never received this much attention in life. The Bogarts came into the house through the back door. Turning into their usually quiet street, Bogart saw in addition to patrol cars a swarm of reporters and photographers and exploded with a series of expletives. He maneuvered the car into an alley that led to the rear of his house, followed by Hammett and Hellman in Hammett's unprepossessing roadster. Villon with Hazel at his side drove right up to the front of the house and immediately fielded a barrage of questions from the newsmen. "Men and ladies, you know as much as I do. I just got here. Let me through, damn it!" He elbowed his way through the mass of reporters while Hazel paused to tell a sob sister she knew, "Love your hat."

Inside the house, Mayo stared down at Hannah with a pained and sorrowful expression. Bogart gently patted Mayo's shoulder and she heaved a dry sob. Hellman stared at the sorrowful tableau in the foyer and then switched her attention to the mess in the living room. The overturned chairs, the open drawers with contents spilled out on the floor, the broken wall mirror—which Lillian didn't know was not the fault of the ransacker—a sideboard from which had spilled a variety of dinner linens. Hellman said to Hammett, "Mayo's one hell of a housekeeper."

"Come off it, Lily. Save the wisecracks for the gang back at the Garden of Allah," meaning the small hotel on Sunset Boulevard that mostly housed refugees from New York and had once been the elegant residence of silent star Alla Nazimova. Bogart joined Hammett.

"What an effing mess. Jack Warner ain't gonna like the

attendant publicity. I wonder if the countess and her help have solid alibis. Mayo! Don't go upstairs alone! There might be somebody up there."

"Just me," said Jim Mallory as he appeared on the top landing. "Come on up, Mrs. Bogart, and check if anything's missing."

"That's just what I intend to do." She hurried up the stairs followed by Hazel Dickson.

Hellman said in an aside to Hammett, "I don't suppose she had much in the way of expensive jewelry."

"Why not?"

"Well, that story of the boyfriend who worked at Tiffany's. It sounded a bit wistful to me. I don't see Bogie as being a man who showers a beloved with expensive gems."

"I see Bogart as a man who's practical enough to keep from drowning in a sea of unnecessary debts." He reintroduced himself to Herb Villon, having met him several weeks earlier when there were several break-ins at the Garden of Allah, but Villon most assuredly remembered him. Bogart was at the desk checking for damage. It was one of the few good antiques in the room and he envisioned a good price for it if he should ever have the misfortune to liquidate, something to contemplate if Mayo continued her spending sprees. He saw a man kneeling and examining Hannah Darrow. Obviously a medical examiner. Bogart turned his face away as the examiner removed the knife from Hannah's chest. The knife was placed in a plastic bag and as far as Bogart and his weak stomach were concerned would forever remain in exile. Bogart joined Hammett and Villon and asked Villon, "You know about the countess?"

"From Hazel."

"Then you know everything."

"When Jim Mallory paged me at the restaurant I had him ring the Ambassador at once. The secretary answered the phone. Then the boyfriend got on the phone and last but not least, the kid herself, la Contessa. All present and accounted for."

"How convenient," said Bogart while Hammett wished

Lillian would get off her knees and stop nosing about in the Bogarts' dinner linens. God forbid there should be no damask napkins. Apparently there was. Hellman was holding one up to the light with a look of surprise on her face, and then rubbing the napkin with her fingers to test the quality of the material. From the look on her face, it was a damned good and expensive cut of damask. Poor Lily. Foiled at last.

Mayo came marching down the stairs with Hazel in tow. "Nothing's missing. Everything's there, including my good Cartier earrings."

Damn fool, thought Hellman, she could have lied through her teeth and collected some insurance.

Mayo said to Bogart, "I think we'd better check into a hotel tonight. Upstairs it's a nightmare."

Bogart suggested roguishly, "I'm sure we could get into the Ambassador."

"Why not our place?" asked Hammett.

"Allah be praised," said Hellman, joining them and lighting a cigarette. "Poor Mayo. This is just awful. It'll be on every front page across the world in the morning."

"Oh, no, it won't!" The one and only, the inimitable Jack Warner had entered unseen by his star, the star's wife, and their friends. He stepped over the corpse to enter from the foyer and the coroner gave him a sharp and unpleasant look. Two of Warner's high powered publicity men accompanied the mogul and also hopscotched over the body. Warner said to Hazel, "Thanks for phoning me, Hazel. It's worth five exclusives."

"Ten," countered Hazel. Warner ignored her.

"Come off it, Jack," said Bogart, "what makes you think you can keep this out of the papers? Murder in Humphrey Bogart's house."

"If it was Humphrey Bogart who was murdered, I'd have a lot of trouble," said Warner, "in fact, I'd cause a lot of trouble, wouldn't I boys," this addressed to his press reps, who had brought their cameras and were photographing everything in sight including keyholes. "But when the corpse is only a housekeeper . . ."

"What an epitaph," murmured Hellman, who made a mental note never to work for Jack Warner no matter how much money he offered, even if he threw in the services of Errol Flynn.

Mayo had built up a full head of steam. "Only a housekeeper! She was a person! A human being! She was our friend!"

"No offense meant," said Warner amiably and then he exploded. "I've got hundreds of thousands of dollars invested in Humphrey Bogart! He starts a major motion picture in a couple of weeks and there's three more lined up for him!"

"What three more?" asked Bogart.

"They're a surprise," swiftied Warner.

"Sure. Like a big increase in my take home."

Warner asked winsomely, "Are you referring to salami sandwiches?"

"No, I'm referring to cheese."

Warner glared at him and then asked, "Who's in charge of the investigation?"

"You've got to be kidding," said Herb Villon. "I'm not window dressing."

"Oh, of course! Herb!" He crossed to Villon and put an arm around his shoulder. He said to the room, "L.A.'s greatest detective! Say, Herb! Why don't you collaborate with Hazel on your autobiography? I'll buy it for Bogie."

Bogie said, "He'll pay you in salami sandwiches."

"I don't like salami," said Herb Villon, and refrained from adding, and I also don't like Jack Warner and if he doesn't get his arm from around my shoulder I just might be tempted to break it.

"Say, Jack," said Bogart, a quixotic tone to his voice, "how do you plan to keep this quiet? Cross everybody's palm with silver, and I mean cash, not the Lone Ranger's horse."

"Just leave it to me and my boys!" To an amused Hammett he sounded like W. C. Fields describing how he cut his way "through a solid wall of Indian flesh." Hammett, like everyone with Hollywood connections, knew Jack Warner considered himself sophisticated and urbane and possessed of a distinct and unusual wit. But like most of his peers, he was crass, vulgar, and about as funny as an infant's funeral.

"Not so fast, Jack. You may be losing out on yards of free publicity for *The Maltese Falcon.*"

Warner raged, "This kind of publicity we don't need and I won't have."

"Supposing I tell you the subplot of this murder case is practically synonymous with Dash's story."

"How so?"

Bogart told him of the pursuit of the mysterious cornucopia.

"That's plagiarism!" shouted Warner.

"It's cold facts," said Bogart. "That's why our place was destroyed and poor Hannah murdered, and the least you can do is send lots of lilies to Hannah's funeral."

"She liked gladiolas," said Mayo.

"You!" cried Warner. "You and your father!"

"Go no further with my father," warned Mayo. "And my mother and I are just innocent victims."

Warner's publicity men took him to one side for a conference.

Bogart said to Villon, "If Warner ever bought the rights to your life story, the son of a bitch would assign it to Jimmy Cagney. Don't you write it!"

Warner emerged from the brief huddle with his toadies. "Maybe this is a blessing in disguise. As my blessed mother used to say, 'Every cloud has a silver lining.' "

"If it was your mother, I'm sure she said velvet," said Bogart.

"I'm going to hire Adela Rogers St. John to write our news releases!"

"That figures," said Bogart. Miss St. John was Hollywood's most respected, most prolific dispenser of news and gossip. Even the major columnists deferred to her. Her father had been the notorious, hard drinking criminal lawyer Earl St. John. Adela fashioned a story about herself and her father into *A Free Soul,* starring Norma Shearer and Lionel

Barrymore and a young Clark Gable whose impact as a sadistic gangster made him an "overnight" success after seven years of struggles.

"Adela has class and respect. She'll make sure this isn't turned into a three-ring circus." Hannah Darrow's body was being removed from the premises, covered with a sheet and strapped to a stretcher.

"Say Jack," said Bogart impishly, "why don't you consider the life of Hannah Darrow?"

"Hannah Darrow? Any relation to Clarence Darrow?"

"That might be arranged." Hammett's expression openly admired Bogart and his total lack of respect for his employer. Lillian Hellman was busy hunting for the Bogart's obviously secret stash of liquor which apparently hadn't interested the intruder.

"Who is Hannah Darrow?" asked Warner.

Bogart pointed to the stretcher being carried out of the house. "There goes Hannah Darrow. Our housekeeper. A hell of a part for Marjorie Rambeau."

"Bogie," said Warner with a sudden attack of piety, "that's sacrilegious."

"How would you know? You never met her."

"Let's get out of here!" Warner barked at his press reps. "And you," pointing a finger at Bogart," tomorrow you rehearse."

"Tomorrow I don't rehearse. Huston cancelled it. Tomorrow I take my wife for a ride on a carousel. Want to join us? Maybe you'll catch the brass ring." Warner advised him to do something both unprintable and physically impossible and then left the house with his flunkies in his wake. Outside, he paused to pose for the photographers and let himself be questioned by the reporters. Bogart appeared in the doorway. "Hey, Jack!" he yelled, "tomorrow send over a crew to straighten out my place! If Mayo and I have to do it, I'll be too tired to rehearse the day after tomorrow!" He shut the door while Warner's face reddened and he clenched his fists.

In the house, Bogart returned to the living room. The indestructible Lillian Hellman had found a bottle of scotch and glasses in a kitchen cabinet and had poured for herself and Hammett. Mayo was in the kitchen fixing a pitcher of gin martinis with Jim Mallory and Hazel Dickson aiding and abetting. A crew of plainclothes officers and forensics experts were dusting down the room and would spend the better part of the night and possibly the next day working on the rest of the house.

Bogart said to Villon, "I don't suppose the countess and her supporting players did the actual ransacking. It's a long schlepp from the Ambassador to here and then back again. I don't think they could have managed it."

"It's an even longer schlepp from Venice Beach," said Villon.

"What do you mean?"

"The countess said they were out visiting the Old Curiosity Shop."

"Well, what do you know about that!" He stopped to think. "I wonder if old man Dickens and Nell know the cornucopia story."

"By tomorrow or the day after, the whole world's going to know it. Miss St. John packs a mean typewriter. Say, Hazel, are you going to let her scoop you?"

Hazel smiled and fluttered her eyelashes. "You may not have noticed, but I have been on the phone with Louella and Hedda and Jimmy and Sidney and Harrison and my sister Clara to tell her I won't be home tonight."

"Why? Where you shacking up?"

She glared at him. He said, "Oh," and returned his attention to Bogart. He took him by the arm and away from the others as Mayo returned with a pitcher of martinis and Jim holding a tray of glasses. Mayo said to Hazel, "Where'd you disappear to?"

"I had some phone calls to make."

Mayo shouted, "Bogie! Martinis!"

"In a minute," he shouted back.

"Why are you two shouting?" asked Lillian Hellman as she added more scotch to her glass.

"It goes with the territory," said Mayo.

Villon said to Bogart, "It's my theory the countess isn't the only one hunting for the whatchamacallit."

"I'm glad you said it. I've been thinking the same thing but couldn't figure out who it might be."

"It could be any number of people," said Villon. "Collectors, dealers, all very unscrupulous people. Like autograph hounds. You know what they're like."

"Vultures with fountain pens and autograph albums. But to commit murder!"

Villon's hands were outstretched with palms open and facing upward. "So what? Maybe the killer thought the house was empty. She didn't live in, did she?"

"No. She has an apartment in West Hollywood. Lives with an unmarried daughter. Christ. She's got to be notified. Mayo! Where's Hannah's home number? Call her daughter before she reads it in the papers. She's probably worried Hannah's not home by now." Mayo went to the desk where she kept their personal phone book. It was an assignment she didn't relish.

Bogart resumed with Villon. "Sometimes Hannah stayed late to do some chores she couldn't do if we were at home. That's what she probably did tonight, poor soul, working in the kitchen, the rest of the house dark. She probably heard the bastard breaking in . . ."

"Skeleton key," corrected Villon. "She probably heard the racket and ransackers make one hell of a racket. It's my guess she came into this room, made a racket of her own and then started for the front door, got caught in the foyer and you know the rest."

"I know the rest. I wish I didn't, but I know the rest."

They heard Mayo talking on the phone. "Call your aunt, honey. Tell her to come stay with you. I'm so sorry, darling." She listened. "They've taken her to the morgue." She listened. She put her hand over the mouthpiece and said to Bogart. "This is sheer agony." She removed her hand from the mouthpiece. "What, darling? Her purse?"

Jim Mallory said, "There's a handbag on the counter next to the refrigerator."

Mayo said into the phone, "It's in the kitchen. It's safe." She listened. "We won't be here in the morning. We're staying at a hotel tonight. Wait a minute." She asked Bogie if they were staying at the Garden of Allah or the Ambassador.

"Allah," shouted Hellman, "the apartment next to us is vacant. And why am I shouting?"

Mayo instructed the daughter to come to the Garden of Allah for her mother's handbag as it was conveniently located in West Hollywood near her apartment. When she hung up, she said to anyone who might hear her, "That was so awful. That poor woman. She was devoted to Hannah."

Bogart said to Villon, "Slugger and I are going out to Venice tomorrow, I think with Hammett and Hellman. Care to join us?"

"Why, Mr. Bogart," said Villon cozily, "I don't mind if I do."

SIX

While the melodrama was being played in the Bogart house, la Contessa di Marcopolo, wearing a housecoat decorated with peacock feathers, stormed back and forth in the living room of her suite shouting epithets in Italian, French, English, and a few in Lithuanian which she had picked up during a brief affair with an ambassador from that country. "The housekeeper should not have been killed!" Neither Marcelo nor Violetta agreed or disagreed. They were playing Chinese checkers. "Clever burglars never commit murder. Now this catastrophe at the Bogarts will be headlines! Headlines! Do you hear me? Headlines!"

"I'm sure they hear you in Pasadena," said Marcelo.

"Don't mock me!"

"Don't shout. We're just a few feet away from you. My nerves are frayed. I need champagne." He reached out to a bottle in a metal bucket and poured some bubbly into the glass at his elbow. He sipped and then studied the label. "Presumptuous. But it will serve until champagnes can come flowing again from Europe."

The contessa sank onto the couch, which groaned for mercy. "A treasure hunt! Hollywood loves a treasure hunt! Ha!"

"Hysteria dulls the mind, cara."

"So now you're a philosopher!"

"You're not thinking clearly. If we can't locate the cornucopia, let someone else locate it for us. And then we step in and appropriate it."

"I can't claim it's mine without the letter!"

"There is no letter. It does not exist. My instinct tells me it is a fabrication of Captain Methot's. If there is a cornucopia, it will surface. Remember what this Dickens person told us.

This city crawls with dealers and collectors. This is a country in which everything is collected and treasured. Baseball cards! Can you believe that? Baseball cards! Movie star autographs! Some said to be worth hundreds of dollars! Comic books! They collect everything!"

"Including wives," said Violetta, a student of fan magazines.

Marcelo asked la Contessa, "Have you ever seen a baseball game?"

"As a matter of fact, on several occasions." She was holding a cigarette. "Violetta!" The secretary crossed the room, lit the cigarette and then returned to the Chinese checkers. La Contessa was still ruminating about baseball. She said, "Loathe the game." A small smile. "*Adore* the players." Then her face darkened. "Do you suppose this Dickson person deliberately sent us on a wild goose chase to Venice?"

Marcelo said, "I think not. I think she sincerely was trying to be of service."

"That was certainly a strange lot," said Violetta.

La Contessa said thoughtfully, "There was something familiar about the proprietor, Mr. Dickens. I don't think he is descended from the Dickens family as he so flagrantly claims. I think I've seen him before."

"Possibly in England when you lived there as a young girl," said Violetta.

"We did not rub shoulders with literary people. The only people welcome in our mansion were the Woolfs, Virginia and Leonard. They bored me." She was deep in thought for a moment. "Dickens's look is very Mediterranean," she sighed. "It will come to me. It always does." A stricken wail escaped her mouth.

"Now what?" asked Marcelo.

"Nobody murders a housekeeper! You fire a housekeeper! But murder one! Oh God, what is the world coming to?"

As Villon intimated he'd be joining the excursion to Venice, Bogart snapped his fingers. "The basement! That's where we've got the captain's papers." He hurried into the kitchen where there was the door leading to the basement. Hammett, Villon, Hazel, and Jim Mallory were close on his heels. Mayo remained in the living room with her martini and Lillian Hellman.

Hellman asked in a monotone, "Aren't you joining them in the basement?"

"I've seen the basement."

Hellman studied the sad face and the way she hungered for the martini and then asked, "Why don't you get out of it?"

"Out of what?"

"Your marriage."

"It's the only marriage I've got."

"You can tell me it's none of my business, but it won't help. Why don't you go back to Broadway?"

"Nobody's asked me."

"Go back and make them know you're back, I saw you in *Torch Song*. You're a good actress."

"Why Miss Lillian Hellman, there does exist a kind word in your vocabulary."

Hellman sat up. "I simply don't understand my reputation for being a flaming bitch on wheels!"

"Because you are, dear. You are."

In the basement, Jim Mallory looked with interest at the wall decorations. Posters of all of Bogart's films to date, including the ones in which he had minimal billing. Mallory couldn't figure out what Gary Cooper's *Mr. Deeds Goes to Town* was doing there and asked Hazel. She told him Mayo had a small role in it, but Mallory couldn't place it.

There was a bar with wicker stools and a Ping-Pong table and over the bar was a large photograph of the Bogart's boat, *Slugger*, with the Bogarts at the rail. They both wore sailor suits and were laughing and waving and looked genuinely happy unless they were even better actors then he knew them to be. Behind him Hazel Dickson said, "Four short years can make a century of a difference."

There was a storage space to the right of the bar. The door was open and Bogart stood in the center of the room with his hands on his hips. "Doesn't look as though the place has been disturbed." He knelt beside the large carton that contained Jack Methot's papers. The strong cord with which the carton was bound was undisturbed. There was no sign of an attempt to cut it. Hammett was at a shelf examining scripts of Bogart's earlier films. "For crying out loud, did you really do something called *The Return of Dr X?*"

"Yeah. I was a ghoul back from the dead. It died." He smiled. "I did a Western with Cagney that year. *The Oklahoma Kid.* Can you imagine me on horseback popping a six-shooter? Scared hell out of the horse. Scared hell out of Cagney, too." He surveyed the rest of the room. "Nothing's been touched here."

Hammett stared at his fingertips. "Nothing's been dusted here either."

"Don't be a fussbudget. We rarely come down here." He exhaled. "I don't know why, but this space always gives me the creeps. I don't like this house." He led Hammett back to Villon and the other two. Villon was behind the bar while Mallory and Hazel were still occupied with the photograph of the *Slugger.* "Never did like this house. Never knew what attracted Mayo to it. It's got no personality."

Hazel turned on hearing Bogart's voice, "You both look so happy and content here, Bogie."

"That's history. What have you found, Herb?"

The detective held up a faded St. Valentine's Day card. "This relic."

Bogart took it and read it. "I remember this. I sent it to Slugger the year we were married. When I was still sentimental." He placed it on top of the bar. "Let's get out of here. I wonder if the press creeps are still hanging around outside."

Upstairs in the living room, Mayo was saying to Hellman, "Might there be something for me in your new play?"

"What you should be asking is, is there a new play? I've just finished one. Something about a liberal on the run from the Nazis."

"Sounds grim."

"These are grim times." Bogart and the others entered

from the kitchen. "Find anything of interest?"

Hammett said, "A lot of well organized dust."

Bogart said, "Let's get out of here. I'm parked behind the house. If the creeps are out front, Herb, keep them amused until Mayo and I make our escape. Dash, Lily, see you at the Allah. Come on, Slugger."

"Wait a minute! I need some things. Don't you want your pajamas? Your shaving things?

"Be a sport, kid. Pack them for me." She looked on the verge of saying something nasty, but then thought better of it and hurried up the stairs. He asked Villon, "Your forensic guys find anything interesting?"

Villon held up a cellophane bag in which nothing appeared visible. "A long, blonde woman's hair. Single strand. Not visible to the naked eye."

"Can't be Mae West's. She does another kind of ransacking. Besides, she's never been to the house."

Villon said, "It doesn't mean it belongs to the ransacker. Mayo's hair is blonde."

"Occasionally."

Hellman said as she applied a lipstick to her petulant mouth, "Bogart, you're all heart."

Hammett was at a window that looked out at the front of the house. Two fingers separated two slats of the venetian blind. "The dogs are still baying around a dead carcass."

"That's pretty good, Dash," said Hellman, "why don't you use it?"

"I have."

Mayo came hurrying down the stairs carrying an overnight bag.

"That was pretty quick, Slugger," said Bogart.

"I needed to get out of there fast. It was giving me the creeps. I don't like this house. I never did like this house."

"Then why'd you urge me to buy it!" shouted Bogart.

"Because it was a bargain!"

"There's no such thing as a bargain!" countered Bogart.

"Oh God, let me out of here!" cried Hellman and headed for the front door. Bogart shoved his hands into his jacket pockets and hurried to the kitchen and the back door while Mayo exchanged a hasty good-bye with Hazel and the detectives.

Hellman opened the front door and stared down at the reporters and photographers. Hands on hips, she asked, "I suppose you're wondering why we asked you all here?" Hammett came out behind her and then Villon, Hazel, and Mallory. The detectives were under siege from a barrage of questions. Any leads? Any clues? Any suspects? Anything stolen? Where're the Bogarts?

Lillian Hellman preceded Hammett to his roadster slowly and with difficulty. Flashbulbs blinded her eyes and several members of the press tried to block their escape. She shouted, "I don't know anything! I'm just a friend of the Bogarts."

"Say where the hell *are* the Bogarts?" cried a reporter.

Hammett said, "I think those are their taillights disappearing in the distance." Villon growled orders to some of his men assigned to guard the exterior of the house to make sure none of the press would enter the house. While some people were ransackers, others were scavengers and the contents of the interior were sufficiently damaged that there was no need to add insult to injury. He hoped Mayo had remembered to pack her jewelry in the overnight bag.

Hammett and Hellman finally made it to the roadster. "Christ," said Hellman, "I hope they don't follow us."

"If they do, I can lose them," he reassured her. "Jackals and hyenas. I've seen nothing like them before. Not even in New York."

"When we get to the Allah, drive straight into the bar." Hellman looked out the rear window as they drove off. "Who said Hollywood goes to sleep early?"

Hammett turned on the radio and found a news program. The newscaster didn't tell them anything they didn't already know. Hellman asked, "Can't you find something cheerful? Like the invasion of Paris?"

Bogart finally parked the car in the Garden of Allah lot. Across Sunset Boulevard from the Allah was director Preston Sturges's Players Club but the Bogarts were in no mood for it. They made their way into the hotel and to the front desk. Lillian Hellman had thoughtfully phoned ahead and the suite next to hers and Hammett's was awaiting them. The lobby was quiet, unusually so at 11 P.M. Hollywood might go to bed early but the Garden of Allah didn't. Bogart wasn't ready for either the arms of Morpheus or his wife. After he signed them in and a bellboy captured the overnight bag, Bogie said, "You go ahead, Slugger, I'm going to case the bar."

"And case a case?"

"You can always join me there once you've used the john. Here, take my hat." She snatched it and followed the bellboy down the hall. Bogart hoped she had some silver with which to either tip the bellboy or betray him.

The bar wasn't as lively as Bogart expected to find it, but there was a pleasant array of familiar and friendly faces. The first person he encountered was Sidney Greenstreet seated at the bar on a stool that seemed inadequate to his size. Greenstreet was with comedian Charles Butterworth who spotted Bogart first. "Ah! Here's Bogie! Why'd you do it?"

Bogie cracked a grin for this droll and loveable little man as Greenstreet beckoned to him. "Come closer. I want to talk to you."

"Be gentle, Sidney. I'm feeling a bit delicate. It's been quite a night."

"This murder at your house. Is it a setup?"

"You don't use a genuine corpse in a setup, Sidney." He ordered a dry gin martini. "And no garbage, bartender. It leaves more room for gin." The bartender understood. Mr. Bogart wanted a glass of iced gin and may the Lord have mercy on his head tomorrow morning.

"How bizarre," said Greenstreet, "and how tragic. I'm glad we're not working tomorrow, it'll give you the chance to rest and compose yourself."

"You might never see me as composed as I am right now. If you see Dash Hammett and Lily Hellman, Charlie, point them in my direction."

"Point them yourself," said Butterworth, "they're right behind you."

"Bartender," shouted Hellman, "I'll drink anything. It's been a rough night."

"She'll have the same as me," said Bogart. "And Mr. Hammett, too. And keep one in reserve for my wife."

Hellman said, "There's Dotty Parker. She looks very sloppy."

"Not as sloppy as usual at this hour," said Hammett. "We're not sitting up all night with her and the husband."

"Hell no. We've got a rendezvous in Venice tomorrow. The wrong Venice, but nevertheless, Venice. I don't see her less-than-better half. Probably out cruising Hollywood Boulevard. That looks like Bob Benchley with Dotty."

"It looks like Bob Benchley," said Hammett, "because it is Bob Benchley. I'm not in the mood for him."

"Who are you in the mood for?" asked Hellman.

"Marcel Proust."

"You don't speak French."

"Sure I do."

"Baloney! I've never heard you speak French."

"There's never been an occasion for me to speak French."

"Dash Hammett, you're so full of it it's coming out of your ears!"

"Lily!" shouted Dorothy Parker, "Don't you agree with me? Aren't men a load of horseshit?"

"It's going to be one of those nights," said Hammett to Bogart. "Look at Benchley. To quote nobody in particular, probably myself, his eyes are stagnant pools of despair."

"I hear he's not been well."

"He's making pots of money."

"What's that got to do with the state of his health?"

A waiter said to Bogart, "You're wanted on the phone, Mr. Bogart. At the bar."

"Thanks," said Bogart, excused himself and went to the bar. It was Mayo and she was upset. "I'm coming to the room. Tell me the number again."

In the room, Mayo had laid out Bogart's pajamas and a

change of shirt, underwear, and socks. "Bogie, I'm going to Portland."

"How come all of a sudden?"

"I just spoke to Mother. I had this feeling something might be wrong. She's very upset and frightened. I told her I'd come up and stay with her. Anyway, she said she'd feel better if I was out of this town. Hannah's murder and the break-in were on the radio and she's fearful of my life."

"You really want to go?"

"She's my mother."

"I'm your husband."

"You can take care of yourself."

"So can she, for crying out loud."

Mayo was firm. "I'm going to her. She's all the mother I've got."

"And I'm all the husband you've got."

"Please drive me to the house. Or else give me the keys and I'll go alone."

Expletive followed expletive and then Bogart snapped, "Come on!" She followed him out of the room. In the lobby, they met Hellman on her way to the ladies'.

"What's going on?" she asked.

"My wife is going home to Mother." Hellman watched the Bogarts hurry out the door, shook her head from side to side, and then hurried to the ladies' room to avoid embarrassment.

Shortly before midnight, the Bogarts hurried to the platform where the last express to Portland was ready to depart. At the gateway, Bogart said "Here" and pressed what cash he had into her hand. "I'll wire you some more tomorrow."

"You don't have to. I'll get it from my mother."

"Get going or you'll get it from me."

She smiled. They kissed. She picked up the suitcase she had none too carefully packed and hurried down the platform and boarded the train. A conductor shouted "All aboard!" and the engineer blew his whistle. Steam began to cloud the platform and the attendant at the gate recognized Bogart as the actor was lighting a cigarette.

"Mr. Bogart?"

"Yeah?" one eye cocked in the attendant's direction and waiting for the expected request for an autograph.

"In the immortal words of the Bard," said the attendant mellifluously, " 'Parting is such sweet sorrow, until we meet again on the morrow.' "

"Oh yeah? I don't think we'll be in the same vicinity tomorrow. I'll be out in Venice Beach."

The attendant smiled. "I'll be at my mother-in-law's funeral."

"Some guys have all the luck."

Back at the bar in the Garden of Allah, Dorothy Parker announced it was time to go to bed. "Every Cinderella has her midnight."

"Where's Prince Charming?" asked Hellman referring to Parker's husband, Alan Campbell.

"Out somewhere getting himself beat up, I suppose. He's going into the army." She didn't notice the variety of upraised eyebrows. "And I'm sure vice versa." Nobody understood why so womanly a woman as Dorothy Parker chose to marry a homosexual. "He supposes he'll be assigned to the Signal Corps. I hope he is. He's awfully good at giving signals."

Parker along with Hammett and Hellman, Charles Butterworth, Sidney Greenstreet, and Robert Benchley were seated at a round table. It in no way duplicated Parker and Benchley's long departed, infamous Algonquin Round Table back in New York, but there was enough wit and bitchery to stir dormant memories.

"I'm glad Alan's been conscripted," said Mrs. Parker as she signaled for a fresh drink, conveniently forgetting her midnight had paused briefly and then passed on. "I'm real glad the army's taking him. Now I can get to wear my dresses again." This convulsed her and nobody else. Then came the fit of coughing accompanied by soothing noises from Benchley, the one man Dorothy Parker had ever really loved. Hellman stared at the two of them with undisguised disapproval. She didn't believe in unrequited love. It was a bore, just as the Ira Gershwin lyric had claimed back in 1930 in *Girl Crazy*. Hellman went after what she wanted tenaciously, and so she was in full possession of Dashiell Hammett despite his wife and daughter cooling their heels in parts unknown.

Charles Butterworth asked with his usual fey cock of the head, "Has anyone noticed Bogie is missing?"

"Over an hour ago," said Greenstreet. "He was called to the phone and then hurried away."

Hellman said, "Mayo is going home to Mother," she pondered. "Maybe it was something to do with his housekeeper's murder."

"I've had a few housekeepers I'd like to have had murdered," said Mrs. Parker. Then, "When was Bogie's housekeeper murdered?" Hellman told her. "Dash and I saw the body."

Parker said smartly, "The privileged few. How come you get to get invited to places that I never do?"

Hammett recapped the evening for the benefit of those of his companions interested in listening. All were interested. By the time he reached the conclusion, Bogart returned and picked himself up a martini at the bar before joining them.

Hellman asked, "Mayo safely on her way home to Mother?"

"Yeah," said Bogart, "the return of the native. But Venice is still on for tomorrow, at least for me."

Said Hellman, "I wouldn't miss it for the world. I can't wait to explore this Old Curiosity Shop."

"I've been there," said Charles Butterworth, "it's awfully coy."

Mrs. Parker interrupted, "Your poor housekeeper. What an awful way to die."

"Is there a good way to die?" asked Bogart.

"I haven't found it yet," said Mrs. Parker, "and nobody's attempted suicide as often as I have. So some burglar did it."

Hammett said softly, "Burglars never commit murder. In my years as a private dick, I've seen this proven too often to refute." He repeated, "Burglars never commit murder." Little realizing this would be all he would ever have in common with la Contessa di Marcopolo, not that he would ever give a damn. "A burglar might hit you over the head."

"Charming," said Mrs. Parker.

"But that's only if you walked in on him and surprised him."

"And burglars loathe surprises," commented Hellman.

"Burglars are very clever and very ingenious. I'm not discussing the ordinary upstart breakings and entries, small-timers who have neither taste nor finesse, you know, the window smashers, the lock pickers. The professional has his selection of skeleton keys. He knows how to smartly unseal a window. He plans his burglary very carefully. He cases his victim for days before pulling the job. He knows his victim's habits. When he comes and when he goes. I've dealt with a lot of burglars in my time and most of them have my deepest respect."

"Dash, you're a pervert," said Mrs. Parker.

"Mind your tongue, Dottie," said Hellman with a loving look at Hammett who cared less about Parker's comment than the look on his paramour's face.

"What we've got here is a classic case of a hunt for treasure," said Hammett, "and treasure hunters are a very mean-spirited lot. They're obsessed with greediness."

"Well aren't burglars?" asked Greenstreet.

"Hell no," said Hammett. "Burglars are out making a living. They know exactly what to steal. You notice when you read in the papers the police are perplexed the burglars left untouched a stash of diamonds or some emerald earrings. Well if they'd learn to check the marketplace in the demand and supply of diamonds and emeralds, they'd find there's little demand and too much supply and the burglar only takes what he's pretty sure he can fence."

Bogart said, "I read someplace that there are unscrupulous dealers and collectors who hire burglars to pick up some things they're after."

Benchley said wistfully and from out of an alcoholic haze, "Doesn't anyone care to steal Mrs. Benchley?"

Mrs. Parker patted his hand. And returned her attention to Hammett.

"As I said, treasure hunters are a mean-spirited lot obsessed with greediness."

"Like archeologists," insisted Mrs. Parker.

"Well they can hide behind the respectability of historical research," said Hammett. "But archeologists don't kill."

"Not that we know of," said Hellman. "I don't trust any of them."

"They're pretty trustworthy, Lily. Anyway, Bogie. There's more bloodshed ahead."

Bogie had lit a cigarette and was fanning the smoke from his eyes. "You think so?"

"Inevitable."

Parker rejoined, "As death and taxes." She smiled, "Which, as you will all recall, was the title of one of my collections of poetry, now available in a Modern Library edition."

"I'm chilled," said Hellman eerily.

"Maybe somebody walked over your grave," said Bogart.

Hellman embraced herself and said, "Damn rude of them."

SEVEN

At nine in the morning, there weren't many patrons in the Garden of Allah's coffee shop. Those who were indentured to the studios had driven to work and those who were unemployed lay in bed, staring at the ceiling and wondering if the phone would ever ring with a promise of employment. Bogie's coffee was growing cold, his toast was largely untouched, and the eggs sunny-side up stared at the actor with yellow, runny eyes. Bogart was engrossed in the *Los Angeles Times* and the front page story of Hannah Darrow's murder. It was illustrated with a recent photograph of Bogart and a not so recent one of Mayo. There was a bonus photograph of Hannah Darrow's body after the knife had been removed. Bogart thought it was obscene and in bad taste. The story was fairly accurate and there was a boxed story devoted exclusively to the legend of the cornucopia. Bogart folded the newspaper and put it aside. He looked at his wristwatch and then got the waitress's attention. He asked for a fresh cup of black coffee. He also asked if she knew Hammett and Hellman and had they been in for breakfast yet. She knew them and they hadn't, adding it was a tad early for them. It was a tad early for Bogart, too, but Mayo awakened him at eight to let him know she had arrived safely and having thought it over, decided maybe she should return to L.A. and her husband and resume the role of dutiful wife. Bogart suppressed a guffaw and urged her to stay with Evelyn. Mayo seemed relieved and said she and her mother were going shopping. Bogart's eyes crossed and then they said their good-byes.

Bogart picked up the newspaper and found yesterday's racing results, pleased to see he had had a couple of winners and wondered if it was too early to phone his bookie. It could wait. He hadn't won a phenominal sum. Lillian Hellman entered briskly wearing white slacks and a blue blouse, a jaunty sailor's cap perched perkily on her head and dangling from a chain around her wrist, a blue and white handbag. Bogart eyed the getup and said, "I don't know whether to salute or to kneel."

"Just get me some OJ and coffee, lots of coffee." Bogart repeated her request to the waitress who brought his coffee and then asked, "How's Dash?"

"Dashed." She had seated herself across from Bogart who wondered if the lines under his eyes were as unhealthy looking as those under hers. "Whatever you do, don't tell me I look well. I couldn't tolerate dishonesty at this ungodly hour." She rummaged in her handbag and found a pair of dark glasses which she promptly secured to her nose and ears. "Why did we stay up so late and drink so much?"

"Force of habit. Here's Dash. He seems to be walking at a very strange angle. Good morning, Dash, or do you prefer not to be spoken to."

"Not at all," he said huskily. "Tell me, Bogie, is this still the Garden of Allah?"

"Oh yes." Without being instructed, the waitress brought two orders of orange juice and black coffee and placed them before Hellman and Hammett. Hammett gently patted her backside in gratitude and then recognized Hellman. "Lily, is that you?"

"It's not Dietrich."

"Why Lily, my dear, you look like the finale of *Hit the Deck*." He stared down at his coffee. "This coffee is black."

"You prefer it black," Hellman reminded him.

"Yes. Of course. I prefer it black." He took a sip. "I'd prefer it hot, too. But oh well, mine not to reason why. Anything special in the paper?"

"My house was ransacked and my housekeeper was murdered. And here comes Lucy Darrow."

"Ingenue?" asked Hammett.

"My housekeeper's daughter. I've got her mother's handbag in my room. Good morning Lucy." He introduced Hammett and Hellman who expressed condolences. Lucy thanked them and Bogart hugged her. "Sit down. Have some coffee."

"No thanks, Mr. Bogart. I have to shop for Mother's laying out." She didn't notice Hellman shudder. Lucy was a spinster in her mid-thirties who while not unattractive, wasn't attractive enough. Bogart asked the waitress to get a bellboy which she promptly did. Bogart gave him the key to his room and instructions to bring him the blue handbag on the coffee table. Lucy continued, "They're performing an autopsy this morning which I think is so completely unnecessary. I mean she was only stabbed to death, wasn't she? There was nothing elaborate like maybe she was raped or something." She found a tissue in her handbag as her eyes began to dampen. Bogart assured her her mother hadn't been raped. Lucy said to Bogart, "You saw her body, didn't you?"

"The three of us saw her body."

"Oh I'm so glad she was in such good company." She sniffled and dabbed. "Oh Mr. Bogart, she absolutely adored you and your wife. She was sorry there was only one cup left in the tea set but she said it was an ugly tea set to begin with."

Hellman said in an aside to Hammett, "I haven't felt this touched since Little Eva was hauled up to heaven."

Bogart said to the woman, "Lucy, I'm taking care of everything."

"What do you mean?"

"I'm paying for everything. The casket, the flowers, the grave site, everything."

"Now that's damned decent of you," said Hellman.

"It's more than decent," said Lucy, "it's Christian. But it's not necessary, Mr. Bogart. Mother arranged everything for herself only last year, like I'm beginning to think she might have had a premonition or something." She said to Hellman and Hammett, "Mother was very psychic and had visions."

"I can believe that," said Hellman, "working for the Bogarts."

"You see, Mr. Bogart, mother bought a family plot and arranged her own funeral and paid for it. The only thing she didn't prearrange was what she would wear as she predicted styles would change and they sure have, so I have to go choose one for the laying out.''

The bellboy returned with the blue handbag, returned Bogart's key and Bogart slipped him a couple of dollars.

Lucy took the handbag and opened it. She was sniffling again and dabbing at her eyes. ''It's all here. Her keys and all. Would you recognize the one to your house, Mr. Bogart? You should take it. She'll never need it again.'' Hellman resisted the urge to suggest burying the key with Mother by way of tribute to the Bogarts but was sure the suggestion might be taken as thoughtless frivolity. Bogart retrieved the key and Lucy retrieved the handbag. ''When the services are set, Mr. Bogart, I'll let you know.''

''You be sure to do that. My wife's up in Portland but I'll positively be there.''

Lucy asked shyly, ''Mr. Bogart, would you perhaps say a few words? I know it would mean so much to Mother.''

''Sure, Lucy. If Mayo was here, we'd arrange a fight for old time's sake.''

''Oh wouldn't that be splendid!'' said Lucy. ''I'd better be going. It takes me forever to pick out a dress for myself. God knows how long it'll take me to pick out one for Mother.'' She was standing, Bogart standing with her.

He said to Lucy, ''Too bad there's not enough time to get Orry-Kelly at the studio to design one.''

''Oh wouldn't that have been wonderful. But, we can't have everything, can we?'' She said her good-byes to Hellman and Hammett and confirmed to Bogart she'd be in touch and then compulsively threw her arms around him and kissed his cheek and then hurried out of the coffee shop.

Bogart sat as the waitress poured fresh coffee for the three of them. Hammett announced he was suddenly hungry and wanted a bowtie Danish, Hellman spoke up for a prune Danish, and Bogart asked for some aspirin. He looked at his wristwatch. ''I wonder what time the shop opens. It's about an hour's drive out there and it'll be another half hour before we finish here.''

"When we're ready to go, why don't I lead and Dash, you follow me."

"Blindly," said Hammett. "Bogie, from the look on your face you're having maudlin thoughts."

"Didn't you know that under this tough exterior there lies a sentimental slob? I was thinking of Lucy Darrow and her having to do all the arrangements on her own. Hannah has a sister somewhere downtown. Mayo tried to get Lucy to get hold of her last night. I guess she didn't."

"Bogie, has it occurred to you that our Lucy absolutely revels in all her tragedy? She is the bereaved and therefore the center of attention. How often do you think she's been the center of attention. She'll hold the spotlight until the last mourner has departed, and then back into the oblivion of spinsterhood. That's the fate of all the Lucys of this world. Sad. She has excellent features. If she'd only learn how to do her face correctly, she'd be very attractive."

It fascinated Bogart, how anyone as homely as Lillian Hellman could dare suggest improvements to another woman. He caught Hammett's eye. Hammett winked, Bogart grinned and Hellman's eyes darted back and forth between the two men. "What's going on here?"

"Why what do you mean, Lily?" asked Hammett innocently.

"That look that just passed between the two of you."

"Why Lily," said Hammett, "we realized we've fallen in love."

"Go to hell!" cried Hellman.

The waitress was distributing the pastries and the aspirins. "Will there be anything else?" she asked.

Hellman said, "Some artificial respiration for my two friends here." She poked her prune Danish with an index finger. "This thing looks stale."

"Lily," said Hammett wearily.

"What?"

"Shut up and eat."

* * *

Herb Villon and Jim Mallory were on their way to Venice Beach in an unmarked police car. Jim was driving while Villon read the morning newspaper. Jim asked Villon, "What happened to Hazel? I thought she'd be tagging along this morning."

"Don't we get enough of Hazel?"

"You getting bored with her?"

"It's not a matter of being bored with her, it's just that there are times when one needs a rest from Hazel. She's at the beauty parlor. An earthquake couldn't tear her away from the beauty parlor. Especially when the roots are beginning to show. I'm not happy with what forensics turned up at the Bogarts."

"They didn't turn up much."

"That's why I'm not happy."

"I wonder why they didn't rummage through the basement."

"Probably discouraged by what they found in the rest of the house." He whistled atonally for a few moments which meant Villon was thinking. "Christ but detective work is boring. It's even worse when we don't have a clue except for that strand of blonde hair." His voice went up an octave. "We don't even have a decent set of suspects. An adipose countess, her gigolo, and something that passes for a secretary."

"What's an adipose countess?"

"A big fat slob."

"Where do you find words like *adipose?*"

"First in a crossword puzzle and then in the dictionary." He resumed whistling. Jim thought he detected a tune that sounded like it might be "The Music Goes 'Round and 'Round" but then he thought it might be "America the Beautiful." "You ever been to the Old Curiosity Shop?"

"Haven't even read it."

"Prepare yourself for eccentrics. I don't mean movie type eccentrics I mean eccentrics so far out they're on another planet."

"I've drunk at the Garden of Allah's bar."

"That's rehearsed eccentrics. New York transplants. Dottie and Alan and Lily and Dash and Prancer and Dancer and Donder and Blitzen. An endangered species. They're getting old which is unavoidable. What's sad is there's no new generation to provide replacements. The war's going to thin the herd. Some awfully talented kids are going to be robbed of their chance to be heard from."

Somewhat shyly, Mallory said, "I wish I had a gift."

"Why? It's your birthday?"

"A talent. Something special."

"For crying out loud, you're a good detective. And by the time you retire, you might be a great one. And in my books that's one hell of a gift."

"Sometimes I want to write a screenplay."

"Why bother? It'll only be rewritten. Let's talk about the ransacking murderer. We can discount a professional burglar. This one's a mean killer and has bad manners. The very idea of murdering Hannah Darrow. So damned unnecessary."

"Maybe it was someone she recognized."

Villon smiled. It was his first smile of the day. It pleased him. It was a very welcome smile. *Maybe it was someone she recognized.*

"Jim, I could kiss you," said Villon.

"Please don't. I promised my father I'd stay heterosexual."

"Who the hell could she have recognized? She never met the countess and her motley crew. The Bogarts have airtight alibis and are hardly about to wreck their own place. Any number of celebrities have been to the house but who among them ever heard of a cornucopia?"

"Or can spell it."

"Right. Now where does that leave us?"

Jim Mallory stared ahead, deep in thought, his hands relaxed on the wheel. "For starters, it leaves us with dealers and collectors . . ."

Villon sang, "Alive alive oh!" He sank into thought and

almost immediately reemerged. "I wonder if Hannah Darrow had any occasion to visit art galleries or meet some dealers. What art I saw on the Bogart walls wasn't exactly Matisse or Modigliani."

Mallory was impressed. "You know Matisse and Modigliani?"

"Not personally. But I get around to museums and exhibits. Hazel scrounges a lot of invitations to opening night cocktail parties. Especially when that crazy antenna of hers tells her there'll be lots of celebrities and lots of gossip."

Mallory had been thinking. "I'll bet the Bogarts have had the Edward G. Robinsons to the house."

"Probably. So what?"

"Robinson's supposed to have a great art collection, worth millions."

"So?"

"So he's a collector. Hannah Darrow would have recognized him."

"Oh for crying out loud. Robinson a ransacker? A killer? What the hell would he want with a cornucopia?"

"If it's our cornucopia he'd want what everybody else wants, the jewels inside."

"Scrub Robinson. He doesn't have a drop of ransacker killer's blood in him."

"There's Hearst."

"Let him stay where he is. Let's consider the more likely candidates."

"Such as?" asked Villon.

"Collectors. Dealers." And after a pause. "Fences. And we've got a lot of fences in L.A. who need mending. Aren't we in Venice yet? I see nothing but ramshackle huts and broken down shacks."

"We're in Venice. Forgive me for not taking the scenic route, but this is faster." In the distance they heard the calliope strains of Venice's celebrated carousel playing "On the Good Ship Lollipop."

Herb Villon scratched his jaw. "Hazel might come in handy after all. She knows lots of dealers and collectors. I'm sure she knows who are the shady ones. Hazel is a connoisseur where that sort of thing is concerned. Why you making a turn?"

"You can't drive on Ocean Front Walk. I'm taking a wild stab that this is the area of the Curiosity Shop."

Hammett and Hellman tailed Bogart in his car. Bogart was listening to the news on the radio and liking none of what he heard. Britain under bombardment, the U.S. escalating conscription. In World War I Bogart had been in the navy. He hated it. He was a seaman second class on the *Leviathan* and became a master at swabbing decks. An accident scarred his upper lip resulting in his slight lisp which had already become his trademark. Now he was just past forty and didn't think he'd be called up. The country was not yet at war but it was inevitable. There were rumors that President Roosevelt was listening with interest to the overtures of the British to come on in, the water's just fine. But there were the isolationists in D.C. who promised their constituents that they would see to it the United States would never participate. Let the Brits and the Axis fight it out between them. There was already Bundles for Britain and Battleships for Britain though these were just a few steps away from being condemned as scrap metal. Bogart thought about his fellow actors at Warner Brothers. He couldn't see Cagney, Paul Muni, George Raft, Pat O'Brien, Alan Hale bearing arms. The younger ones would be called. Bill Lundigan, Herb Anderson, and, with any luck, that pain in the backside Reagan who kept insisting one day he'd be president of the United States. Bogart had advised him, "First learn how to act. The presidency is a great part. It's almost as good as *Hamlet*." Next he tried to envision Mayo as a war wife. It wasn't easy. Mayo baking him cookies? She'd need a compass to find the oven. Mayo knitting him sweaters. It was easier envisioning her shearing sheep for the wool. Mayo collecting his life insurance accompanied by a swelling score by Max Steiner or Erich Wolfgang Korngold. From behind, he heard Hammett bearing down on his horn. Bogart looked to the right and saw a street that led to Ocean Front Walk. He beeped in reply to Hammett and then swerved to make the turn. He'd been advised there was a small parking lot at the end of the road on the left. The Old Curiosity Shop was to the right. The parking lot was empty. Villon and Mallory had not yet arrived. Bogart and Hammett pulled into the lot and parked adjacent to each other. Hellman emerged from the roadster and inhaled luxuriously. "Ah! That magnificent sea air! The Pacific Ocean!"

Hammett said to Bogart, "She will now erupt into a fit of coughing."

Hellman erupted into a fit of coughing. Tears welled up and she struggled in her handbag for a tissue. Hammett said to Bogart, "By law there should be a large billboard erected here, proclaiming breathing fresh sea air can be injurious to your health. I just might write to the Chamber of Commerce."

"If you do," said Bogart leading the way to the Old Curiosity Shop, "don't take any bets there'll be somebody there who can read."

EIGHT

The Old Curiosity Shop was two stories high. The store occupied the bottom half and the top half contained the living quarters. The entrance was centered between two large display windows that contained relics and curios and various assortments of oddments that would probably bring a paean of joy to the lips of a pack rat. On the walk in front of the store, there was a variety of junk furniture, bins with used books and magazines and a rack of T-shirts, one of which appealed to Hammett. On it was the legend: I OWE, I OWE, SO OFF TO WORK I GO. Hellman was several feet away from Bogart and Hammett, still recovering from her fit of coughing. She did not hear Hammett's comment as he and Bogart admired a cigar store Indian. "Startling resemblance to Lily, don't you think?" The facade of the store was a fair replica of the Old Curiosity Shop in London near the Tower of London. Bogart hoped it hadn't been bombed out of existence.

Hammett was asking, "Lily, you all right?"

"I'm just dandy." She slowly walked in their direction while rudely staring at the variety of Venice denizens that were at large. There were the ever-present body builders with their abnormally developed pectorals and biceps. There was an assortment of women, young and old, in various stages of undress and overdress. Some girls wore bathing outfits that emphasized their humongous breasts, while others emphasized their oversize buttocks. Legs ran the gamut of unusually shapely to varicose veins. Peddlers hawked souvenirs or ice cream or custard or cold drinks. One could purchase souvenir scarves and gloves and anklets. There were any number of shops and cafés along the sea front and there were wooden tables and benches for picnickers. There was the usual quota of musicians, some playing reeds, some playing accordions, and one sturdy individualist sat at a portable organ belting out hymn after hymn, with a female companion banging a tambourine and a small boy, presumably their son, worked the strollers with hat in hand soliciting contributions.

Bogart was the first to enter the Old Curiosity Shop. The doorbell chimed the opening bars of "The Land of Hope and Glory." Bogart left the door open for Hellman and Hammett who were slow in joining him, so caught up were they in the spectacle outdoors. Bogart was captivated by the charm of the premises, the thousands of items on display, their tackiness. There was a lot of art work and referring to most of it as art was an uncommon generosity. There were lots of Indian heads painted on wooden boards; there were lots of bad copies of a variety of the masters; there was a plethora of Art Deco items that Bogart figured were of value to certain collectors. He remembered as a child a woman friend of his mother's who collected salt shakers, one of which was decidedly obscene. There was a tray of Indian arrowheads and a display of old weapons; knives, pistols, swords, sabers, and cutlasses. Behind the display stood an elderly man who was Bogart's height. He had a voluminous shock of white hair and a white goatee. Bogart guessed his age as anywhere from the late sixties to the mid-seventies. On the bridge of his nose was a pince-nez attached on each end to a ribbon that hung around his neck. He wore a sleeveless shirt and slacks tied around his waist with a rope. There was certainly nothing ostentatious about this person, thought Bogart, so he must be terribly rich. Bogart indicated the weapons on display.

"That's quite an arsenal you've got here, sir."

"These? A mere bagatelle. I've many more impressive items in the basement."

"Oh? Some really good stuff?"

"All my stuff, as you put it, is good stuff." He removed the pince-nez. "It's been a long time since you've honored us with a visit, Mr. Bogart. Where's your delightful wife?"

"This week she's doing her shopping in another city. You might have heard about the recent unpleasantness we've suffered."

"I have indeed. So tragic about Miss Darrow."

"You knew her?" It was Villon who had just entered with Mallory. Hammett and Hellman were still, outside, Hellman suffering from a slight case of biceps fever.

"Hello Herb," said Bogart, "meet Edgar Dickens. Edgar, this is Detective Villon and Detective Mallory of the downtown precinct."

"How do you do," said Dickens affably. "Yes I did know Hannah Darrow. A lovely person. Terribly tragic, her death. I must remember to phone her daughter Lucy and commiserate."

Hellman and Hammett had entered. Bogart introduced them to Edgar Dickens. Hellman gave Dickens a thorough going over. "Perfect type," she said to Hammett.

"For what?"

"Courtly Southern gentleman, what else?"

Bogart reminded them, "Mr. Dickens is of British descent, isn't that right?"

"Most assuredly," said Dickens. Hellman wondered why did so many British sound so affected. It seemed that everytime they left the United Kingdom for destinations overseas, their accents became more pronounced and exaggerated, especially actors. Then she said under her breath, "Jesus Christ, now what?"

From the rear of the store, through a set of beaded curtains that tinkled softly as she rustled through, there arrived Nell Dickens. Bogart had commented when he first encountered her that to fully appreciate Nell Dickens one had to be perfectly sober. She was five or six inches over five feet in height. She wore a calico dirndl that revealed surprisingly shapely legs. Her shoes were a simple variation of ballet slippers, laced at the ankles. Her blouse was a frilly piece of froufrou that Hellman decided had once wrapped a large box of imported fancy candies. But the face. The hair. On each of her cheeks was a perfect circle of blood red rouge. Her lips matched her cheeks in color. Hellman thought she'd been slaking her thirst at somebody's neck. Her eyelids were outlined with heavy black kohl. The lids were painted a deep blue and her eyebrows were two slashes of black mascara. They looked like they had been shaved. Her hair was something else. It was egg yolk yellow and carefully coiffured long, thick curls hung down to her shoulders. More thick curls crowned her head. She looked like the sort of dolls they gave away as prizes at sideshows. Hellman didn't even try to guess her age.

"Aha! My Nell!" Dickens voice had turned even fruitier. "My enchanting daughter. You remember Mr. Bogart."

Nell advanced toward them slowly. "Of course," she said in a voice surprisingly husky. Hellman had expected the sounds of a lute. "Mr. Bogart is unforgettable. I'm so sorry about what happened in your house last night. We are entering an era of anarchy. The brutes are taking control of the world. I feel the coming of Armageddon. The destruction of the world."

"I hope not too soon, my dear," said Hellman, "I've got a screenplay to finish."

Nell's eyes embraced Hellman, and it made the writer uncomfortable. Dickens introduced Nell to the others. "Ah! Detectives! It's been so long since we've had detectives." Nell's curls shook and it seemed to Hellman they had lives of their own. She wondered if they had ever suffocated anyone Nell had slept with. Nell seated herself at what was purportedly an antique desk, and found a cigarette in a musical box that played "Yes! We Have No Bananas." Mallory hurried to her with his lighter at the ready and prayed it wouldn't betray him. As he lit her cigarette, she said seductively, "I am always looking to the comfort of strangers, Mr. Detective."

Villon interjected, "How long's it been since you've had detectives?"

"You mean in the store?" she asked alluringly to the accompaniment of fluttering eyelashes, also coal black.

Villon chose to ignore the double entendre, while Hammett and Hellman exchanged glances. They'd be dining off little Nell Dickens for many nights to come. Hellman couldn't wait to describe her to Dorothy Parker. "Do detectives visit here often?"

"Every time there's a robbery of any consequence," said Dickens. "After all, I buy. I don't ask where the object for sale originated unless it arouses my suspicion. But according to reports, Mr. Bogart, nothing was stolen from your place."

"Only its dignity. And a good person was murdered."

A tragic wail enveloped them. Little Nell was clutching her ample bosom. "Our poor Hannah! How could this have happened to our poor benighted Hannah?"

Hellman whispered to Hammett, "I may scream."

He replied, "If you don't, I will."

Villon said, "Have you got much in the way of cornucopias?"

"Oh not again!" It was an unfamiliar voice coming from the back of the store. From a wing chair there arose a slender man of slight height, with squinty eyes protected by rimless glasses and crew cut hair that made him look like a military brush. He wore a blue apron over faded blue jeans and a brown tee shirt.

"My God," said Hellman, "could it be Roland Young?"

Edgar Dickens laughed. "A reasonable assumption as Mr. Young portrayed Uriah Heep in *David Copperfield* and this is my shop assistant who laughingly enough is called Sidney Heep."

"I'm sure no relation," said Hellman, "as Uriah Heep was fictional."

Sidney Heep laughed. "There are those who think *I* am too. Ha ha ha. Actually, I'm the only Heep on this side of the ocean. There's a heap of Heeps back in Blighty. We're not in touch." He came closer to Villon and Mallory. "You're detectives. I can tell by the way you slouch." He turned to Hammett and Hellman. "You're both literary. I can tell by the snide asides." Hammett introduced himself and Hellman to Sidney Heep who recognized the names with delight. "Capital! Capital! Two fine writers!" He concentrated on Hellman. "I didn't much like your lesbian play. I don't like lesbians. They worry me. They make me feel weak and ineffectual. You're not a lesbian, are you?"

"Not lately," said Hellman wishing for a breath of fresh air despite the possible threat of a coughing fit.

Sidney Heep turned to Villon and Mallory. "Yes we have cornucopias, but not the one you're looking for. Heh heh heh." He sidled to a space next to Nell Dickens. "A crazy fat lady was here yesterday with two minions looking for cornucopias. We showed her everything we had, didn't we Nell?"

"Well yes," said Nell on the verge of another double entendre, "we showed her everything we had in the way of cornucopias, that is. Her boyfriend should have a frame built around him and be put on exhibit. He's the sort of man who makes a woman glad she's a woman, if you know what I mean."

Bogart was wondering if that strand of hair Villon found in the house might be one of Nell's. Villon was apparently reading his mind. Bogart heard him asking Nell, "Were you by any chance in the vicinity of Mr. Bogart's house last night?"

She smiled a rather vague smile. "There's nothing very subtle about you, is there Mr. Villain."

"Villon. As in François Villon."

"The poet?" asked Sidney Heep somewhat shrilly.

"The poet," said Villon.

"Well there's nothing very poetic about you, sir. There's never anything poetic about detectives. At least not the ones we've been getting. They're poor imitations of Tommy Dugan and Fred Kelcey."

Bogart explained Dugan and Kelcey were actors who specialized in fumbling comedy detectives.

Villon repeated his question to Nell.

"We shut the shop a little before ten and went upstairs for some supper and a couple of rounds of Monopoly."

Villon indicated Heep. "He live here, too?"

Edgar Dickens said, "And most welcome. He's an old friend and associate and there's plenty of room."

Villon asked Nell, "Miss Dickens, have you ever acted anywhere beside this store?"

For a moment her face froze. Then it relaxed as she rubbed out her cigarette in a tray. "Years ago, I was with a stock company back East. It was just a whim. I can't act."

Oh yes you can, thought Bogart, you're doing one hell of a job right now. If I could see what you've got under all that makeup, I might recommend you to Jack Warner.

"I don't trust that fat thing," said Sidney Heep, "claimed she was some kind of contessa."

"La Contessa di Marcopolo," said Bogart.

"You've met her?" screeched Heep.

"No, but my wife has. Seems her father and the contessa's father were buddies some time back." He quickly recapped the story of the Baron di Marcopolo's fatal voyage.

Villon said to Edgar Dickens, "Sound familiar?"

Edgar Dickens replied, "Actually yes. The hunt for the cornucopia is an old story. It's been dormant for quite a while. Actually Mr. Bogart, I thought its revival might be a publicity ploy for your new version of Mr. Hammett's old story."

"Now don't be mean," said Bogart affably, "Mr. Hammett's old story is a hell of a lot better then any so-called new stories I've read in the past ten years." He said to Villon, "If the countess has already examined their cornucopias, no need for us to waste any time."

Edgar Dickens interrupted. "Surely you mean to speak to other collectors? There are several unscrupulous scoundrels at large in this city."

"Yeah. Mostly they produce movies," said Bogart.

Villon asked Dickens, "Any suggestions?"

"Well sir, you can't expect me to be pointing a finger!"

"Why not?"

"That would be unscrupulous!"

Villon and Mallory exchanged glances. Villon asked Dickens, "You wouldn't by any chance have some scissors on the premises?"

"Oh I have some incredible scissors. One dating back to the Revolutionary War."

"It doesn't have to have a history. Just any old pair of scissors will do. I only wish to borrow a snippet of Miss Dickens's hair."

Nell glared at him. She opened a desk drawer and produced a pair of scissors and handed them to Villon. Then she snatched the wig from her head and said, "Here, help yourself." She had a close mannish bob.

"Sorry to see you snatch yourself baldheaded," said Villon.

"I'm not bald. I happen to wear my hair close cropped as a convenience for the wigs."

"You have more?"

"I have dozens. They're upstairs in my bedroom. Care to look?"

"I believe you." He snipped a strand of the wig and put it into a cellophane bag he kept in his pocket.

"Now really, Mr. Villon, you don't think I wear this thing outside of Venice." She shook the wig vigorously and then fit it back over her head. "Voilà!"

Hellman said to Hammett, "Fascinating morning. Why can't I have more of them?"

"Mr. Dickens." Villon's tone of voice told Bogart he meant business. Dickens stared at him while running a hand through his thick mane of hair. "Was yesterday the first time you've met the contessa?"

"Yesterday was her first time in Los Angeles, or so she told us."

"You might have met her in Europe."

Dickens smiled. "Europe is a long time ago in my life."

"So you're British."

"Yes."

"You don't look particularly British. You're so dark. Mediterranean."

"Actually I'm from Wales. There's a strain of Welsh that could easily be mistaken for Mediterranean. For instance, there's Ivor Novello. He's a famous star in England. He's Welsh. He's very dark and very swarthy."

"And incredibly handsome," said Hellman. "I've seen him on stage in London. But he happens to have Italian antecedents."

"A great many Italians emigrated to the U.K. and settled in Wales."

Sidney Heep chirruped, "And tons of them landed in Australia."

"Why?" asked Hellman, "faulty navigation?"

Villon zeroed in on Nell. "You don't look anything like your father."

Hellman said, "How can you tell?" Her remark was ignored out of kindness.

Bogart was wondering what the hell was going on. It was obvious Villon had taken an instant dislike to the inhabitants of the shop. He attributed it to the grotesquerie of Nell, though the weird Sidney Heep wasn't all that easy to take.

Nell was working on a fresh cigarette. Mallory made no effort to light this one for her. He was afraid that while bending over Villon would kick him square in the butt, and where Villon kicked, no grass grew ever. Nell exhaled a perfect smoke ring in Villon's direction by way of telling him to stuff it. "I favor my mother," she said. "She was light-skinned, light-haired, and light-headed. She lit out, so Dad brought us to the States. Fate brought us to Venice. Anything else?" The two words were more a challenge than a question. Bogart was wondering if she could beat every man in the store at Indian hand wrestling. Sidney Heep and probably Dash Hammett for sure.

"You've got the silliest damn look on your face, Bogie," commented Hammett.

"That's because I'm entertaining some damn silly thoughts," he said with a sly grin.

Villon said to the Dickenses, "Who referred the contessa to you?"

Nell Dickens crossed her legs and said smoothly with a tinge of venom, "A friend of yours, she said. Hazel Dickson.

She spent some time with the contessa yesterday. Mrs. Bogart was there too. The contessa is a very dedicated woman."

"I think a very determined woman is a lot more like it," said Bogart. "For a new arrival, in under twenty-four hours she certainly has stirred a hornet's nest in this town. Herb, maybe it'd be safer to have her deported." He saw the look Nell and Edgar exchanged. "Just kidding, folks. Lily, see anything you want to buy?"

"My freedom." Hammett took her by the arm and guided her outside. They called their good-byes over their shoulders as they left.

Edgar Dickens said, "Oh dear. I had so wanted to show them my collection of literary autographs. I have George Eliot, Louis Bromfield, Booth Tarkington, Mary Roberts Rinehart."

"You seem to have a lot of hidden treasure here, Mr. Dickens," said Villon.

Dickens said with a sigh, "I keep promising myself to do an inventory. But every time I plan one I keep putting it off." He stretched his hands out expansively. "Just look at what I've got here. And look what's outside. And you've no idea what there is in the basement and the upper floor. I know, I know. I should stop stalling and get down to it. Who knows, I might find I have enough with which to retire. Are we ready for retirement, my dear Nellie?"

His dear Nellie said with a rasp, "I haven't even had breakfast. Sidney, go upstairs and fix something."

"What's broken?"

She shot him a look that dripped with menace and he hurried to the back of the store and the door that led to both the upper floor and the basement.

"You got any more business here?" asked Bogart of Villon.

"Probably, but there's always tomorrow." He turned to Mallory. "Who knows Jim when I might next suggest we go to the Dickenses." Without saying good-bye, he headed for the front door followed by Mallory who mumbled good-bye to father and daughter.

"It was nice seeing you again, Mr. Bogart. Remember me to your wife." Edgar Dickens stood near his daughter, looking like the grandfather in *Heidi*, smiling benevolently.

Bogart said, "Sorry you couldn't sell us anything. Maybe next time." He made his exit to the chimes of "The Land of Hope and Glory" and wondered why he was feeling so dispirited.

As the door closed behind Bogart, Nell jumped up, tore the wig from her head and flung it on the floor. "Temper, my dear, temper," cautioned Edgar Dickens.

"Oh bugger off!" snarled Nell, hardly very Dickensian in talk or demeanor.

Outside, Hammett had spotted an outdoor café where the waiters looked fairly presentable, not always the case with Venice restaurants. They were usually unemployed actors or writers whose capabilities as waiters were usually restricted to filling glasses with water and distributing menus and then disappearing to the backyard for a smoke.

Bogart was recognized by the management and the few patrons at other tables but no special fuss was made and nobody asked for an autograph. Only tourists asked for autographs and the population of Venice was determined not to be mistaken for tourists. There was a young man in uniform, probably home on leave with a middle-aged couple who were probably his parents. The woman smiled at Bogart who nodded and then gave his attention to his four companions.

Bogart spoke first. "That little visit left me a little depressed."

"A *little* depressed," said Hellman, "one more minute in there and I'd have attacked my wrist with one of Mr. Dickens's ancient razors."

"I didn't see any razors," said Hammett. "Lily, you're always seeing things I never see."

"There was a tray of them next to a pile of what looked like opera gloves."

Villon said, "I didn't like that threesome at all. Dickens put me in mind of a defrocked priest."

"He put me in mind of another Dickens character," said

Hammett. "Magwich in *Great Expectations*. You remember him, Lily."

"Why sure, we were old buddies." She was lighting a cigarette and wondering what kind of bribe it would take to get the attention of a waiter.

Hammett reminded the others, "He was the escaped convict who was young Pip's benefactor."

"I *loathe* young Pip. A parvenu upstart." Hellman was staring at four waiters deep in conversation near the entrance to the main dining room. She snapped her fingers at them. "Yes *you*. The U.S.C. Hadassah." A waiter tore himself away and came to the table. He brought with him menus and the personality of a porcupine in heat. When he recognized Bogart, he became suddenly mannerly.

Bogart took command. "Bring us pots of hot coffee and some muffins and bread and jam and butter. Can you manage that?"

"Doesn't anyone want lunch?"

"Look, son," said Bogart with the look usually reserved for the actor on screen he was about to bump off, "just bring what I ordered and if you can't cope with it send over the manager."

The waiter's face reddened. "Yes sir. Right away, sir." He hurried to the kitchen.

Villon said with a faraway look in his eye, "The escaped convict who was young Pip's benefactor. I saw the movie. Henry Hull played Magwich. Magwich lost. What about the other two?"

"They're unreal," said Jim Mallory.

"Are you always given to understatement?" asked Hellman. "Little Nell was bizarre to say the least, and I'm being kind which doesn't happen very often."

"She looked like a drag queen," said Mallory.

Bogart disagreed. "Too off the wall for a drag queen. And I'm a drag queen maven. I used to know a lot of them in Greenwich Village when I was playing those 'Anyone for tennis?' juveniles on Broadway. The really good ones have a lot of class. They have to fight for what little respect they get so they dress expensively and act so subtly that you can't tell what gender they are. Nell's just an angry woman sticking her finger in the eye of the world and thumbing her nose for good measure. She was probably the meanest kid on her block. Caught flies, tore the wings off them, and then ate them.''

"How disgusting!" exclaimed Hellman while Hammett chuckled.

Bogart resumed. "Nell's a Venice fixture. She revels in her notoriety. It's probably all the identity she's got. What else is there for her? A junk shop and the apartment upstairs. *Bleak House*. More Dickens. She's probably hugging forty and reluctantly.''

"Unmarried," said Mallory, conveniently forgetting there was a moment when the lady held some allure for him.

Bogart asked, "Is unmarried a crime?"

"That wasn't meant as an insult. I meant maybe she's frustrated that the only men in her life seem to be her father and that creep Heep."

Hellman folded her arms and said, "I don't believe for one minute those are their real names. Not for one minute."

Bogart said, "You might be right. There are an awful lot of aliases out here in Southern California."

"But not nearly enough alibis," said Villon.

The waiter returned with another waiter bearing pots of coffee, baskets of bread and muffins, butter, sugar, cream, plates, napkins, and utensils. Hellman murmured, "Greeks bearing gifts. Beware them." The waiters exchanged glances. Neither one of them was Greek, though each in his own mind thought he was an Adonis.

Villon said to Mallory, "Jim. Hate to ask you to do it now but we should check the precinct."

"No problem," said Mallory as a third waiter arrived with pots of jams and jellies. Mallory grabbed a muffin, split it open, slavered strawberry jam in it and set off for the parking lot.

Villon said, "Venice is notorious for its anonymity. I had a homicide out here once and it was hell. Took months to nail the guilty party when it should have taken days. What do you think, Bogie? You're the actor. Are the Dickenses and Heep performing?''

"I think what we're seeing are masks. Those people are hiding from something. I always felt that from the first time Mayo took me there. But you see, when I first met them, I liked them. They were charming. Nell wasn't all that grotesque. She didn't wear a wig. She had her own hair. Not blonde, by the way.''

"I couldn't tell what color her hair was when she tore off the wig,'' said Villon.

"It's dyed,'' said Hellman, "henna. Has anyone tried this blueberry jam? It's absolutely gorgeous.''

"I'm so glad you're happy,'' said Hammett.

"Who the hell said I was happy? I'm just asking if anyone's tried the blueberry jam?''

"They also brought peanut butter,'' said Bogart with undisguised distaste. "Did we order peanut butter? I can't stand peanut butter especially when somebody else is eating it.''

"Off with their heads,'' said Hammett regally.

Bogart was removing the peanut butter to an adjacent table when Hellman cried out, "Hey! I like peanut butter. Bring it back!''

Bogart placed the peanut butter back on the table. "There's perverse and there's perverse.''

"Listen, smart ass,'' said Hellman, "you know who else likes peanut butter? The Lunts.''

Bogart asked, "What Lunts?''

"And Tallulah Bankhead. Though I dread to tell you how she eats it.''

Hammett said to Villon, "None of this pointless banter is getting you anywhere, is it Herb?''

"You know, Dash, it's sometime the pointless banter that is the substance of some surprisingly solid substance. Bogie thinks we've seen masks. That threesome might be hiding from something. Banter, but very interesting banter. *Are* they hiding behind masks? Is it possible they're not what they're trying to look like? I happen to think that's a pretty damned good observation. They been in Venice a long time, Bogie?"

"Search me," said Bogart, pouring himself more coffee. "Mayo and I got hitched in August of thirty-eight, three years ago. She started her shopping sprees that Christmas. Of course I wasn't suspicious I had a demented woman on my hands because Christmas time almost everybody goes berserk with shopping for gifts. But a couple of weeks later Mayo is off and running again and running up bills and conning me into going with her when I wasn't needed at the studio which isn't too often. Jack Warner gets his money's worth out of all of us. He makes Shylock look like a shrinking violet. Anyway, Mayo had been tipped about the Curiosity Shop so there we went. It looked then like it had been around a long time. They seemed to know everybody who patronized the place. I know this: Heep is local. Told Mayo he used to teach drama. I'd hate to see his results but who knows, who can tell."

"Maybe he's having an affair with Nell," suggested Hammett.

"Why?" asked Hellman.

"Because she's there," growled Hammett, "and she's not getting any from the old man."

Hellman said, "He could be an old goat, you know."

"Well if he is," said Hammett, "he's probably happier sniffing around some other assortment of nannies."

Villon said to Bogart, "Am I right in assuming Hannah Darrow was brought here by your wife?"

"Oh yes. Hannah went along with Mayo lots of times because I urged her to in order to try and put a rein on Mayo. Sometimes I wonder if Mayo's a wife or a bad habit."

"Don't get maudlin on us, Bogart," chided Hellman, "what we need is more helpful banter for Mr. Villon."

Villon said, "I think I know why they skipped searching the basement."

"They?" asked Bogart.

"There had to be more then one. Jim Mallory hit on an idea on the drive here. He suggested Hannah Darrow was murdered because she might have recognized the ransackers."

"I like that very much," said Hammett, "very much indeed."

Bogart snapped his finger. "Hannah went with Mayo to some of the galleries. She's met some dealers. She was always giving out her special recipe for pineapple cheesecake."

"Oh yes?" asked an alert Hellman. "How does it go?"

Hammett suggested a seance. "Why don't we touch fingers and try to reach Hannah Darrow. It's a lovely day for it."

"Why don't you take a flying hop?" countered Hellman.

Jim Mallory was back. The look on his face told Villon there was trouble. "Out with it."

Mallory sat. "There was another murder last night. An interior designer named Joshua Trent."

Bogart whistled.

Villon said, *"The* Joshua Trent?"

"Could there be others?" asked Hammett innocently.

"When was it reported?" asked Villon.

"This morning. It was reported by his associate, someone named Ned Aswan."

"Oh yeah," said Bogart. "His protégé."

"You mean his lover," said Hellman.

Bogart said, "Mine not to reason why. You're so quick, Lily."

Hammett said, "Around Lily it's essential to be a moving target."

"Aswan's a very pleasant fellow," said Bogie. "Very devoted to Josh Trent."

Hellman said, "Well I hope Trent left his buddy well fixed."

"Dear Lily, always the pragmatist." Bogart winked at Hellman. "I'll have to phone Mayo and tell her. She was very fond of Joshua. Played bridge at their place quite frequently. Mayo's been after me to redo the house and so she heard about Joshua from Kay Francis and got in touch. Nice guy, Josh, real nice guy. And Herb. He was a very heavy collector.

He bought and traded with others. He also did work for some of the studios when they were doing period pieces. I remember he was out at the studio a lot when they were doing *Anthony Adverse.* Poor Ned must have been wrecked by this."

Villon asked Mallory, "The precinct say when he was murdered?"

"Like I said, last night."

"So how come it wasn't reported until this morning? Don't the guys live together?" He asked the others, "Don't they usually?"

"It's a matter of taste and preference," said Hellman.

Bogart said, "They lived together and they worked together. It's a big place above Hollywood Boulevard in the hills. A section of it is their showroom and workroom, the rest is where they live, and I might tell you, quite lavishly."

Villon asked Mallory, "So how come Aswan waited until this morning to report the boyfriend's death?"

"He was on a job in Santa Barbara. He didn't get back until this morning when he found him."

"You've left out something."

"What?"

"Wasn't it ransacked?"

"Ransacked? It was practically wrecked."

Hellman said, "Why are some people so unthoughtful?"

NINE

Villon drove with Bogart to the Joshua Trent house in the hills above Hollywood Boulevard. It was a treacherous drive, the roads here being narrow and winding. It's as though the area had been laid out haphazardly and at the mercy of a city planner who had taken to drink. There were many magnificent mansions to be admired and Bogart was able to identify some of them, almost all dating back to the silent screen era. "That's Falcon's Lair behind the gates on the right. Valentino built that one."

"I know it. I've been there. Wife beating. Not nice."

Villon studied Bogart's face. He wasn't all that tough looking in person. Bogart grinned. "Approve of what you see?"

"Always have. Nice of you and your friends to tag along on this case."

"Nice of you to let us. Besides, I've got a personal interest. My place was ransacked. My housekeeper murdered. I hope Warner got a studio crew over to my joint to fix it up. Not that I'm looking forward to moving back in. You sure you don't mind Hammett and Hellman?"

"Not at all. They're the comedy interest. Can always use a few laughs even when they're labored."

Bogart said, "They are not happy people."

"Aren't they a solid twosome?"

"What's a solid twosome?"

"Aren't they madly in love with each other?"

"Why Herb Villon, you sentimental *momser*. They're a convenience for each other. They're used to each other. They can just about read each other's mind. I mean take a good look at them. Lily's as homely as a can of shoe polish."

"But she's got style."

"That's for starters. She's got a great mind. She's a suc-

cessful playwright. One of these days she'll get rid of her husband if she hasn't already on the quiet. She's also one hell of
a cook."

"Oh yes? She doesn't strike me as the type."

"She's the type. She's Jewish. Southern Jewish. They're
even more the type. She's perfect for Hammett. Back in the
twenties he was a private eye, a Pinkerton man."

"That's the elite."

"I've heard he was pretty good. That was in San Francisco.
That led him into short stories and he was pretty successful
in magazines like *Black Mask*. That led to book offers and a
move to New York without his wife and child. After a couple of potboilers, he hit it big with *The Maltese Falcon*. He
topped that with *The Glass Key*. And *The Thin Man* dropped
all the pins in the alley."

"And since then?"

Bogart smiled. "The slow descent. The continuity for a
comic strip. The script for a cheesy movie shot in New York.
Some radio series. He's not a well man. Lungs or something
like that. Lily takes good care of him. They're pretty straight
with each other from what I can see. To tell you the truth,
I'm a little surprised they're tagging along today. Hammett's
always interested in police procedurals, of course. Keeps the
hand in. You never can tell when he'll start up again. As for
Lily, she'll do anything to keep her away from a screenplay.
She likes the money but she hates the work. She'd rather be
in her house on Martha's Vineyard working on a play and
baking bread." He turned and looked out the rear window.
"Our little caravan's intact in a row."

"Ahead!" shouted Villon.

Bogie swerved and by a hair avoided colliding with an oncoming Ford. "These damn roads! Why don't they do something about broadening them! See if they're okay behind
us."

Villon looked out the back window. "They're okay.
Bogie, haven't you learned never to look out the back window when you're driving?"

"Joshua Trent. Mayo took it hard when I phoned her

from the restaurant. And it's really got her frightened. I told her to stay put until I signal an all clear. 'Such stuff as dreams are made on.' Supposing we don't find this cornucopia?''

"Still have to find the murderers. I hope we're not entangled in a chain reaction. From Hannah Darrow to Joshua Trent to someone else and then further and so on."

"L.A. will be suffering a serious shortage of art dealers and collectors. We can't have that. The town is suffering enough deficiencies as it is."

"I'm going to suffer a lot of flack from Trent's murder. He was a heavy hitter. Very big connections."

"He overcharged."

Villon laughed.

"Sure! You can laugh! You've never received a bill from him. I won't even ask you to guess what he charged me for a consultation. I almost took to my bed for a week. That's it up ahead past that row of cedars of Lebanon. Lots of police cars."

"That's just for show. For crying out loud will you look at that mansion. I mean talk about ostentation."

In Hammett's car, Hellman said, " 'Last night I dreamt I went to Manderley again.' How do you live in a place like that?''

"Luxuriously."

"If you sat in a lap of luxury you'd slip between its legs."

"I'm willing to risk it."

"If you'd get back to some serious work . . ."

"Skip it, Lily. I guess I'll pull in behind Bogie. There's more room for a fast getaway." He braked to a halt and then sat saying nothing.

"Well? Are we getting out?"

"Villon intrigues me."

"Why? He's just another everyday homegrown detective."

"He's different."

"I find him a bit pretentious. He name-drops a lot."

"There are a lot of names out here to drop. I admire his nuances, his subtleties. That bit about 'banter.' It's what I did with Nick and Nora, except I didn't really carry it off all that well. They did it better in the movie. Villon's right. Let people chat away and they'll not realize how much they might be giving away."

"Christ, you've got to be an awfully good listener for that, and I'm not a good listener. None of the Algonquin bunch were good listeners except maybe Heywood Broun. They were all too busy waiting for an opening to jump in with a wisecrack."

"You've got to be a good listener to be a good writer."

"Are you taking a swat at me?"

"No, Lily, I'm not. You didn't mean it when you said you were not a good listener. You say something like that be- cause you want me to say 'Oh Lily you're a perfectly won- derful listener. Why it's such a pleasure to watch you listen- ing. I can see you absorbing everything with your wonderfully unique ears.' "

"How would you like a crack in the jaw?"

Jim Mallory was saying to Bogart as they walked toward the graceful, superbly designed front porch, Villon leading the way, "I thought you guys were goners back there on the road."

"I was looking out the back window."

"And Herb didn't chew you out?"

"No, he was fairly understanding. He had to be. I'm a movie star." He turned and asked Hammett and Hellman, "What do you think of the place?"

Hellman said, "I'm interested if it's priced right."

"Nothing would get you to relocate to this town."

"I'll tell you Bogie, if this town had Times Square and Fifth Avenue, the Champs Élysées and Shaftesbury Avenue, I'd give it a chance. But all it has is ratty palm trees, tatty Hollywood Boulevard, and is nothing but a couple of dozen suburbs in search of a city. We are about to be besieged by photographers and reporters. Why don't I just tell them that Hammett and I don't really belong here, that we're doing a survey for the United Jewish Appeal." They managed to make their way up the stairs of the front porch relatively unscathed. Hellman said to Bogart, "For some reason I'm feeling some sort of guilt. Is it right, our trespassing on this protégé's privacy?"

"His name's Ned Aswan."

"I mean shouldn't he be allowed the privacy of his grief?"

"Nobody grieves in Hollywood. They reminisce."

In the front hall, Villon was getting information from a detective. Aswan had found the body in the showroom that occupied most of the first floor. The living quarters were on the next two floors and according to the detective looked as though it had taken a direct hit by an enemy bomber. Joshua Trent had been stabbed in the heart and probably died instantly. The body had not yet been removed and was still being examined by the coroner, the same man who had done Hannah Darrow's honors. Hellman averted her eyes from the body although she could tell the trousers and lounging jacket had that distinctive cut of London's Bond Street. Several of Trent's employees hovered about mostly distraught upon arriving at work to find the police on the premises and their employer murdered. Ned Aswan had spoken to each of them offering them comfort and solace when it was he who was sadly in need of them. The employees set about trying to bring order to the chaos created by the ransacking while tears ran down cheeks and there was lots of snuffling and the expected array of expletives. Bogart spoke to some of the employees he knew and they appreciated his kindness while remembering to commiserate with him on Hannah Darrow's death. Jim Mallory conversed with a detective who had been at Bogart's house the previous night and said the Bogarts got off lucky. Villon was told Ned Aswan was on the next floor checking for any missing valuables. Villon headed up the rather grand staircase imported by Joshua Trent from a castle in Scotland. Villon gestured for Bogart, Hammett, and Hellman to follow, while Mallory continued talking to the detective.

Hellman was impressed. She wasn't easily impressed, but now she was impressed. The grand staircase, the imposing crystal chandelier suspended from a ceiling two stories above. The superb and some not so superb art that hung along the walls.

"Tamara de Lempicka," Hellman told Hammett, identifying a large oil of an aristocratic woman, with, sweetly enough, one breast exposed. It was a beautifully formed breast and Hellman admired it, while, Hammett was positive, envying it.

"And who is Tamara de Lempicka? Or who was Tamara de Lempicka?"

"In the twenties, Dash, she was the darling of Parisian high society, especially those with low morals. I'm surprised to see her work here. In Europe, she's fallen into disfavor. Her work doesn't sell anymore."

"Is she dead?"

"No, she's still alive. She's not old. No more than about forty or so. I met her at a cocktail party in New York a couple of years ago. I like her work. I wish I owned one. I think someday she'll be very very valuable."

"Maybe."

"Dash, remember how they scoffed at Modigliani? How I wish I owned a Modigliani." Jim Mallory was taking the stairs two at a time. Hellman snapped, "Have you no respect for the dead?" Mallory flashed her a look and then chose to ignore her, continuing his ascent.

The grand staircase led to an even grander reception hall that had been famous as the site of so many stupendous cocktail and dinner parties. There was more imposing artwork on the walls, all of them hanging askew, as though visited by a small army of house maids who wanted to impress the master of the house with their skillful dusting. Bogart was heartsick at the damage. He had enjoyed this room as a guest on several occasions, a warmly welcomed guest not because he was a celebrity but because Joshua Trent was a caring man who liked people and never discriminated.

From his right he heard Ned Aswan's familiar voice. "Oh Bogie. Shambles. At last we have something in common. If Josh was alive and saw this he'd drop dead." They embraced.

Then Bogart introduced him to Hellman and Hammett and then to Villon and Mallory.

Aswan's face lit up. "Lillian Hellman and Dashiell Hammett. Joshua will never forgive himself for missing the chance to meet you two. He knelt at the feet of genius."

For want of anything better to say, Hellman said, "We're sorry we missed him, too. Bogie has told me so many wonderful things about him."

"Just about everything about Josh was wonderful. His capacity for friendship, for loving and spreading love among his friends, his superb taste, his Toll House cookies." Ned Aswan was of medium height and in his late thirties with a handsome face that stopped short just this side of decadence. When he had just passed his eighteenth birthday, Joshua Trent discovered him working at a gasoline station. As the legend goes, it was something about the way he handled the gas pump that caused Trent to swoop the young innocent into his Cadillac convertible and brand him as his own. Ned Aswan never looked back because he never cared to. Here was the very reasonable facsimile of a fairy godmother who was also incredibly rich and decently attractive and offering to train him in interiors with Ned proving in time to be a very worthy apprentice.

"I don't know how I'll survive without him," said Ned.

"You'll do just fine. My money's on you, Ned."

"You're so generous, Bogie. Oh my God! Where's Mayo? Does she know?"

"I phoned her. She's at her mother's in Portland. Couldn't cope with our own disaster."

"I don't know if I can cope with this one. Does her mother have another spare bedroom?" And he suddenly exploded. "What the hell kind of madmen could do a thing like this? Murder poor Joshua! Murder him! Not just tie him up and stuff a gag in his mouth! But murder him! The monsters! May they roast in hell!"

Villon said, "Maybe he made the mistake of fighting back."

"*Joshua?* Joshua fight back? How? Oh God. When the smoke has settled I must think of a memorial service." He righted an overturned chair and sat on it. "I don't understand this! I just don't understand this! As far as I can tell so far, nothing's been taken. The wall safe hasn't been broken into. It's behind *Whistler's Uncle.* One of his lesser known paintings. There's not a scratch. There's so much in this house they could have stolen, I'm insulted they haven't made off with a thing." Mallory had provided chairs for the others and even found some ashtrays in the wreckage on the floor. Bogart and Hellman promptly lit up while Villon positioned himself next to Aswan.

Villon began, "Tell me Mr. Aswan . . ."

"Please call me Ned. I loathe Aswan. It's a perfectly awful name. I once thought of changing my name to Ned Hepburn because I adore Katharine Hepburn. But at the time Josh wouldn't let me because she was box-office poison. Now she isn't anymore but I haven't the strength to think of anything but getting this house back in order and oh Christ getting in touch with Josh's family . . . one of the secretaries can do that . . . and oh my God will somebody give me a cigarette?"

"You don't smoke," said Bogart.

"I do now." Bogart gave him a cigarette and lit it for him. Aswan puffed but didn't inhale. Neither Bogart nor Hammett relished hearing another fit of coughing.

Villon was speaking. "Ned, I believe you spent last night in Santa Barbara."

Ned's eyes widened. "You're questioning me! Oh my God! I can't possibly be a suspect!" He asked Bogie, "Am I?"

Bogie said, "It's just police routine."

"Oh God, I can't face questions now." The look on Villon's face told him to face questions. "Yes I spent the night in Santa Barbara at Mr. and Mrs. Samuel Potter's. I was doing an estimation for redoing their villa which is a monstrosity. I stayed for dinner and by the time we'd polished off a lot of port it was too late for me to head back to L.A. and I was in no condition to drive anyway. I left early this morning and got here around eight. Our employees don't get in until half past nine and that would give me time to shower and breakfast with Joshua which is a ritual with us so we can plan the day." His eyes were misting and Hellman was suddenly feeling maternal with an urge to take him in her arms until a cooler head prevailed. "I came in from the garage which is behind the house. It's a six-car garage except we only have five cars." He shrieked. "The kitchen! What they did to the kitchen! I was terrified by what I saw! I shouted for Josh. I ran from room to room until I was in the showroom and there he was, stabbed in the heart. So much blood, so much blood. What's that line from *Macbeth?*"

Jim Mallory provided it. " 'Who would have thought the old man to have had so much blood in him?' "

"Aren't you clever. Except he wasn't all that old. He was only fifty-three and he'd kill me for telling you." He bit his lower lip. "I'm sorry. I'm not behaving well."

Hellman said sincerely, "I think you're behaving beautifully. If it was me I'd be shrieking the house down with hysterics."

Ned said, "If you care to stick around, wait until you hear me later when all this really sinks in."

"Ned, you know what a cornucopia is?" asked Villon.

"Of course I do. They're absolute kitsch. Only a grandmother would own one."

"Do you own one?"

"Oh years ago we had one. From the Henry B. Walthall estate. You might have heard of him. Joshua told me he was in *Birth of a Nation.* When he died about five years ago Joshua bought some of his effects. We didn't really want them but the family wasn't too well off and it was Joshua's way of helping. He was always doing sweet things like that."

Villon told him, "We think the killers were after the cornucopia."

"That cheesy thing?"

Bogart told him the cornucopia story. At the finish, Ned exclaimed, "You mean we had those jewels under this roof and didn't know it?" He thought for a moment. "It was quite an interesting piece, come to think of it. Samuel Goldwyn bought it from us."

"Sam Goldwyn? Maybe it was for his wife, Frances."

Hellman interjected. "Nobody gives Frances Goldwyn a cornucopia. A necklace of matched pearls or a bracelet studded with star saphires. But a cornucopia? Never."

Bogart was laughing. "I doubt if it was intended as a gift."

"It wasn't," said Ned. "It was for a movie, that awful thing Gary Cooper did a couple of years ago. *The Adventures of Marco Polo.*" He paused. "This sudden quiet. You could hear a pin drop. Anyone got a pin?"

TEN

Nobody had a pin and nobody wanted to hear a pin drop. Hellman said with irritation, "Of all the producers in this town to be involved with the cornucopia, it has to be the man I'm working for. He's probably been to my office by now, and, finding me missing, yelling his head off all over the lot."

"Screw him," said Hammett.

"You have no taste," growled Hellman. "Wipe that silly grin from your face, Bogie, it's totally incongruous."

"I grin when I'm amused. And I'm amused. I did *Dead End* for Sam four years ago. He didn't give me any headaches. I got along with him just fine. Lily, you've got to learn to curb your temperament."

"I am not in the least bit temperamental. Dash, am I temperamental?" He was lighting a cigarette so Hellman continued. "I can't stand interference. Sam's always interfering. When he hires a gifted person such as I am he should trust me. Let's go give him a hard time."

"About what?"

"About the cornucopia. He's got a fortune under the studio roof, the very thought of it might bring on a stroke."

"If it's the one we're looking for."

Villon asked Bogie, "You game to take on Goldwyn?"

"What the hell," replied Bogie. "He's got a great liquor supply. I could use a drink."

Ned Aswan nimbly leaped to his feet. "Let me see what I can find."

"Oh no. Don't you bother yourself," said Bogie. "You're in mourning."

"Oh no," said Ned softly. "I'm not mourning Josh. I'm celebrating him. I know this will sound maudlin, but he gave

111

me my life. My opportunity to become somebody." He smiled. "Now it's my turn. Now I pick up the torch and run with it. I shall help someone make something of themselves the way Josh helped me." He happened to look at Mallory and smile. Mallory's face went ashen. Ned looked at Bogie. "I know there's champagne in the refrigerator."

Bogart said, "Forget it, Ned. Herb here's got a heavy schedule and he's kind enough to let us participate. You might have heard I'm about to start a new movie from a book by our friend Hammett here. A detective named Sam Spade. I'm getting a lot of pointers from Herb."

Villon smiled. He was feeling good. Bogart getting pointers from him. He heard Hellman say, "Another silly grin! It's epidemic!"

"Bogie," said Villon, "you've made my day."

Hammett was at a window that overlooked the front porch. "They're taking the body away."

Ned howled. "Oh no! Not until I've said good-bye!"

Villon stopped him from running downstairs. "Ned. He's being taken for an autopsy. They'll let you know when to claim his body. Probably some time tomorrow."

"Autopsy," echoed Ned. "What an awful word."

Villon said to Bogart, "I repeat, you game for Goldwyn?"

"Don't you have to stick around here?"

"To do what? My men are all over the place and I trust every single one of them. My forensics team is one of the best in the country. Let's get going." He put a hand on Ned Aswan's shoulder. "I know you'll be all right."

"I'll be just dandy." His voice was flat and morose. He looked around the once lavishly appointed room now in a pitiful state. "I never realized how big this place is. When you're happy, size doesn't matter."

Hellman spoke the thought that had just come to her. "Ned, why don't you come back to the Garden of Allah with Dash and me. It's crazy for you to stay here by yourself until some sort of order is restored."

"I'm not afraid. I know Josh is looking after me." Hellman felt her skin crawl but said nothing. She foresaw an awful lot of conversations between Ned Aswan and the shade of Joshua Trent. Well why not. He would find it comforting.

Bogart said to Hellman, "You and Dash jumping ship?"

"I relish no confrontation with Mr. Goldwyn at the moment. Okay with you, Dash? We grab some lunch someplace and go sit by the pool and splash everyone?"

" 'Whither thou goest,' my love," said Hammett as he bid Ned a warm good-bye and led Hellman to the grand staircase. Over his shoulder he called to Bogart and Villon, "You know where to find us if you get lonely."

Mallory wished Ned well and Villon and Bogart took more time with him. Villon handed him a card. "If you think of something or if you need me, here's my card."

"I'm so grateful. You're so kind." He pocketed the card. "It's hard to believe the gossip about police corruption." Villon winced while Bogart took Ned's arm and squeezed it reassuringly.

"Now I don't want you in this place getting depressed all by yourself."

"You mean I should invite a few friends over to get depressed with me?" asked Ned airily. "Actually, 'Butch' Romero and some friends are coming by later to take me to dinner. It'll be more like a wake." He paused and smiled. "It's like I said. We'll celebrate Josh's memory."

"Drink one for me," said Bogart as he released Ned's arm. He hurried down the stairs with Villon and Mallory in pursuit. Mallory caught the eye of a pretty secretary who at some other time might have signaled encouragement. He made a mental reminder to return with some trumped up excuse to see Ned Aswan and another go at the handsome woman. Villon said to Mallory, "Call the precinct and let them know we're off to the Goldwyn studios and not for screen tests. I'll stay with Bogie and make sure he keeps his eye on the road."

Mallory trotted to the unmarked police car leaving Villon to field questions from the reporters who were still milling about. The photographers concentrated on Bogart while reporters wanted to know what was his connection to the investigation. Bogart reminded them he'd been victimized the previous evening and continued the myth of studying Villon for his new picture. He figured the least he owed Jack Warner was some gratuitous plugs. Villon said, "Should we maybe phone ahead and let Goldwyn know we're on our way?"

"Don't worry. He'll be there. Sam's one landlord who can always be found on the premises and that often includes Sundays." At Hollywood studios before unionization, it was a six-day working week. Very often it was a seven-day working week with no overtime, something about which Bogart did a lot of grousing.

In the car, Bogart said, "I better refill the tank." Villon suggested a station at Hollywood Boulevard and Fairfax Avenue which was conveniently en route to the Goldwyn studios on Santa Monica Boulevard. They passed Mallory who was talking into the car radio and Bogart maneuvered carefully down the drive past badly parked police and press vehicles, unaware the departure was being watched by Ned Aswan from an upstairs window. Ned's face was tear stained. He hadn't lost a friend and a lover, he'd lost a father. He covered his face with his hands and whispered, "Help me. Please help me."

In Bogart's car, Villon said, "It's better to have Hellman as a friend, isn't it."

"So you noticed. I don't think she realizes she's so mean and ornery. It's second nature to her. Dash says it's her protective armor."

"Protective from what?"

"Everything and anything. She and my wife are sisters under the skin. Everybody's against them. Everybody's out to get them. Be on the offensive before they get a chance to attack you. This business is loaded with their carbon copies. Crawford. Connie Bennett. Boy there's a bitch on wheels if ever there was one. Like I said before, Cagney and Davis. On the other hand, there're the sweethearts. Barbara Stanwyck for instance. A broad from Brooklyn and doesn't forget it. Irene Dunne. A real lady with a great sense of humor. Joan

Blondell. She's my angel. If both of us were free I'd ask her to marry me, but she's stuck with that putz Dick Powell. Glad Lily and Dash pulled out?"

Villon shrugged. "People don't bother me. If they're here, they're here, if they're not, they're not. I've taught myself to tune out. That's mostly thanks to my beloved Hazel who by now is finished at the beauty parlor and has her antennae out trying to track me down."

"You ever going to marry her? I don't notice her wearing an engagement ring. If you *are* engaged, let me tell you something I once overheard my mother telling one of my sisters. 'Long engagements are hard on short tempers.' One of the few times she ever gave them any advice that I knew of. She didn't like them. Hey! There's the gas station!" He pulled in, rolled down his window, said to the attendant "Fill it up!"

The goggle-eyed attendant asked, "Are you really him?"

"Yeah," said Bogart, "I'm Stan Laurel."

"Ah g'wan," said the attendant, while Bogart groped for his wallet.

Villon said, "Be nice to him. He might be the next Ned Aswan."

After they left the filling station, Bogart asked Villon, "What do you think, Herb? Although I suppose it's too early to tell. There being only two ransackings so far. Do you suppose it's the start of a pattern?"

"Like I said, it could very well be. Your mother-in-law and you were ransacked because Captain Methot was the start of the Yellow Brick Road. That's the countess and her bunch. I'm convinced they did the job in Portland and did it badly. Your wife pointed out what a cinch it was for them to make it here from Portland with plenty of time for tea. As for doing your place and murdering Hannah Darrow, their only alibi is each other. But somehow, I can't buy them as killers."

"Why not? Marcelo Amati strikes me as being hot-blooded."

"That's because he's your stereotype hot-blooded Italian and as an actor you're always dealing with stereotypes. But let me tell you, Bogie, in my experience with so-called hot-bloods and hot tempers it usually turns out they've mostly got piss in their veins. As to Joshua Trent, whoever did your housekeeper did Trent. Same modus operandi. Same kind of violence. Same kind of anger. This person is very familiar with the world of L.A. dealers and collectors. With Joshua Trent they were starting at the top. Big bucks and big contacts. They'd be in a position to get their hands on hidden treasures. Most of these people are duplicitous. Most of them are always suffering a slow cash flow. They live high off the hog because they're expected to. But it's a rough go. The trick is, did Joshua Trent know the origin of the cornucopia story or was he as much in the dark as Ned Aswan appeared to be?"

"I think if Josh suspected he had a hidden treasure, he'd have unsealed it and looked."

"Maybe he did," said Villon.

Bogart was lighting a cigarette. "Ned would have known."

"You're right. So if they had the treasure, they didn't know it and sold it to Goldwyn for of all crazy coincidences, *The Adventures of Marco Polo*."

They were nearing the studio. Bogart bore down on his horn as a teenager on a bicycle cut across him and sped into a side street. Bogart was furious. "And I suppose if I had hit him, you'd have booked me for manslaughter!" He turned into a dirt road that led to the studio entrance. He pulled into the gate. The guard recognized him and smiled.

"Hiya Bogie! Long time no see! Gonna be doin' a pitcher with us?"

Bogart remembered his name. "No Isaac, I don't do quickies."

"Ho ho! Let the boss hear you say that. I don't have you on my visitor's list." Villon flashed his badge. "Say! Who you after?"

"Goldwyn," said Villon.

"No! What's the beef?"

"Just after some information."

Isaac looked from left to right and back again, as though

there might be some danger of being overheard. He asked conspiratorially, "Morals?"

"I don't know," said Villon, "I suppose he has some."

Isaac guffawed. He said to Bogart, "He's still in the same building."

"Thanks Isaac." Slowly, Bogart drove ahead and carefully. There was unusually heavy pedestrian traffic. "Sam must have rented a lot of space this month. A lot of independent producers use Sam's lot. He offers top facilities and a good dining room. On the other hand, a lot of producers steer clear because Sam is always sticking his two cents in. Ever cross paths with him?"

"Oh yeah. Back in twenty-nine. A series of killings involving Diamond Films. Remember Alexander Diamond?"

"Sure. 'If It's A Good Film, It's a Diamond.'"

"Goldwyn was a friend of Diamond's." He chuckled. "Diamond was having trouble with an actress who was forever forgetting her lines. Goldwyn is supposed to have suggested she might be suffering from magnesia."

"It makes for a good joke," said Bogie, "but all those Goldwynisms were and still are dreamed up by a smart press agent. You don't get to the top of the heap where Goldwyn is by being a Mrs. Malaprop. There's a parking space. God is on my side. I've never seen the lot this crowded."

Sam Goldwyn had been presiding over his kingdom for almost two decades, when he broke away from Metro-Goldwyn-Mayer to go it as an independent. He let them keep his name and they let him keep his integrity. He had only a few stars under contract, but they were top drawer. His major asset was Ronald Colman who he nursed successfully from silents into talkies. He developed Gary Cooper into a major star. His only serious misjudgement was the Russian actress Anna Sten who was very beautiful and a very good actress but not in English. She cost him a lot of money, a blow he was a long time recovering from. Goldwyn's near-implacable taste in film properties was now legendary. Most importantly, he invested his own money. He earned millions and poured it back into his own productions. He happened to be standing at a window that overlooked the entrance to his building, hands folded behind his back, deep in thought, when he saw Bogart and Villon approaching. He was pleased. The man with Bogart seemed familiar but he couldn't place him. Goldwyn went to his desk and signaled his secretary on the intercom. "I'm available now." He was positive Bogart and his friend were coming to see him. Who else would a star like Bogart come see at his studio? The secretary announced Bogart and Villon.

Goldwyn was standing, arms outstretched as the door opened and Bogart came in with Villon. Magnanimously, Goldwyn cried, "Hungry Bogart! What a nice surprise!"

Bogart winced. "Sam, you old gonif." They shook hands. "This is Herb Villon. He's a detective with the downtown precinct. You might remember him from those Alexander Diamond murders."

"Of course! How could I forget such a clever detective!" He hadn't the vaguest remembrance of ever having had met Herb Villon. "Sit down, boys, sit down. Terrible thing that happened to you, Bogie." He said to Villon, "I assume you're heading the case and tracking the murderer. That's why you come to me? Maybe I'm the murderer?" He laughed. "They write stories about how I murder the English language. Believe me. I'm not all that exclusive. I also murder French and Spanish." He winked at Bogie. "Something tells me you could use a little schnapps. How about you, Herb Vilson?"

"Villon."

"So what did I say."

"You said 'Vilson'," said Bogart, knowing Goldwyn had mispronounced his name deliberately.

Goldwyn said, "Maybe I was thinking of Woodrow Villon." He was at his well-stocked bar.

Villon said, "I never drink while on duty."

"So make believe you're not on duty. You're in Sam Goldwyn's office, so have something. Some bourbon? Some rye?"

Villon said, "Have you got some seltzer water?"

Goldwyn snorted. "You heard of a Jewish producer who doesn't stock seltzer? By us it's better then a blood transfusion. Bogie?"

"Scotch'll be fine."

"I've got a great brand here. Smuggled to me exclusively from Mexico. You can imagine what the war is doing to the scotch industry. War." He shook his head from side to side. "Everything's rationed. What I go through getting film stock!"

Bogart smiled. "But you get it."

"Of course I get it. We all get it. We need entertainment and the movies are the number one entertainment in the world next to sex, and it's less energetic. Talk about sex, how's your wife Mamie."

"Mayo."

"Mayo?" He was pouring the scotch. "When did she change it?"

"Come on, Sam, we're here on serious business." He brought Bogart his drink and then found a seltzer bottle and squirted a glass full for Villon.

"So get serious. I'm stopping you?"

"There's been another murder. Maybe you haven't heard about it. Joshua Trent."

"My God. I wonder if my Frances heard. Joshua Trent? But how? Why?" Bogart told him the how and the why.

"And I bought this cornucopia for *Marco Polo?* Maybe I did and maybe I didn't."

"You did. Ned Aswan says you did."

"If he says I did, then I did." He buzzed his secretary. She entered immediately, a handsome middle-aged woman named Sarah with a pleasant smile and a no-nonsense look that bespoke efficiency.

"Sarah. You know what's a cornucopia?"

"Yes, I do."

"Do we have one?"

"We had one."

"What happened to it?"

She sounded as though he should remember what happened to it. "It was sold at the auction!"

"Aha! The auction. So the auctioneer would have a record as to who bought it." He told Bogart and Villon, "Last year I set up an auction to get rid of a lot of junk that accumulates. Made a nice profit. That's because at a Sam Goldwyn auction people bid more than at an ordinary auction. You remember the auctioneer?"

"How could I forget. It was my cousin Herman Zabin."

Goldwyn said to Bogart and Villon, "See. We keep everything in the family. If it isn't her family, it's my family. Sarah, phone your cousin and tell him to look up the cornucopia and to who did he sell it." She nodded and left. "While we're waiting, let's discuss a movie, Bogie."

"You got a movie you want me to do, you discuss it with Jack Warner. He's very particular when it comes to lending actors."

"From Jack Warner I wouldn't borrow a cup of sugar."

"He probably wouldn't lend it. It's rationed."

Sam Goldwyn was back on the track with murder. "Joshua Trent murdered. What won't they think of next?" He asked Villon, "You got any clues?"

"I haven't got much besides my suspicions."

"I can tell from looking at you that your suspicions are good suspicions. Just like my Frances. She's very good with suspicions." He rambled on about his wife and his son and Bogart and Villon refused refills. Sarah returned at last with a paper in her hand.

"Sorry it took so long. Herman had to dig in his files. Here. I've written down the buyer's name, address, and phone number."

Villon took the paper and read aloud, "Mrs. Angelica Harper."

"Oh boy," said Goldwyn.

"That sounds like you know her," said Bogart.

"By the way," said Sarah, "there's a Mr. Mallory waiting for you."

Villon asked, "Why didn't you show him in?"

"Well actually," said Sarah, "I was going to announce him but he said he'd just as soon wait."

Villon went to the door and opened it and said to Jim Mallory, "You suddenly shy or something?"

"Well through the door I heard Mr. Goldwyn going on about his wife and son and I didn't want to interrupt."

"Okay, we're about to leave."

Bogart asked Goldwyn, "Who's Mrs. Angelica Harper?"

"You never heard of her? Well, she's an artist. Not just an artist, but a highly eccentric one. In fact, she's crazy. It would be just like her to bid for a cornucopia. Maybe she doesn't have it anymore. You better call her. Here, use the phone."

Villon dialed and by the fifth ring Mrs. Harper answered. Villon introduced himself and explained about the cornucopia she'd bought at auction.

"The cornucopia! Of course! You're a detective? Wonderful! You can help me. Do you have my address? Come right over!" She slammed her phone down.

Villon said to Goldwyn, "She sounds a little off center."

"Not just a little, believe me. My Frances bought one of her paintings. She wanted to come stay with us for a few days until the painting adjusted to its new home."

"I see," said Villon. "One of those. Well Bogie," he looked at the address on the paper, "she's not too far from here. Down the road a piece on Fairfax Avenue. Thanks for your help, Mr. Goldwyn, good to see you again."

"Anytime. Now that you know the way, don't be a stranger. Tell me Bogie, maybe you can break your contract with Jack Warner?"

ELEVEN

The Hollywood grapevine crackled with the electricity of hot news. Joshua Trent's murder was definitely hot news. Even as Sam Goldwyn entertained Bogart and Villon, Trent's murder was a special flash on local radio stations. The former screen queen Marion Davies heard it at her palatial beach house in Santa Monica while sharing martinis with Mary Astor. Both women had known Joshua Trent. It seemed that every woman connected with films was acquainted with Joshua Trent. They were sitting on a veranda that overlooked the beach, though the house itself was surrounded by a ten-foot high protective wall atop which were layers of barbed wire that could cause instant electrocution if touched. Armed guards patrolled the premises with trained police dogs. It seemed to Mary Astor there was a small army of these guards. She was tempted to ask Davies how she lived this way, wasn't it uncomfortable, wasn't it scary and then she looked at Davies leaning over in her chair to catch every word coming from the console radio. The woman's face was a blank, a heavily made-up blank.

"A knife in his heart," said Davies, "just like Bogie's housekeeper. Mary, I think there are maniacs on the loose."

"What's so special about that in this town?" Astor sipped her martini reminding herself to restrict her intake to two glasses as the martinis served in the Davies household were notoriously potent and there was a dinner engagement in Holmby Hills that night awaiting her attendance.

Davies said, "I think I'll ask Bill to hire more guards. Double what we've got."

"Seems to me you've got a good-size private army as it is."

"Them? Them on the beach? They're on the lookout for

Jap invaders in case there are any on the way. Bill says there's going to be trouble with Japan.''

"Why?"

"Why not?"

Bill was the powerful newspaper tycoon, William Randolph Hearst. Marion Davies had been his mistress for close to twenty-five years, he having plucked her from the chorus of a Ziegfeld Follies, determined to possess her physically and to make her a major star of motion pictures. Both of his ambitions where she was concerned cost Hearst millions of dollars. Surprisingly enough, Davies turned out to have a delicious sense of humor which worked well for her in several films, and for over two decades. She even succeeded in talkies despite a pronounced stutter which she learned to control and finally retired in 1938 after a succession of flops. On her retirement, she had millions of dollars, owned real estate on both coasts, including an office building on the southeast corner of Park Avenue and East 57th Street. Her jewelry collection, of course, was impressive and blinding.

The newscaster signed off and Davies turned off the radio. "Mary?"

"Yes, Marion?"

"You're a pretty smart kid, right?"

Mary Astor smiled. "Sometimes too smart."

"There's no such thing as too smart," said Davies, stirring the pitcher of martinis on the table next to her and then refilling her glass. "You know a lot about everything. What's a cornucopia?"

Astor told her.

"A horn of plenty? What the hell's a horn of plenty?"

Astor gestured with her hand. "All this. You live in the midst of a horn of plenty. Of course all your wealth is a metaphor."

"What's a metaphor?"

"An example. A horn of plenty and great wealth are often synonymous."

"What's synonymous?"

"Let's go back to cornucopia."

"This horn of plenty." Davies was getting warmed up to the subject. "Is it anything like a ram's horn?"

"I don't think I've seen a ram's horn."

"Oh sure you have. It's what the Jews blow on Yom Kippur eve. That's their highest holy day. I had a Jewish lover who taught me all this stuff. The Jews call the ram's horn a shofar. You know when my lover said he had to go to shul that night . . . shul, you know is a synagogue . . . because they were going to blow the shofar. I misheard what he said and thought they were going to blow the chauffeur which near convulsed me . . ."

"Marion?"

"What."

"That's an old one."

"Yeah, but it's still good. I pulled it on Bill before you got here and he went *heh heh heh*. For Bill, that's a belly laugh. He called me from the castle. He's up there for a couple of days. He says we had a cornucopia someplace. If it's up at the castle, they'll never find it. So much damn junk up there. Y'know, there's crates of stuff Bill's brought from abroad that have never been opened?"

"I know. You showed me the last time I was there."

"Oh I did?"

"You did." She could tell the martinis were having an effect. Lunch had been promised but there was not a sign of it.

"Well if it's not up at the castle, it must be here someplace. And say ! . . ." She sat up and looked like an obscenely evil child, "if it's the same one that has them ransacking and murdering, I've got a hidden fortune." She contemplated what she had just said. "And I need a hidden fortune like I need a third tit. And I don't relish the thought of being ransacked or murdered."

"You've got nothing to worry about what with your guards and their dogs."

"Honeybunch, believe me, there are ways of getting in and out of this place without being caught. I know. I've done it. Often."

"What about the high wall and barbed wire?"

"Mary, do you know how often this dump's been broken into? Bill keeps it out of the papers when it happens to discourage any copycats. But they keep on coming. This joint's a real challenge. A good crook, and by good I mean a crackerjack, a whiz, a topnotch professional can get into and out of any place if he sets his mind to it. When I was in the Follies I met a lot of shady characters and from them I learned plenty."

"I can pick a lock," continued Davies.

"You can't."

"Sure can. With a bobby pin. Bill gave up locking me in my room because I was as good an escape artist as Harry Houdini." She suddenly went all dreamy. "God Harry was a great lay." A butler materialized. "What do you want?"

"Luncheon is served."

She said to Mary, "It's always luncheon. It's never lunch. And it's never ever 'Soup's on' anymore." She said to the butler, "Okay, okay, Jeeves. We're coming." She struggled off the chaise longue on which she'd been reclining.

"His name isn't really Jeeves, is it?"

"How the hell should I know? Never saw him before this morning. Boy, war sure is hell. Can't hold on to the help anymore. They're going off to factories and shipyards where they get paid a fortune." She took Mary Astor's arm. "Let me help you, dear, you're a little unsteady."

"Which way do we go?" asked Astor.

"Straight ahead and turn left at the Rembrandt. Christ, I hope it isn't chicken à la king again." She brightened. "Maybe it's a big fruit salad. All laid out in a cornucopia. Hmm. I wonder if we have that effing thing. So you're signed to Warner now. Son of a bitch ruined my career. That last stinker, *Ever Since Eve*." She shook her head. "I hear they're still fumigating the theaters."

"Do you miss making movies?"

"Nah! I only made them because Bill wanted me to. There's only one thing I miss about making movies."

"What's that?"

"Screwing my leading men. Ha ha ha ha ha!"

Fairfax Avenue was one of the cosier streets in West Hollywood. It was predominantly Jewish and also famous for Hollywood High School which produced a good share of movie personalities. Bogart and Mayo in their happier days came here at least once a week on a Friday, a few hours before the start of the Jewish Sabbath to shop for such goodies as smoked salmon, smoked whitefish or carp or sturgeon, challah bread, onion rolls, pickled herring in sour cream or au naturel, chicken noodle soup, matzo balls (Mayo, on her first time here with Bogart asking in all innocence, "What kind of balls are matzo balls?"), stuffed derma, gefilte fish, brisket of beef. Bogart's mouth was watering.

"Say Herb, how's it if I pull into Canter's parking lot?"

"I'm all for it, but first let's attend to Angelica Harper. She sounded a little frantic on the phone." Bogart had driven a block past Fairfax Avenue's commercial area. Villon was looking ahead through the windshield. "There's a very strange-looking house ahead on the left on a very large lot."

"Where?"

"You blind? The gray thing with the turrets. Looks like an imitation castle."

Bogart laughed. "Oh sure. I've passed it dozens of times. Do you suppose that's Mrs. Harper's?"

"Pull over. There's a mailbox with an address printed on it."

Bogart pulled over. The address on the mailbox confirmed this was the residence of Angelica Harper. There was a short road behind a locked gate that led to what seemed to be a moat over which there lay a drawbridge. "There's a speaker in the gate," said Bogart. "I'm going to park here. It looks safe."

They left the car and went to the speaker. There was a button that Villon pressed. No response. He pressed again. Bogart was staring up at a turret and said, " 'Rapunzel, Rapunzel, let your hair down.' "

They heard what they supposed was Mrs. Harper's voice. "Yes?"

"Mrs. Harper. I'm detective Villon!"

"But mais oui! Le gendarme! Au secours!" They heard a buzzing noise and the gate clicked open. "Entrez! Entrez! Bienvenue or whatever the hell you're supposed to say."

Bogart and Villon looked at each other. Bogart said, "This is not real."

"This is Hollywood," said Villon. "For Hollywood, this is real." They passed through the gate and walked to the draw-bridge. Bogart looked in the moat. "Real water." He grimaced. "And lots of dead things."

Villon said, "The drawbridge is a fake." At the end of the drawbridge was a wooden door. Villon tried the knob and pushed it open. They walked into what was probably a reception room, though it held very little furniture. There was a long wooden table that Villon tested by shaking it. It was quite sturdy. Around the table were about a dozen wooden chairs that Bogart thought were probably fifteenth century in design. There were tapestries on the walls depicting medieval knights jousting and hunters stalking deer and wild boar and to Bogart's delight, the fairy tale heroine Rapunzel with her mile of blonde hair floating down from a window at the top of a turret where she was imprisoned.

"I know," said Villon. "It's a movie set." There was a circular wooden staircase that led up a long flight to a balcony that seemed to lead to a hall and other rooms. On the opposite wall just past the balcony was a double door. From behind the double door came the unlikely sounds of a harp being plucked. Bogart recognized the melody, "I Dreamt I Dwelt in Marble Halls."

"Most inappropriate," said Bogart, "there's not a slab of marble in sight."

"I think we're supposed to go through the double doors," said Villon.

"I hope we're not interrupting a recital," said Bogart.

Villon pushed open the double doors. They entered a studio that was two stories high and aglow in sunshine pouring through the glass roof overhead. There was indeed a harp and playing it was a very thin little lady of an indeterminate age with a beatific expression on her face. Several feet beyond her was a platform with an easel and canvas and daubing at the canvas wearing a smock and a beret with a devil-may-care attitude was undoubtedly their hostess, Angelica Harper, holding a palette in her left hand and a brush in her right. She was probably sixtyish, but, as Bogart noticed, she had very shapely legs. Bogart was known to be a sucker for a shapely leg. Her smile was beguiling, enticing. "Mes amis! Vous avez arrivez! Which means, My friends, you have arrived at last!" She laughed. "I'm terribly pretentious! In time you'll get used to it." She said to the harpist, "That was just fine, Letitia. Absolutely splendid." She said to the men, "Letitia is practicing to be an angel." Having divested herself of her painting appurtenances, Mrs. Harper slowly walked down the six steps that led from the platform, while Letitia curtsied and then scampered out a door that in a flash Bogart saw led to a kitchen.

Villon introduced himself and Bogart.

"Of course I recognize Mr. Bogart," said Mrs. Harper. He took the hand she extended and shook it. She seemed disappointed. Hand kissing was an art that had eluded Bogart. Likewise Villon who shook hers lightly. She indicated a sofa and some easy chairs in another corner of the room where apparently she occasionally held court. "I can offer you port or chablis." Both men refused. "It's just as well. The glasses are a bit dirty." She looked at four glasses on a nearby table that held the bottles of port and chablis. "In fact, they're filthy. I must have a word with Letitia. In fact, I shall have several words with Letitia. She keeps house for me in addition to providing mood music that I require when I'm working. I'd say she was a treasure but she isn't. She's been with me for years, ever since my husband died." She was seated in an easy chair that resembled a throne. "My husband built my castle. He designed it."

"He was an architect?"

"He was an idiot," she said with a charming smile. "But he

was rich rich rich!" Her arms were outflung and there was a lascivious look of ecstasy on her face. "Archibald Harper was a rogue, but never a peasant slave. He based this castle on the one Douglas Fairbanks had designed for his *Robin Hood*. Doug was a good friend, he visited often. These are all my creations." One of her hands was making lavish circles in the air drawing their attention to the walls which were crowded with framed canvases of varying sizes and dimensions. Angelica Harper's works covered a broad canvas of their own. There were still lives and portraits of celebrities from the historical past. There was one of a nurse who Bogart assumed was probably Florence Nightingale though he found the leer on her face somewhat confusing. There was a pretty good one of Rasputin, the mad monk with a soulful expression that seemed somewhat out of place.

Villon seemed mesmerized by a huge canvas of nymphs and satyrs cavorting in a forest glen with the god Pan tootling his pipes and it was all refreshingly pornographic. All the while they studied her work the artist rewarded them with a monologue about herself and her art.

"On the far right you have Marie Antoinette in the kitchen at Versailles icing the cakes for the poor. Just below her is George Washington crossing the Delaware and he is violently seasick. To the right of George is Alexander Graham Bell phoning information for a number and below him is Betsy Ross tearing the flag apart because she's displeased with the color arrangement." She stopped speaking. They stared at her. She shut her eyes and after a few beats, reopened them slowly. "Gentlemen. I am psychic. There is a sword of Damocles dangling over both of your heads. There are ectoplasms of death surrounding your bodies." Bogart considered screaming but didn't want to alarm Herb Villon. "I know the tainted history of the cornucopia you're looking for. It may be mine. It's sealed. I've never tried to open it. I like things to be left intact. It's depicted in a painting I sold to the Goldwyns. I know about your house being ransacked and your housekeeper murdered, Mr. Bogart. Quelle tragedie. And Mr. Villon, I know about the ransacking at Joshua

Trent's and his tragic death. Un autre tragedie." She smiled. "I've taken up studying French. You'll forgive my occasional Gallic interjections. Mr. Bogart, do you perhaps speak any French?"

Bogart said, "Un peu."

"Oh you do, you do! How clever you are." She had crossed to a wall behind them and stood in front of the portrait of a handsome man who seemed rather effete, or that was how Mrs. Harper had caught her subject. "This is Joshua Trent." The portrait nowhere resembled the grotesque corpse they had seen earlier in the day. "The mouth is not as good as I wanted it to be because he never shut it. Talk talk talk a mile a minute. Gossip gossip gossip. But a kind man and a generous one. Of course you know he was murdered."

"I'm assigned to the case. Remember the cornucopia."

"Indeed. As there are those who remember the Maine." She walked slowly back to them. "Then you've met Ned Aswan. I assume he inherits everything." She smiled. "Being men of the world, we accept that they were a homosexual relationship." She paused for a moment. "Thank God I never married a homosexual. They're so fussy about their kitchens. In the kitchen I'm a slob. My husband Archibald wouldn't let me near it. His was the magic touch with aspics and kasha varnishkas. After his death, Letitia inherited the responsibility. She wields one hell of a can opener. But I have not digressed too far from the cornucopia to lead you back." She was back in the chair. "Such a lovely design."

"May we see it?" asked Villon.

"Mais c'est impossible."

"You don't have it?"

"I loaned it to a friend who admired it so and wanted it for the centerpiece of her Thanksgiving table. For weeks I've been trying to reach her by telephone but she doesn't seem to be answering the phone. She's a bit on the private side, a little reclusive I'd say though given to the occasional Thanksgiving gathering. She's a bit of a mystic like me and given to long days of meditation. You know what the French always say, Cherchez la femme!''

Bogart groaned inwardly. He was hungry. He wanted to be seated at a table at Cantor's and munching on a half sour pickle while making a selection from the vast menu that promised monumental indigestion. "I'll phone my friend again." She went to a sideboard where there was a telephone hidden under a doll wearing a voluminous eighteenth-century ball gown. First she opened a drawer for her address book. She found the number and then raised the doll revealing the telephone. Villon looked at Bogart and shrugged, and Mrs. Harper dialed. She hummed "La Marseillaise" while she waited and then spoke, "Kito? It's Mrs. Harper again. I *must* speak to Mrs. Brabin." Her sigh was one of vast exasperation. "I am tired of indulging your mistress. I'm sending two gentleman to collect my cornucopia. One is Mr. Villon who is a detective with the Los Angeles police department and with him is a very famous movie star, Humphrey Bogart." They heard a screech coming from the phone. Mrs. Harper said, "Kito, control yourself. It's only a movie star. It's not the second coming of Christ. They'll be there shortly." She slammed the phone down. "Kito's a fan of yours, Mr. Bogart."

"I heard. I'm only a movie star."

"I'd love to paint you, Mr. Bogart. You have a most revealing face."

"Oh yes. What does it reveal?"

She said mysteriously, "Much more then you do. It was so nice having you." She told them Mrs. Brabin's address.

Villon said not without a trace of irony, "It was so nice being had by you. We'll find our way out."

Her voice sang in their ears as they left. "Remember! Those swords dangling over your heads! 'Forewarned is forearmed.' ''

Letitia had made her way back to the harp and plucked away at the strings. Villon recognized "I'll Be Glad When You're Dead, You Rascal You."

They hurried outside and into the car. Bogart lit a cigarette. He exhaled some smoke, turned on the ignition, let the engine warm for a few seconds and then said to Villon, "Eh, mon vieux, peut-être Cantor's?"

Villon exploded. "For crying out loud stop the frog crap and let's go to Canter's!"

TWELVE

The look on Bogart's face was sheer bliss, as he and Villon waited to be seated. The hostess was a tall, vastly overweight bleached redhead with a fixed smile and incredibly long, ominous looking fingernails. Villon thought in her spare time she might be a professional wrestler. As she advanced on them standing behind a velvet rope, the fixed grin broadened into a smile that revealed a slash of purple gums. There were also teeth but the gums predominated. Bogart recognized her from earlier visits.

"It's been so long since we've seen you, Mr. Bogart. Remember me? I'm Pearl. I'm sure you don't remember my name, nobody does." She smiled at Villon. "And you are?" head cocked slightly like a nearsighted pouter pigeon.

"Hungry," said Villon taking no pains to mask his impatience with oversized and overaged coquettes.

Bogart intervened. "This is Detective Villon, he always gets his man."

Pearl asked with a sly smile, "Does he always get his woman?"

Villon stared at her. "Does he maybe get seated and a shot at the menu?"

"Would you prefer a booth or a table?"

"A booth. How about that one straight ahead next to the one holding some people we know." Bogart nudged Villon with an elbow. Bogart's eyes directed Villon to the booth in question. He saw Sidney Heep with a woman he didn't recognize.

"Who's the broad?" asked Villon as Pearl unclipped the velvet cord and indicated they follow her.

"Her name's Lucy Darrow."

"Any relation to your housekeeper?"

"Her daughter."

"Well now isn't this a how-dee-do," said Villon.

"How-dee-do," repeated Pearl, "I recognize that. It's Gilbert and Solomon."

Sidney Heep saw them coming and under the table nudged Lucy Darrow with his knee. This annoyed her and she looked at him questioningly. His eyes led her to Bogart and Villon. Bogart now saw both were nursing draught beers. The dish of sour pickles, sour tomatoes, red peppers, and sauerkraut seemed untouched. Bogart hungered to attack it.

"Well Lucy, what an unexpected pleasure seeing you twice in one day. Meet Mr. Villon. He's a detective. He's trying to find your mother's killer."

Pearl said, "I've left menus on your table. Enjoy your lunch." Bogart thanked her and she favored him with gums again as she walked away.

"Mr. Heep," began Villon, "you're a long way from home."

Heep squinted up at him from behind his glasses. "I'm making my rounds. Today I see dealers and collectors. See what they've got to sell. Find out what they might be interested in buying."

"Come across any cornucopias?" asked Villon.

"No," snapped Heep. "I'm having a bad day. A very bad day. It began with you people this morning and then Joshua Trent is killed and we were old friends. The only nice thing to happen to me today was running into Lucy and she's in mourning for her mother."

"Say Heep," asked Bogart, "you know an artist named Angelica Harper?"

"She's nuts."

"So you know her. You deal with her?"

"Her stuff's too expensive. She thinks she's Mary Cassatt reincarnated."

"Some of her stuff is pretty good, I think," said Bogart. "She's got an interesting portrait of Joshua Trent. He was a pretty good-looking guy."

"Pretentious."

"The portrait or the subject?"

Heep said, "I knew Joshua Trent when he was a snotty hustler trying to work some of our richest boobs."

"I guess he succeeded," said Bogart.

"He certainly did."

"I thought you said you were old friends."

"We most certainly were. Joshua bought a lot of tchotchkes from us. So? I don't mince words. He began as a snotty hustler and became terribly pretentious. Terribly grand and terribly rich. I'm not telling you anything I didn't tell him." He said to Villon. "Are you assigned to Joshua's murder, too?"

"It all comes under the umbrella called cornucopia," said Villon. "Got any theories?"

"About what?" asked Heep.

"About who's the crazy behind these ransackings and the killings?"

"I'm not one given to theories. If I was, I'd be in detective work."

"How about Dickens and Nell? They discuss it with you after we left this morning?"

"You were very rude to Nell. You shouldn't be rude to Nell. Just because she's so garish and otherworldly. Nell's an original. She's very clever. A very smart businesswoman."

Bogart asked Lucy, "You find a dress for your mother, Lucy?"

"I've seen some potentials." She indicated a notebook on the table. "I've jotted them down. I suppose I'll be at it all day. Maybe tomorrow, too. Mr. Villon, when can I find out when my mother's body will be released? I've made a reservation for her at Utter McKinley's funeral parlor. It wasn't easy. They're very heavily booked. They've given me a selection of times for the chapel. I've got a priest standing by. Everything's set. All I need is my mother." Heep patted her hand. She gave him what Bogart supposed was a grateful look. "It was Mother who introduced me to the Curiosity Shop. I found it very curious. Mr. Heep has been very kind. I'm so glad we ran into each other today."

Bogart said, "We'll let you get on with your lunch."

"It's taking an awful long time," said Lucy. "The restaurant's very crowded."

Bogart nudged Villon. "Let's order." They said their good-byes and went to their booth. Bogart attacked the dish of relishes and selected a half sour pickle. He munched contentedly as he opened the menu. Villon was preoccupied. "What's bothering you, Herb?"

"Lots of things are bothering me."

"Such as?"

"Those two in the next booth, for instance."

"Careful, they might hear you."

"With all this din going on around us? They're lucky if they can hear each other."

"What about them?"

"They didn't happen to run into each other."

"You're positive?"

"No, I'm not positive. But I trust my instincts."

"What are you going to eat?" asked Bogart.

"Whatever it is, I'll regret it." Villon studied the menu. Bogart saw Lucy and Heep leaving.

"They're leaving."

Villon peered around the edge of the booth. "I don't think they ate any lunch."

Bogart said, "I don't think they ordered any."

"Then why come to Cantor's?"

"Because it's one of those places where they don't expect to run into anyone they know." Bogart smiled. "What's the matter, Herb. Didn't you ever make dates with women you didn't want to be caught seeing?"

"All the time," said Villon with the air of a practiced man about town. "I never thought of meeting a date in this place."

"Why? You an anti-Semite?"

"Oh shut your face. Me an anti-Semite. I like that a lot. Hazel Dickson is not Hazel's real name."

"No kidding. What's her real name?"

"I can't pronounce it. Neither can Hazel. That's why she

took Dickson." A waiter stared down at them. He had a large Adam's apple and his ears stuck out. He reminded Bogart of the comic strip character Happy Hooligan. He stood with pad and pencil poised for their orders.

"Are you ready to order?" asked the waiter in a thick, middle-European accent that made Bogart curious.

"Where you from?" asked Bogart.

"Don't ask," said the waiter with a sigh.

"You're a refugee, aren't you?"

"Everybody on earth is a refugee. We are all looking for a safe harbor. Some of us will find our safe harbor and the less fortunate won't. That is Kossow's law."

"Who's Kossow?" asked Bogart.

"Me."

Bogart laughed and order a triple-decker special. Villon decided on a sardine and mayonnaise on white bread and heard the waiter say under his breath, "Goy."

Bogart asked the waiter, "You an actor, Mr. Kossow?"

He hit the right nerve. "An actor? Am I an actor? You want to know who I am? You have heard of Stanislav Kossow?" He held up a hand. "Don't speak! Of course you have not heard of Stanislav Kossow. You have not had the glorious opportunity to see him! My Hamlet! My Macbeth! My Romeo! My etceteras! In Czechoslovakia I am their Laurence Olivier. You asked where I come from and I said 'Don't ask,' well now you know why I warned you. Mine is another of the hundreds of thousands of tragic stories that cross the thresholds of this free world. Yes, Mr. Bogart. I recognize you. Don't look so modest. You're a star. Make the most of it." He leaned forward with his eyes popping. "Because it won't last forever?"

"He's giving me the creeps," said Villon in an aside.

Kossow looked over his shoulder to ascertain if Pearl was within hearing distance and scold him. "Mr. Bogart, I will do anything. Bits, extras, walk-ons." He smiled. "Perhaps you can arrange a screen test?"

Bogart said, "Call me at the studio tomorrow. I'll leave your name at the switchboard. Stanislav Kossow."

"You remember my name?"

"Why not? I only heard it a minute ago."

Villon pleaded, "Kossow, will you please place our orders?"

"Immediately! At once! Mr. Bogart, I kiss your hand!" He hurried off.

"Who knows?" said Bogart, "he might be the next 'Cuddles' Sackall."

Villon asked Bogart, "You think Heep and Lucy Darrow are what the columnists might call 'a thing'?"

"Maybe. What if they are. What's it got to do with the case?"

"How do I know? I'm open to all suggestions. I've got a clueless case to deal with."

"What about that strand of hair from my place?"

"Unreal. Useless. That's why I thought it might match that wig of Nell's. But I don't think she wears that thing anyplace but in the store. She'd stand out like the red light over the entrance of a whorehouse. I also think there's more to the Curiosity Shop than meets the eye."

"Such as?"

"Edgar Dickens. That trace of an accent. I've got a good ear for accents. I come up against them all the time and I know how to identify them."

"Always on the nose?"

"Give or take. Dickens's accent is not Welsh. Because the Welsh, they have a lovely lilt to their voices. A cousin to the Scotch brogue."

"The brogue is too thick for me."

"Okay, then an Irish accent. I mean a real homegrown Irish accent, not an exaggeration like Barry Fitzgerald's." He speared some sauerkraut. "I'm telling you Dickens is from somewhere on the Mediterranean Sea. Italy's my guess."

"I didn't notice any statues of Christ or nuns or crucifixes in the shop."

"They're there," he stated positively. "Upstairs someplace or in the basement."

"What's all this got to do with the cornucopia?"

"I don't know. I'm shadowboxing. I'm catching flies. That's how it always is with me at the beginning of a case. It's like running into an alley and finding there's no way out at the end. You got to turn around and go back and follow something else. Very frustrating. Very aggravating. Very stimulating. By God here's Kossow with our order. How'd you get it so fast, Stanislav?"

"I promised they would cater my big party!" he told them eagerly as he placed their sandwiches on the table.

"When you having this big party?" asked Bogart.

"When I sign my contract with Warner Brothers! And you are both positively invited!"

Bogart didn't know whether to laugh or cry.

"Now this is a very impressive piece of real estate," said Villon to Bogart as they pulled up in front of the Brabin estate in Brentwood.

"Why does a dame who lives in a palace like this have to borrow a cornucopia for a Thanksgiving dinner centerpiece?"

"That's why she lives in such splendor and elegance. She's thrifty."

"Or has a rich husband."

"Who is also thrifty." Villon suggested Bogart drive up the circular roadway and park next to one of several impressive pillars at the front of the house. Bogart drove in and parked under a shade tree.

"Mrs. Charles Brabin," said Villon. "That name strike a bell?"

"I don't have any bells for it to strike. There's somebody peeking out at us from an upstairs window. Feel like playing Living Statues?"

"Let's not horse around. I've got to be taken seriously." They were now standing at the most impressive front door with its sculpted panels and an immense door knocker that might have been silver. "I don't think I can lift this knocker," said Villon.

"You don't have to. There's a bell button." Bogart's index

finger connected with the bell button that was in a side panel to the right of the door. More chimes. Villon thought just about everyone in Hollywood must have a set of chimes attached to their door. These chimes played "In the Hall of the Mountain King," and from behind the door, though slightly muffled, sounded ominous and foreboding. The sky was clouding over and Bogart feared they were about to lose their bright, sunny day. They heard the pitter-patter of what might be tiny feet hurrying to the door. The door was pulled open by a diminutive Japanese man who was smiling from ear to ear and, thought Bogart, beyond the ears.

"Welcome, Humphrey Bogart, welcome." He bowed several times. "It is an honor to welcome you to my house!"

"You're Mrs. Charles Brabin?"

"Oh no. She is meditating but will soon be finished. I am Kito, a most important member of the household without whom the Brabins could not survive."

Modest little devil, thought Bogart. Kito ushered them into the downstairs hall, shut the door and then scurried in front of them, leading the way to a huge, rococo furnished and decorated living room. The clock had been turned back, and this was at least two decades ago. Everything was brocades and velvet and a grand piano with a Spanish shawl draped across it. An original Tiffany chandelier hung from the ceiling and across an oversize divan was thrown a leopard skin. There was a polar bear skin on the floor, the bear's head oversize and its mouth open, revealing ferocious teeth. There were several end tables that held lamps with bases that were the heads of saints or Egyptian houris with legs extended and quaintly enough, Bo Peep with her crook looking not for her sheep but as though she was dying to get laid, or so thought Villon. He was given to flights of erotic fancy on the rare occasion he found himself in such exotic surroundings. This was a touch of old Hollywood, the Hollywood that was once so gloriously outrageous. The Hollywood of the woeful scandals that brought down such celebrities as "Fatty" Arbuckle, William Desmond Taylor, Wallace Reid, Mabel Normand, and countless others.

A strange, sickeningly sweet odor attacked their nostrils. Bogart looked around and saw Kito lighting a stick of incense protruding from the belly button of a statue of Buddha in the corner of the room. Bogart noticed an exquisitely wrought marble staircase leading up to a pair of blood-red drapes that hid, probably, a hallway. At the foot of the staircase was a good-size gong.

Bogart realized he hadn't identified Villon and corrected the oversight. Kito bowed to Villon who was wondering if the little man's name was on a secret roster of Japanese names compiled by the FBI for immediate round-up and detention in the event of a war with Japan. Bogart, among others, was perplexed as to why in some quarters Japan was seen as a possible threat to the nation's security. He studied Kito. This little man a threat? He realized Kito was holding a pen and an autograph album under his nose.

"Please Mr. Bogart, would you sign my album?"

"Sure," said Bogart, and scribbled his name.

"Oh sir, please. Above your name please write 'To my good friend Kito.' "

Bogart smiled. "No problem."

"Oh sir, you are truly my most favorite actor in all the world. I see your pictures many times. I have seen *High Sierra* eight times."

"No kidding? By now you should have built up an immunity to it."

Villon glanced at his wristwatch. He was anxious to get on with it. "How much longer will Mrs. Brabin be at her meditation?"

From upstairs, they heard a bell tinkle.

"Aha!" said Kito. "The meditation is completed. Madam will be preparing to descend." He hurried to a cabinet, opened its doors and exposed a Victrola. He wound it up hastily and then placed the arm holding the needle into the starting groove. They heard the haunting strains of "Pale Hands I Love Beside the Shalimar." Kito hurried to the gong and struck it three times very slowly. It reverberated through the room. Kito hit a light switch at the foot of the stairs that were now enveloped in a clear, pink light. At the head of the stairs, a woman's hands parted the bloodred drapes. They saw a middle-aged woman wearing a black dress that reached her ankles and covered her arms. Her rich raven-colored hair was pulled tightly back from her head ending in a lavish chignon. Her face was alabaster white. Her lips were richly ruby red as were her fingernails. Slowly she descended the stairs staring down at Bogart and Villon. They heard Kito declare, "Gentlemen, Mrs. Charles Brabin."

Of course, thought Bogart, of course. Charles Brabin had been a film director but it was his wife who had garnered the celebrity. Mrs. Charles Brabin. I'll be damned. He wondered if Villon recognized the greatest vamp of the silent cinema, Theda Bara.

THIRTEEN

"How nice to welcome you to my home, Mr. Bogart."
Her voice was a mellifluous contralto. She was smiling at Villon. "And Mister . . . ?"

"Detective Villon."

"Oh my. Is there some fine I've forgotten to pay?" The men shook hands with her and Bogart marveled at how youthful she looked until he realized she couldn't be much older than him. She'd made her last film fifteen years earlier and at the time was not quite thirty years old.

Villon said, "Angelica Harper sent us. She phoned to let you know we were coming."

"She spoke to your servant, Kito," said Bogart.

She was draped across the sofa on the leopard skin. Bogart and Villon sat in chairs opposite her. Bara snapped her fingers at Kito and told him to shut off the Victrola and to kill the blue light on the staircase. Without asking if either man cared for some, she told Kito to bring tea. Kito bowed and backed his way out of the room still grinning at Bogart who didn't quite know how to respond or if he was expected to.

Mrs. Brabin said to Bogart, "Don't be discomforted by the perpetual smile. We never know if he's happy or if he's dyspeptic. At times we wait, after Kito has left the room, if the smile remains behind like Alice's Cheshire cat. Kito can also be terribly forgetful. He did not give me the message. I don't scold Kito because then he sulks and the atmosphere becomes unbearable." She smiled at Villon. "Are you selling tickets to the policeman's ball? My husband and I don't socialize very much but we're happy to give donations for widows and orphans."

"I'm not selling," said Villon, "I'm investigating."

"I see," her voice was subdued but her face showed curiosity. "And for some reason your investigation has brought you to me."

"You borrowed a cornucopia from Miss Harper," Villon reminded her.

"Yes. This past Thanksgiving, an interesting object. I wanted it that one time for a table decoration. I knew I'd never use it again and there was no point in buying one of my own. So I borrowed hers. All terribly simple. Oh dear. I suppose she's still irked I didn't invite her to the dinner. I couldn't. There were ten guests and my husband and myself. That's twelve. Had I invited Angelica, that would have made thirteen at the table. As you know, superstitious people consider thirteen a very unlucky number. Kito is terribly superstitious. He won't serve a table holding thirteen people. Kito is priceless." Her smile was a tacit request for understanding. "Angelica isn't."

"There's always somebody who's expendable," said Bogart. "Especially in Hollywood."

"Yes, in time it happens to many of us." There was a warm twinkle in her eye. "I think you recognize me, Mr. Bogart."

"You haven't changed a bit. You look the same. Maybe my friend here doesn't recognize you. Herb, the lady was very famous once. Theda Bara."

Villon brightened. "That's who you are! I knew I'd seen you somewhere before."

Mrs. Brabin leaned forward. "Tell me, is there a connection with the murder in your home, Mr. Bogart, and that of my dear friend Joshua Trent to Angelica's cornucopia?"

"Do you know the legend of the cornucopia?" She didn't and Bogart told her. Kito brought the tea and served it along with some excellent petit fours.

"And you think when you find the cornucopia you will have found your murderer?" She was nibbling a biscuit and knew she shouldn't be. She had gained weight and had been advised by her doctor to lose it. She loathed advice.

Villon said, "I don't know that at all. If you have the cornucopia, I don't think you murdered for it."

"Why not? I was famous for my interpretations of monstrous vampires. Sometimes life imitates art." She laughed. "Quite honestly, I wouldn't know how to commit a murder. I'm a nice Jewish girl from Detroit who had fame thrust upon her by a ruthless producer named William Fox. But unlike the fame, the name Theda Bara lives on. I'm always in crossword puzzles! 'Vamp Bara! Twenty-one Across.' " A troubling thought assailed her. "Mr. Villon, if I were in possession of the cornucopia, I'd be in danger of being ransacked and murdered."

"It's a possibility," said Villon.

"Well what a relief. I don't have the cornucopia."

"Where is it?" asked Villon.

"As far as I know, it's back with Angelica."

"But it isn't," said Villon, "that's why she sent us here."

Mrs. Brabin was on her feet and pacing. "Now that's very odd. I know I gave it to someone to bring to Angelica. Well, Angelica is so flighty, she might have forgotten it was returned to her. Oh wait a minute! I remember! I entrusted it to Karen Barrett! She lives near Angelica and said it would be no problem to drop it by the next day. Do you suppose she didn't?"

"Looks like it," said Villon.

"Now that's not very nice of her. Do you at all remember Karen Barrett? For a while there she was very successful as a serial queen. You know, like Pearl White and Ruth Roland. Her big success was *The Terrors of Thomasina*. It was fifteen chapters of absolute nonsense in which she disguised herself as an alley cat and went around rescuing people from predicaments they had no right getting themselves into. This is terribly naughty of her." She crossed to the gong and gave it a thumping whack. "Poor Karen's been having a hard time of it. She's been on welfare. I have her for dinner as often as possible though she makes my husband nervous. Poverty tends to give him the hives. Other people's poverty, that is."

Kito entered and of course remembered to bring the smile with him. "Kito, please phone Karen Barrett. I don't remember her number."

"I remember the number, Mrs. Brabin. I remember all your numbers, Mrs. Brabin." He went to the table at the far end of the couch and dialed.

Mrs. Brabin was back sitting on the couch. "Like too many of the silent era, Karen didn't invest wisely. Nor did she marry wisely all four times. Charles and I, as you can see, are among the fortunates. When I was a Fox star I got stock from the old Fox and it has multiplied and now it's Twentieth Century-Fox."

"Not bad," said Bogart.

She shrugged. "The tip of the iceberg."

Bogart said to Villon, "What's that crazy look on your face?"

"Where's Jim Mallory? Where'd we lose him?"

"Maybe he decided to go back to the station. We passed him in the car checking the precinct on our way to Angelica Harper."

"He was probably called back," said Villon. "And no way of telling us. I'll check in as soon as Kito is off the phone."

Kito had been off the phone for a while waiting for a chance to speak. He finally caught Mrs. Brabin's attention.

"Yes, Kito? What about Miss Barrett?"

"I'm sorry to tell you, the phone has been disconnected."

"Oh dear, that doesn't bode well, does it. Perhaps it's just a matter of her being delinquent with her bill. Kito, give the gentlemen Miss Barrett's address." She said to Villon, "I assume you want to check into this."

"Very definitely. Mrs. Brabin, may I use the phone? I'd like to call my precinct. I seem to have misplaced my associate."

"Please do." As Villon availed himself of the phone, Mrs. Brabin said to Bogart, "Is detective work your hobby, Mr. Bogart?"

"No, not at all. I'm with Villon because of the murder and the ransacking in my house. Some other friends of mine were along with us but they dropped out."

"Isn't it rather unusual for detectives to let outsiders tag along with them?"

"Herb Villon isn't your everyday run-of-the-mill detective. He's a maverick. He hears a different drummer. If I was in the way, he'd get rid of me. But Herb likes someone along with him and Jim . . . Jim Mallory. His associate. Nice young man with a tendency to occasionally wander off as like right now. When last seen he was reporting to the precinct on his car radio. Maybe he was called back."

"Maybe he was kidnapped," suggested Mrs. Brabin, as though kidnapping was a common occurrence.

"No, he's quite safe," said Villon, returning from the phone. "He's at Cedars of Lebanon Hospital." Bogart was startled. "Ned Aswan tried to commit suicide." Bogart was on his feet.

"Joshua's Ned Aswan?" asked Mrs. Brabin. When Villon said "Yes," she said, "Oh how terrible! Kito! You must take him some chicken soup." Kito was handing Villon a slip of paper on which he had written Karen Barrett's address. Villon slipped it into a pocket.

"Is it bad?" Bogart asked Villon.

"When is it ever good. He drank poison. Something they use on furniture. He's in a coma but they think he'll come out of it."

"You going over to the hospital?" asked Bogart.

"No need to. Nothing I can do. Jim's got it covered. The place is swarming with reporters and photographers and the big question from them is, did Ned Aswan commit the murder."

"Oh for crying out loud," said Bogart.

"Right," agreed Villon. "He was in Santa Barbara when the murder was committed. Jim checked the people Ned was with. He's got a solid alibi."

Mrs. Brabin said softly, "I had no idea love could be so powerful."

Bogart said, "Maybe it was fear."

Mrs. Brabin said, "Oh. Do you suppose he thought the murderer might come back for him?"

Bogart said, "He wasn't afraid of dying. The suicide attempt is your proof. He was afraid of living. That's my theory and I'm not all that much of a philosopher. Thanks for the hospitality, Mrs. Brabin."

"My dear Mr. Bogart, it was hardly any trouble and very much worth it. I haven't had such a wonderful time in ages. Cornucopias, murders, ransackings, a suicide attempt. I can't wait for Charles to get back. He'll never believe a word of it."

Kito chimed in. "Oh Kito will back you up."

"He'll believe it even less. Good-bye, gentlemen. I do so hope we'll meet again but under happier circumstances." She followed them out and stood in the doorway of the house, waving as they got into the car. Bogart beeped the horn by way of farewell and Mrs. Brabin's face beamed a splendid smile.

Nell Dickens was pacing back and forth in the rear of the shop, puffing a cigarette and sounding very agitated. "You had to meet her at Cantor's. Half of Hollywood eats in Cantor's!"

"Did I know Bogart and the cop would show up?" Sidney Heep was not happy.

"What's the fuss?" asked Edgar Dickens. "You and Lucy are acquaintances. You ran into each other. Cantor's was convenient. Why behave as though a crime was committed?" Nell started to speak but Edgar Dickens cut her short. "You're both making too much of this. So Villon thinks I'm Italian. Well, he's a pretty smart dick but I'm not easy to trace. It's years since I left Italy. I served my sentence. I paid my debt to society or whatever corny phrase you care to substitute. I'm sure Mr. Villon has never heard of Nino Brocco. Why should he? He was a small boy when Nino Brocco was arrested for forging fake art treasures. Nino Brocco has been Edgar Dickens for a very long time now. Edgar Dickens is an American citizen."

"You fraud," snorted Nell.

"The dead man was an American citizen. When I took his name from a stone in the cemetery, I checked on him and he was indeed a born and bred American. Forging the appropriate documents reincarnating myself as Edgar Dickens was child's play.''

Dickens was seated at his desk and Nell stared down at him. "Villon is a very smart cop. If he thinks he's on to something with you and your possible Mediterranean origins, if he needs to he'll try to make something of it. He's got two murders to solve.''

"I didn't kill anybody," said Dickens. "You know I didn't kill anybody.''

Heep piped up. "You're forgetting something.''

"What?'' snapped Nell.

"La Contessa di Marcopolo. For an old lady, she has a very sharp memory.''

"Why not. Decades ago I deflowered her. A woman never forgets the man who took her virginity." He smiled. "She was so easily seduced.''

"She could make trouble," said Nell. "She as much as threatened it yesterday. She worries me.''

"She won't make trouble," said Dickens confidently.

"She will if she doesn't retrieve the cornucopia," said Heep.

"She never had the cornucopia so she has nothing to retrieve," said Dickens.

"She's determined. I think she's dangerous.''

Dickens said, "It's as though this murderer had access to my records. I'm very meticulous about who we do business with. Who sold to us. Who bought from us. Who traded what with us. The Bogart tragedy, of course, is related to the ransacking of his mother-in-law's apartment. That of course had to be Marcelo Amati and Violetta Cenci. But they didn't have murder on their minds. They tricked the woman out of the apartment. But the Bogart ransacking is something else. It wasn't them. They wouldn't have killed the housekeeper. Someone else has taken over. I'm sure Herbert Villon is smart enough to be thinking along the same lines. You know something, Nell?''

"What?''

"At this moment, I don't think it's such a good idea for

anyone in this town to admit to owning a cornucopia. Especially a sealed one. Sidney, give me that green ledger on the table there. I want to see who we've sold and traded the blasted things."

Nell said, "We'd have known if we had the right one. It must be damned heavy."

"True. Lots of sealed cornucopias are darned heavy, filled with all kinds of objets d'art. Who knows? Maybe we had it after all."

Nell said unpleasantly, "You trying to give me a stroke?"

"You're not the stroke type, my dear." He took the ledger from Sidney Heep and riffled the pages. The pages were stiff from age. There were water stain and food stains and little chicken scratches that Dickens didn't bother to decipher because he knew he couldn't. He lingered over a few transactions because they evoked pleasant memories of bargaining and friendly haggling. That's what buying and selling and trading had been about. How shrewdly could you beat the other guy down.

Hannah Darrow. Joshua Trent. There would be more killings. And if he knew it, Herbert Villon knew it. Dickens wondered who beside himself had a register of cornucopia owners. Perhaps it wasn't necessary. Perhaps there was but one authentic one. The one the Baron di Marcopolo entrusted to Jack Methot. Where had Jack Methot stashed it? Had he in turn entrusted it to anyone. His daughter Mayo?

"Such a sigh, Edgar," said Nell, "such a long, long sigh."

"Such an awful predicament. And such fruitless murders, I think." He slammed the ledger shut. "The hell with it. Let Villon do his own solving."

Joshua Trent's secretary, Zelda Sweet, the one who Jim Mallory had given the eye earlier that day, was glad he was back so soon, but sad that he was asking questions about Ned Aswan's attempted suicide. She liked Ned Aswan as well as she had liked Joshua Trent. They were decent employers and not given to innuendo. They were interested in women only as clients. With them you didn't have to worry about sexual harassment or veiled threats if you refused to unveil.

"I think you should attribute his attempted suicide to a sudden case of despondency," suggested Zelda to Jim.

"There's no such thing as a sudden case of despondency," said Jim who had taken some training in psychology when he decided to go into police work. "Despondency has to accumulate and develop until it becomes dangerous."

"You mean like a kid brother? I've got a rotten kid brother."

Jim Mallory wasn't interested in her rotten kid brother. "He always given to moods?"

"Ned? Well, he had a quick temper. And he was abnormally precise about everything. Look Mr. Mallory, Josh was the sun around which Ned orbited. Josh was his life. He was his father, mother, uncle, sister, and brother. Josh's world was all the world he knew. It was all the world he wanted to know. Ned was just plain afraid to continue on his own. This business was Joshua Trent, and underline the name. Ned doesn't know peanuts about business. He knows how to make estimates but it's Josh who knows how to rob . . . figure the costs. You taking all this down?" Jim nodded. "Am I any help?"

"You're lots of help. How long have you worked as Mr. Trent's secretary?"

"Little over five years."

"You happy here?"

"Until this morning. I don't think there's going to be any more business conducted here once the smoke clears. I know the contents of Josh's will. He dictated it to me. Ned gets almost everything except for some small bequests to a few friends and employees and a marble torso of a prizefighter he's bequested to Mae West."

"Nice lady. Was involved in a case with her once."

"Ned has no family. But with the kind of money he's inheriting, he can buy himself one."

"When are you free for dinner?"

"You name it."

"I'd like to do it tonight, but I'm not sure if I can. I have to find my partner and see what more needs to be done."

"You have to find a murderer."

"We'll nail him."

"Maybe it's a her."

"Maybe it's a him and a her. Who knows? That's what's so fascinating about murder. You never know who you're going to find waiting at the end of the trail. So, when do you quit work?"

"Tonight, who can tell. The place is such a mess. Ned had invited company for tonight and I'm still trying to track down some of them to call them off." She wrote something on a slip of paper and handed it to him. It was the office number and her home number. "You'll find me at either place. Unless I'm on a bus in between." She smiled. "You'll find me."

FOURTEEN

Once again back on Fairfax Avenue, Herb Villon asked Bogart to pull over to an outdoor phone. He called the precinct to give them Karen Barrett's address to be passed on to Jim Mallory when he checked in which Villon knew he did frequently. The phone was outside one of West Hollywood's tonier and more expensive beauty salons, Mr. Gwen. Hazel Dickson was at the counter settling her rather exorbitant bill. Hair dyes that obliterated the former color of roots, a facial, a manicure, a full-body massage, a pedicure, and lots of gossip always took their toll. Through the plate glass window Hazel saw, to her joy, her beloved Herb Villon talking on the phone accompanied by meaningless gestures, unless you heard what he was saying. Hazel thrust some bills into the cashier's hand with instructions to distribute them as tips and then hurried out to the street to surprise Villon.

He was hanging up the receiver when he heard the familiar Dickson voice greeting him. He was genuinely pleased to see her and proved it by kissing her cheek. "What are you doing here?" he asked.

She pointed to the beauty salon. "My home away from home. I told you I'd be spending hours here." She looked into the car. "Hi Bogie!"

Bogie lowered a window. "Hello gorgeous, you look good enough to eat."

"Don't talk dirty. There are women with toddlers in carriages who they have a bare memory of conceiving. What have you accomplished, Herb?" It didn't take Villon long to cover the territory he and Bogart had covered. "Theda Bara, for crying out loud. I wish I'd been there."

Herb was glad she hadn't, but didn't say so. "We're on our way to Karen Barrett's, want to tag along?"

"Karen Barrett, for Pete's sake. Isn't there anyone on your list who's made a talkie? Mmmm," she mmmm'd, "Karen Barrett on welfare. Louella will love that one. Back in the good old bad old days she, Karen, and Marion Davies used to pal around a lot. I'll see if I can get Louella to put the touch on Davies for Barrett. Davies is always good for a touch. She has a list of dependants longer then her arm. Where does Barrett live?"

"Down the block past Angelica Harper's dump and a left turn. Where's your car?"

"In the lot behind the salon. Give me a minute and I'll tail you."

Five minutes later, Hazel had rescued her car from the parking lot and two minutes later was tagging Bogart to Karen Barrett's place. Ned Aswan's attempted suicide didn't sit well with Hazel. She liked him and his nutty sense of humor, like the time he came to Cesar "Butch" Romero's Hallowe'en party in drag and passed himself off as his own twin sister, a gag that collapsed when Marlene Dietrich took him aside and advised him to use a depilatory.

In Bogart's car, Villon wondered if it would be appropriate to put his hand over his heart as they passed the Harper castle. Bogart said, "I wonder if I should be hurt she didn't ask me to sit for my portrait. Some of her stuff's pretty good. John Decker once asked me to sit for him in that filthy house of his on Mulholland Drive. I figured what the hell why not and arrived at the appointed hour of ten in the morning. Well let me tell you, never before have I stepped so gingerly into a drunken nightmare. His easel was set up under a gigantic skylight covered with bird droppings and rotting greenery probably blown there years earlier by a Santa Ana. On a podium was a throne chair in which I was supposed to sit, except it was already occupied by W. C. Fields who it was obvious was a bit incontinent. Sprawled on a couch was Errol Flynn and sprawled on Flynn was a nubile sweetie who, I might tell you, now has a stock player's contract at Warner's. They were but a small part of the population in that room. There was at least another dozen alcoholics in various stages of inebriation. Even the houseboy who admitted me had trouble standing erect. It was a scene of such complete perversion that would have appealed to Hogarth's shade had it been haunting the place."

"Where was Decker?" asked Villon.

"He was presumably upstairs asleep. Obviously there'd been an all-night orgy and as Errol's doxy was obviously underage, I made tracks fast and drove to the nearest church. It being Sunday I did not go in but for my own peace of mind I recited a couple of Hail Marys and a Stations of the Cross and then drove home to Mayo, spoiling for a really hot knock-down-drag-out and, bless her heart, Mayo didn't disappoint me. Have I passed Barrett's place?"

Villon was staring past Bogart out the window. "I think this is it here." Bogart pulled over to the curb and parked. Hazel parked in front of him, sparing him a dented fender by a very narrow margin. The three stood on the sidewalk staring at a two-level apartment complex that at one time in its existence must have been a favorable address. Bogart later described it to Mayo as what appeared to be rows of rabbit warrens that were semidetached and undoubtedly semi-inhabitable. Attached to an outside wall was a directory on which Karen Barrett was indeed listed. Hazel said in her usual optimistic way, "I hope Barrett's not our second suicide of the day."

"Bite your tongue," said Villon. "I need her." They climbed the cement stairs to the second level. Villon was in the van. Now they were standing in front of the door to Karen Barrett's apartment. Her name was in a slot over a bell. Villon pressed the bell. They waited. He pressed it again. The door opened a few inches. There was a protective chain.

"I'm a friend of Mrs. Brabin's. She sent me and my . . . er . . . associates to see you."

"Why?"

"To ask some questions."

"What kind of questions?"

"If you'll let us in, I'll give you some samples."

"Don't try to kid me. You're here to dispossess me." The fear and the pathos in her voice affected the three.

Villon's tone of voice was gentler. "Miss Barrett, I'm Detective Herbert Villon. It's to do with the cornucopia Mrs. Brabin gave you to deliver to Angelica Harper the day after Thanksgiving."

"Oh God." She shut the door. They heard the chain removed and then the door opened. Karen Barrett wore what was once a Japanese kimono, held in place by a strip of what might have been curtain material tied around her waist. A worn, tired snood held her hair in place and her feet were encased in scuffs that were frayed at the edges. It was a one-room apartment with two windows on the wall opposite the front door that looked out on a courtyard. There was a sofa that Hazel assumed opened out into a bed, a table, and four kitchen chairs, a half-sized refrigerator, a stove, a sink, and a door that opened onto a small bathroom. On a shelf above the sink Bogart spotted a box of dry cereal, a can of condensed milk, a box of soda biscuits, a few canned goods, and a near-empty gin bottle. Déjà vu, thought Bogart. A replica of the roach-infested studio he lived in when he first came to seek his fortune in New York. There were some bits of clothing strewn on the floor and the couch.

Karen Barrett wore no makeup, and was still a handsome woman despite the evidence of vicissitude. On the table was an ashtray and a pack of cigarettes and a book of matches. "Forgive the mess," she said in a voice tortured by too much cigarette smoke and too much gin and too much talking to herself, "it's the maid's day off." She gestured at Bogart. "You're Bogart, right?"

"Right," said Bogart, managing what he hoped was a friendly and sympathetic smile.

Barrett looked at Villon. "So you must be Herbert Villon. Very fancy monicker, I must say, so I've said it." She looked at Hazel Dickson. "I know, don't tell me. You're the Spirit of Christmas Past, back in the days when there used to be Christmas." Her words were soaked in gin. "Have a seat. Anywhere you like. They're equally uncomfortable." Bogart saw the phone on a small end table at the end of the sofa. He sat on the sofa next to the phone. The sofa was lumpy. "You can't use the phone because it doesn't work. It's been disconnected. How do they expect you to pay your bills if you can't get work and haven't got a dime to call your own?" Mayo's spending sprees were flashing through Bogart's mind. He made a mental note to give her some swift kicks in the behind when next he saw her. Better yet, he might go home and pack all her clothes and send them to Karen Barrett except they weren't the same size, Mayo was petite, Barrett was tall and with an athletic body. Serial screen queens had to be athletic in the silents. They didn't have doubles. They did their own stunts and survived to give interviews about their athletic prowess.

There was a knock at the door.

"Oh shit!" exclaimed Miss Barrett. "That's him. From the sheriff's office with my dispossess. Where the hell do they expect me to go? Griffith Park?"

There was another knock at the door.

Karen Barrett squared her shoulders and shuffled to the door, a brave action more conducive to a brief appearance before a firing squad. She opened the door and Jim Mallory said, "Is Detective Villon here?"

Karen Barrett's smile was like a klieg light at a Hollywood Boulevard premiere. "Who gives a damn if he is or isn't. You're absolutely adorable. Come right in. And you're blushing. I haven't seen a man blush like that since I seduced a teenager who wasn't worth the trouble." Barrett shut the door. "Well, there must be some hope coming out from under the rocks. Mr. Villon, introduce me to this improvement." Villon introduced them. "Mallory. Jim Mallory. Any relation to Boots Mallory? Cute kid who did some features at Fox in the early thirties. I don't know what's become of her."

"I do," said Bogart, "she's Jimmy Cagney's sister-in-law, married to his brother Bill."

"Well what do you know about that," said Barrett. Jim Mallory told her Boots was no relation. "I'm sorry I've got no refreshments to offer you," she said, obviously determined to hold on to what few belts of gin remained in the bottle, "but I'm fresh out. Sit down, Jim. The kitchen chairs are serviceable." He chose to remain standing by the door as though a hasty exit might soon be called for.

"About the cornucopia, Miss Barrett," began Villon.

"I was afraid you'd get back to that." She pointed to a small radio on a shelf above the refrigerator. "I know all about the murders. I was one of the first to give Joshua Trent a break." She paused. "He stopped returning my phone calls. Funny, but just telling you that, it still hurts." The others in the room were veterans of unreturned phone calls, although Hazel tended to get violent about it and send threatening letters to constant offenders.

The silence in the room was broken by Jim Mallory. "Herb, should I check the precinct?"

Hazel said, "You'll have to use drums. The phone's disconnected."

Barrett said with a small laugh, "What's worse, I'm fresh out of drums." She stood in front of Villon and saluted him smartly. "Sir, I'm a disgrace to the regiment and I throw myself on your mercy. I know that somewhere under your skin there beats an understanding heart. But in dire need of food and to pay my electric bill, I hocked the God-damned thing."

"Jesus," said Villon.

"He also existed on handouts," Barrett said. She sat at the kitchen table and lit a cigarette. She asked no one in particular, "I still got some looks. Do you think I could make it on the streets? Maybe I should try Chinatown. There they don't give a damn who they sleep with as long as the price is right."

"Now don't you talk that way," said Hazel softly. "Remember, in every cloud there's a silver lining." Bogart strained to hear a sad violin but no sounds were forthcoming. "You used to be a good pal of Marion Davies's, why haven't you asked her for help."

"I'm too ashamed."

"But you mustn't be!"

"But I am. In those days, I used to pick up the tabs. For

Marion it was a fresh experience and Louella was always a freeloader." She fiddled with the snood for a moment. "Funny how many people drop out of your life when you're no longer picking up the checks." She now wore a tender smile. "I used to love to take people out. Well, them days are gone forever." She shuffled to a table where she kept her handbag. It was the table with the phone next to where Bogart was sitting. "Here's the pawn ticket." She fumbled with the purse. "Leo Bulgari's on Sunset near La Brea. There's three brass balls hanging over the entrance, one more than Bulgari has. Though he's usually pretty fair." She was staring into the purse.

"There's nothing wrong, is there?" Bogart asked with a smile.

She said nothing. Her eyes were misting up. She sat next to Bogart and rummaged in the purse. She was careful not to expose the twenty dollar bills Bogart had surreptitiously slipped into the bag. She didn't want to embarrass either herself or Bogart. She found the pawn ticket, shut the handbag and leaned across Bogart to replace it on the table. She arose and took the ticket to Villon. He studied it.

Villon said, "Bulgari's not all that generous."

She stared him in the eyes. "I had some good meals and saw a couple of good pictures, and if I'm under arrest, you'll have to wait while I get into something glamorous."

Bogart spoke swiftly. "You're not under arrest. Certainly not for hocking some crappy thingamabob." His words were directed at Villon.

"Of course you're not under arrest. Mrs. Brabin would have to file a complaint, and I doubt she'd do that. She sounded as though she's very fond of you."

"Yes, I guess she is even though I outlasted her in pictures. We got our start around the same time, but after five or six years of them, the public grew tired of vamps. They grew tired of my serials too but I was able to move into adventure pictures and Westerns. As a matter of fact, I did some talkies. Cheapies on Poverty Row. I made three for a couple of rats who were lowercase impressarios. The evil of two less-ers." She smiled at Villon. "Mrs. Brabin wouldn't file charges because the thing didn't belong to her. It belongs to Angelica Harper."

"She won't file charges," said Bogart, "or I'll file charges against her for having a musician on the premises without a license."

"I had no idea you were so civic minded," said Villon.

"Neither did I," said Bogart. "I think we've taken up enough of Miss Barrett's time."

Jim Mallory held out a pad and pen to Karen Barrett. "Miss Barrett, may I have your autograph?"

"Oh shit, you've got to be kidding!"

"It's for my mother. She's a big movie fan. I know she'll be tickled pink to have it."

"Well, okay." She took the pad and pen. "What's your mother's name?"

"Mary Bessie."

Hazel crossed her eyes. Karen Barrett wrote a message and signed it with a flourish. She returned the pad and pen to Mallory and then on impulse patted his cheek. "You're too handsome to be a cop. Maybe Mr. Bogart can arrange a screen test."

"No way," said Mallory, "I'm very happy where I am."

Villon said, "Come on, let's be on our way." He was holding the door open. "Thanks a lot, Miss Barrett. You've been very helpful. If you ever need me, I'm at the downtown precinct." Hazel and Mallory filed out.

"Mr. Bogart?" asked Barrett. "Could I see you alone for a minute?"

Bogart said to Villon, "I'll be right down." Villon shut the door.

Miss Barrett retrieved her handbag and extracted five twenty dollar bills. "This is a new experience for me. Usually men took money from my handbag, not put money in it. Mr. Bogart, this is very generous of you and I shall cry myself to sleep tonight and a lot more nights after. It's too much. I can't take all this."

Bogart made a fist. "You want a rap in the kisser?"

"You sound like one of my husbands."

"Get your phone back on again. It can't be all that much."

"It isn't."

"Treat yourself to a new dress. Then phone me at the studio. I'll leave your name at the switchboard. They're always hiring stock players. Lots of old-timers. We've got Monte Blue and Wheeler Oakman and Larry Steers and probably when my time comes maybe somebody will do me a good turn with a stock contract. Only one thing, and forgive me for saying it because I'm sure you know my reputation for downing a few belts, but don't spend too much on gin."

"Oh honest to God, I won't. Now I can go back to bourbon!"

Bogart laughed and hugged her. "Christ but how you gals are made of sterner stuff." He had the door open. "Get the phone back on and be sure to phone me, I want to see you on the set of my next picture."

He shut the door. She stood staring at it. She stared at the twenty dollar bills she was clutching. She replaced them in her purse. She went to the bathroom where she had left the glass in which were dissolved twenty-three sleeping pills. She poured the contents of the glass into the toilet bowl and flushed it. She rinsed the glass thoroughly and placed it on the rim of the sink. She stared at herself in the mirror in the door of the medicine chest above the sink. She removed the snood and stared at her mess of gray hair. "Girl, you're getting yourself a rinse and a dye job and a very fancy set and you're going to phone Humphrey Bogart as soon as the juice is back on and get your tail over to Warners and take whatever they offer you. He's not handing you a line either, honey, and he didn't suggest beddy-bye. He's the real article."

She stripped, ran the shower, stepped under it, and for the first time in too long a time, remembered what it was to be happy.

On the street, the others watched as Bogart rejoined them. He said to Mallory, "That was damned nice of you to ask for her autograph. That was really damned nice."

"But I meant it. My mother's movie crazy. I try to get her all the autographs I can. So help me, it's true!"

Hazel asked Bogart, "How much did you slip her?"

"What are you talking about?"

"I saw you slipping those bills into her handbag. Nice job of sleight of hand if I must say so myself."

"And you have," said Villon.

"Hazel, if I see anything about this in somebody's column, and I read everybody's column religiously, like every other egomaniac in this town, I'll slap you bowlegged."

"She's already bowlegged," said Villon.

"You shut up!" scolded Hazel. To Bogart she said, "I have every intention of telling Louella about Karen's bad luck because I know Louella will help. She's not completely a mean old bitch. And Louella will pass it on to Marion who's a good Joe and will probably invite Karen over to share a fifth of gin."

"Karen prefers bourbon." Bogart looked at his wristwatch. "The day's growing shorter, Herb. What's the name of that pawnbroker?"

"Leo Bulgari."

"Oh yeah. Him with the three brass balls. Let's get going."

Villon was reading Mallory's mind. "You can phone the precinct from Bulgari's. Oh Christ, I almost forgot, there's so much going on with this case—how's Ned Aswan?"

"They expect him to pull through. I had a long talk with Josh Trent's secretary, Zelda Sweet, back at the house. It seems that he's always needed Joshua Trent to stabilize his emotional insecurity."

Bogart asked, "I'm sure Trent left him very well fixed."

"According to Zelda Sweet, more then very well fixed."

Villon asked him, "When you having dinner with her?"

Mallory blushed. "What do you mean?"

"You're blushing so you know what I mean." Villon said to Bogart, "Jim's a sucker for a pretty face. But nothing comes of it. He's still single. He never gets engaged."

"Hell," said Mallory, "engaged means a ring and who can afford a ring on my salary."

Hazel said to Villon, "You earn more then he does."

Bogart asked, "You following us, Hazel?"

"I don't like that smirk, Mr. Bogart."

"I never smirk, Hazel. My upper lip's too stiff. Funny, with my stiff upper lip I don't understand why I'm never offered no British parts. What do you think, Hazel?"

She said as she got behind the wheel of her car, "Scrub it, sweetheart. They've already done *Little Lord Fauntleroy*."

FIFTEEN

"Leo Bulgari." Villon spoke the name with a hint of contempt.

"Your paths have crossed before, I take it."

"Many times. He's so crooked he gives corruption a good name. He's a Turk. We know he's a fence but we've never caught him at it. He calls himself the pawnbroker to the stars. You'd be amazed at the number of names who have utilized his services. He's so greedy, he does house calls. He preys on has-beens like Karen Barrett. Too many silent screen actors had absolutely no business sense whatsoever. The exceptions were Mary Pickford and Charlie Chaplin and some shrewd mothers. Pickford's mother. The mothers of the Talmadge sisters and the Gish sisters. Very clever with a buck and demons at the bargaining table. But ladies like Karen Barrett, they didn't have mothers. They had husbands. Bloodsuckers who bled them dry. You slip her much?"

"A hundred."

"Very nice. It's tax deductible. Charitable contribution."

"Forget it." Bogart added, "And I don't want Mayo to hear about it. Spread the word. Especially to Hazel."

"Tell her yourself. Up ahead, I see three brass balls."

"That's Bulgari's place." He looked out the rear window. Mallory was right behind them, and behind him was Hazel who was more concerned with examining the recent repairs to her face in the rear mirror than she was with the oncoming traffic in the adjacent lane.

Bogart saw a space and parked. Mallory did a U-turn into a small lot that was adjacent to a hot dog stand. Hazel joined him. Traffic was surprisingly light for the late afternoon and Mallory and Hazel were able to make it across the street to join Bogart and Villon in safety. The pawn shop had two display windows offering unredeemed objects for sale. There were items of jewelry, a variety of watches and musical instruments, fur coats and jackets, cameras, radios, dishes, silverware, and linens.

"Look," said Bogart, "the cornucopia."

The cornucopia was set in the center of a display. Bulgari had placed a card alongside it on which he had printed, IS THIS THE HORN OF PLENTY?

"Brazen bastard," said Villon.

Hazel said, "So that's what a cornucopia looks like. I wouldn't give it as a wedding gift to a couple I disliked."

"It's sealed," said Bogart. He and Villon looked at each other. "You know, Herb, at the end of *The Maltese Falcon* when they find what they really think is the bird they're looking for, it turns out to be a fake."

"You trying to tell me something?"

"I'm trying to tell you not to be too disappointed if this thing is filled with crackerjacks."

"Bogie, to me the cornucopia is an afterthought. I'm trying to catch a killer. He's going to kill again. He's undoubtedly gotten his hands on a list of cornucopia owners. This could spread into an epidemic."

They heard a bell tinkle as the pawnshop door was pulled open. "But of course! It is my old friend detective Villon! I thought I recognized you! And my heavens! Do I see before me Humfairy Bogart?" Leo Bulgari was possibly five foot seven inches tall. He seemed taller because he wore a fez on his head with a gold tassel that dangled to just below his left ear. He was fat and his stomach bulged over his trousers belt. He was brave enough to wear an earring at a time when only certain kinds of men favored earrings. Bulgari's earring was a crescent moon worn on his right lobe.

Bogart mumbled, "This, I suppose, is Bulgari?"

"Yeah. The fez is familiar," said Villon.

"I don't go for that Humfairy business. He trying to be funny?"

"Ask him."

Bulgari said to Hazel, "That is a delightful brooch you are wearing."

"And shall continue to wear," said Hazel.

For a man of his girth he bowed gracefully, one hand extended by way of inviting them into his store. Hazel was the first to enter followed by Mallory and Villon. Bogart managed to disguise his distaste as his eyes met Bulgari's. "I am a great admirer, Mr. Bogart. You have given me very many pleasant hours." Bogart managed a smile that Bulgari could interpret any way he saw fit. Bulgari shut the door and offered them chairs and Turkish coffee. Hazel sat. Nobody wanted coffee. "And how may I help, Detective Villon?"

"You know what I'm after. A certain cornucopia."

Bulgari clasped his hands together and his eyes beseeched the ceiling. "What is it all of a sudden with cornucopias?"

Villon said, "Bulgari."

"Yes?"

"You're overplaying." Bulgari unclasped his hands. "That one in the window."

"It is worthless. Unless you care to buy it."

Villon handed him Karen Barrett's pawn ticket. "Is this the ticket for the thing in the window?"

Bulgari examined the ticket. "Ah yes. Miss Barrett. An unfortunate victim of circumstances. Are you interested in redeeming the object? Twenty-eight dollars."

"What! You gave her fifteen dollars."

"In a rash moment of generosity. It has been here a long time and each day the interest on the loan increases."

"That wasn't Miss Barrett's to hock. It belongs to someone else."

Bulgari shrugged. "That is not my concern."

"Take it out of the window. I want to examine it."

"Take my word. It contains nothing of value. It is sealed because I sealed it myself. These things are dust catchers."

Villon said to Mallory, "Jim, get it out of the window, pronto."

Jim reached into the display and removed the cornucopia.

Bulgari hovered behind Mallory. "Careful, careful. Don't throw anything over."

Mallory carried it to a desk. Villon said to Bulgari, "Unseal it." Bulgari shrugged. He took a pen knife from his pocket and with elaborate care unsealed the tin foil that obscured the cornucopia's interior. "Surely your friend could tell by its light weight that it contains nothing as heavy as gems."

Villon pulled back the tin foil. He knew he'd find nothing of value. He was enjoying harassing Bulgari who he seemed to have forgotten was unharassable. Bulgari said, "You see. There is only wads of cotton. So, do you wish to redeem the item?"

"I'll think it over."

"As you wish. It might interest you to know I have had another inquiry. A gentleman inquired on behalf of a royal personage."

"La Contessa di Marcopolo."

"Aha! You know about her. Her emissary tells me this cock and bull about her father and I humored him."

"Were you successful?" asked Villon.

Bulgari shrugged. "He was a most disagreeable person. Very good looking. But very impatient and quick-tempered. Italian. They are usually very quick-tempered, and now that they are allied with the Nazis, I trust them even less."

"Spoken like a true patriot," said Bogart, enough iron in his voice to construct a battleship.

Villon asked, "You've got other cornucopias?"

"Only this misbegotten one. You doubt me? Look around. You will see no other cornucopias."

"You've got a basement."

"There is nothing of value down there. I assure you. No cornucopias."

"I might come back with a search warrant," threatened Villon.

Bulgari clasped his hands together. "How often have you threatened me with search warrants!" Bulgari said to the others, "It is a little game we play, but he never returns with a search warrant."

"You do business with Edgar Dickens?"

Villon's question seemed to catch Bulgari by surprise. "Dickens?"

"You know who I'm talking about. The Old Curiosity Shop in Venice. You guys are always buying and selling and swapping with each other."

"Ah! Of course! Today my brain is like a sieve. Whatever is there tends to slip through. Yes of course I have dealt with Mr. Dickens. And I may as well tell you I've also dealt with Joshua Trent. But this you have probably already surmised. We are a closely knit community here in Los Angeles. We know each other well. We buy, we sell, we trade, we haggle, we threaten, we fight, and then come to an agreement." He added soberly, "But, my friend Villon, we do not commit murder."

Villon's hands were on his hips. His voice rasped. "Bulgari, are you a citizen of this country?"

"Soon. Soon. Very soon. I shall throw a banquet in my honor."

Bogart said to Hazel and Mallory, "The bastard'll probably charge admission." He didn't give a damn if Bulgari heard him or not. He disliked the man and was not about to make any bones about it. "Herb, we have to hang around here any longer? I need fresh air."

"Let's go," said Villon.

"Villon!" The Bulgari charm had evaporated. "Do not threaten me. I will not tolerate being threatened. I conduct my business with decorum. I have no police record. I have never been charged. So do not threaten me."

Villon left without saying a word. Hazel and Mallory followed. Bogart stopped in the doorway, turned, and said to Bulgari, "I don't like the way you pronounced my name, fatso. Get it right. It's Hum*free*. Right?"

Bulgari shrugged. Bogart left. The four huddled on the sidewalk. Bulgari watched them through a window. He wished he could read lips.

Bogart was saying, "That was a very unpleasant experience. I should have decked him. I need a drink. I need a couple of drinks. I'm going back to the Allah and check for any messages. Mayo may be looking for me. And the studio. Anyone care to join me?"

Villon said, "Thanks, Bogie. But Jim and I should get back to the precinct. We've got a lot to do. You going home, Hazel?"

"If that's a hint, I'm not taking it. I'm tailing after you two bums so I can use the john and the telephone and then Herbert Villon, you're taking me to dinner."

"You're taking me. It's your turn."

"Gee," said Mallory, "then I can invite Zelda Sweet to dinner."

"Zelda what?" asked Hazel.

"Come on, come on," said Villon, "let's get going. Bogie, if anything turns up, I'll call you at the hotel."

"Thanks, Herb," said Bogart. He got into his car and was soon heading to the Garden of Allah, which was only a five-minute drive from the pawn shop.

In the bar of the Garden of Allah, Dashiell Hammett and Lillian Hellman were going through the motions of holding court. With the strong-willed characters inhabiting the bar at cocktail time, a favorite sport was jockeying for position. Hellman had been holding somewhat spellbound an audience consisting of Dorothy Parker, her husband Alan Campbell, Robert Benchley, and the portly Sidney Greenstreet. She was telling them about the encounters at the Curiosity Shop and the tragedy at Joshua Trent's estate. She repeated the incidents well and with enough dramatic intensity that there were no inane interruptions with the usual fatuous wisecracks. At one point Mrs. Parker insisted the butler did it but Hellman insisted there was no butler, in Trent's case, only a lover and an assortment of employees. Then surprisingly enough, especially for Hellman rarely given to compliments or kind words, she waxed generously enthusiastic about Herb Villon.

"He sounds absolutely spiffy," said Mrs. Parker. She indicated her husband. "When Alan gets killed in action, I'll look up your Detective Villon." Campbell didn't look kindly on her statement but kept his peace. He had no intention of seeing action. He had wangled himself into Special Services where he would write scripts for army films.

"Seems to me," said Benchley with a chuckle, "what this case needs is your thin man, Dash."

"He wouldn't be of any use," demurred Hammett.

"Your modesty is appreciated but most unbecoming," said Benchley, "Nick Charles would have this case solved in about the time it takes him to drink four martinis."

Hammett said to Hellman, "Here we go again." He said to Benchley, "Thanks to the film series, you're under a bit of a misapprehension. Nick Charles is not the thin man."

"Apple sauce," said Mrs. Parker.

"He's not apple sauce either," said Hellman.

Hammett retrieved the spotlight. "I repeat, Nick Charles is not the thin man. In my book as in the first movie of the series, the thin man is the elongated shadow on the wall of the murder victim. The building janitor tells Nick he saw a thin man, meaning that shadow on the wall. There. You have it from the horse's mouth which is as dry as hay and in desperate need of sustenance. The liquid variety."

Hellman shouted for a waiter and then waved at Bogart who was headed for the bar. He signaled he'd join them as soon as he got himself a drink.

Mrs. Parker asked Hellman, "Any news about the wife?"

"She's no wife, she's a bad habit. As far as I know she's still up north with Mama. For Bogie's sake and sanity let's hope she decides to stay there."

Alan Campbell said, "She won't let go of him. Not now. Not while his career is swinging into high gear."

"Why beloved," said Mrs. Parker, "is that why you won't let go of me?"

"Just say the word," said Campbell, "and you're a free woman."

"Balls."

"That's not the word."

Bogart joined them and sat next to Hellman. "Well, you character assassins, been having a field day?"

"As a matter of fact," said Hellman, "we've been discussing another assassin, the one who did in Josh Trent and your housekeeper. Well don't sit there as though you're waiting to audition for something. What have you guys been doing? What did you find out? Was useless Goldwyn of any use?"

Bogart lead them to Sam Goldwyn and from Sam Goldwyn to Angelica Harper and her castle that had Benchley fascinated and wondered if she'd be a fit subject for the two-reelers he wrote and starred in at M-G-M. Bogart said probably and then went on to Mrs. Charles Brabin, relishing the looks on their faces when he identified the lady as the old silent screen vamp Theda Bara.

Hammett said dreamily, "She used to give me an erection."

"Did she charge much?" asked Hellman.

"This Kito," asked Greenstreet, gratified to finally put an oar in, "was there anything suspicious about him?"

"He grinned. Very big grin. Very big teeth. Why suspicious, Sidney? You think he might be a spy?"

Mrs. Parker contributed, "Possibly a rear admiral on a secret mission."

"He didn't have much of a rear," said Bogart. "And stop interrupting." He moved onward to Karen Barrett and her sad state of affairs, sidestepping his contribution to her of a hundred dollars.

"There's an awful lot of that going on in this town. Even Louis B. Mayer has some of them under stock contract. May McAvoy, Barbara Bedford, Aileen Pringle." Benchley shook his head and sipped his drink.

"In her day Pringle made him millions," said Greenstreet.

"Her day's passed," said Bogart, "so why don't I get on with it?"

"There's more?" asked Mrs. Parker, who was showing signs of fatigue.

"There's a Turkish delight," Bogart told her. He launched into the incident with Leo Bulgari with relish and a side order of venom, describing his girth, the earring, the fez, and the worthless cornucopia.

"It wouldn't be worthless if it had contained the jewels," said Hellman.

"Your Bulgari sounds like someone Eric Ambler might have created. He was very big with Turkish scoundrels," said Greenstreet.

Hellman was on a trail all her own. "Maybe it did contain the jewels and he's got them stashed away some place."

"I do wish somebody wants another drink," said Mrs. Parker, "it's too early to think about breakfast."

"You haven't had dinner," said her husband.

"Oh. I hadn't noticed."

Hellman said to Bogart, "If you haven't got any dinner plans, join us. We're thinking about Musso and Frank's."

"Sure. But listen. Are you in a rush about dinner?"

"Hell, no," said Hellman, "I'd rather hang in here for a few more drinks and wait for Dotty to drop something quotable." Mrs. Parker behaved as though she hadn't heard her. She hadn't dropped anything suitably quotable in a long time. In time it would be discovered that bitchery was more her forte then wit.

Bogart said, "Why don't I meet you back here in a couple of hours. I want to go over to the house to see if the Warner crew's got it anywhere near back in shape."

Somebody might have heard him but he doubted it. They were heavy into a discussion of Theda Bara and her Japanese servant and, wondered Mrs. Parker, do you suppose they might be having an affair right under Mr. Brabin's nose?

In the lobby, Bogart stopped at the desk to see if he had any messages. There was one from the studio to remind him of the rehearsal the next morning and Bogart told the clerk he'd be back in a few hours. He hurried out of the lobby and into the parking lot and was soon on his way to Brentwood.

There was a lot crowding his mind as he drove into Laurel Canyon Road. There were victims and an attempted suicide and an unknown assassin and the Goddamned cornucopia and Villon and Mallory and Hazel Dickson and a silent screen vamp and her Japanese houseman and a ditsy artist and a lady very far down on her luck. He stopped for gas at his usual station near his home and soon he was driving into his street and wishing he hadn't left the Garden of Allah.

There was a blue coupe parked in front of his house and inside the house he saw a light in the foyer. He wondered if the coupe and light connected to one of the Warner crew. He left his car and went up the walk to the front door. He put his key in the lock. It was unlocked. He entered and crossed from the foyer into the living room.

There wasn't a sign of the crime. The Warner's crew had done a superb job. No one ever would have suspected that a murder had taken place. All the place lacked was the little woman to welcome him home with his pipe and slippers in place. He went into the kitchen and then traveled to the den. He went upstairs. His and Mayo's room was immaculate. Also the guest room. At the end of the hall was an unused room, presumably for a live-in servant but Hannah Darrow had used it as a work room for herself and where she kept a few things such as a smock, an extra dress, and extra shoes. It hadn't even been examined to see if it had been ransacked. Bogart saw a light coming from under the door. That was very curious.

Bogart slowly walked down the hall to the door. When he reached it, he listened for a sound from within. He heard nothing. Abruptly, he pushed the door open. "What are you doing here?" he asked.

Lucy Darrow looked startled.

SIXTEEN

She was sitting at what looked like a small desk, but when opened it was a sewing machine. On the desk was a shopping bag into which Lucy was folding garments. "Oh! You frightened me. I phoned you here and at the hotel to tell you I'd like to collect my mother's things, but I couldn't find you." She indicated the shopping bag. "Her smock, her aprons, her slippers . . ." her voice faded away.

"How did you get in?"

"The men from Warner Brothers were just leaving. They let me in. Actually, my mother kept a spare key in the apartment that I was going to return to you, I intended to use it." She folded and packed as she talked.

Bogart leaned against the door with his arms folded. "You find the dress for your mother?"

"Finally. It's in the car. I'm taking it to the funeral parlor. They're delivering Mother tomorrow morning."

"Why did you and Heep leave Canter's without having your lunch?"

"Oh, that. I wasn't hungry. Sidney wanted to get back to Venice. I wanted to get back to finding mother's dress. Is that man a really good detective?"

"Herb Villon? He's aces. You finished here? I've got a dinner date."

"Yes, this is it."

"You could have borrowed a suitcase."

"This shopping bag's fine. Thanks just the same." He held the door open for her. She walked past him and he switched off the light. He followed her to the foyer downstairs. She talked as they walked. "I haven't chosen the time for the services. Probably the day after tomorrow at noon. I need time to notify her friends."

"Why don't you run a notice in the *Times?*"

"That's an idea. Except it's too late to place it today. Mother didn't have that many friends and as to relatives, there's only my aunt and she has no family. I'm an only child. I never knew my father. He died before I was born."

"Sorry about that."

"Oh," she said airily, "you don't miss what you never knew." In the foyer, she rummaged in her handbag for her car keys. "And oh, here's the house key." He pocketed it. "Is Mr. Villon close to finding the killer?"

"He needs the lucky break."

"The lucky break? What's that?"

"What every detective prays for. A phone call with some information that leads to the killer. Or the killer to make a slip and do something suspicious or say something suspicious. Detectives never know where it's going to come from. But sooner or later, it comes."

"And the cornucopia?"

Bogart said, "I wish I'd never heard of the damn thing."

She said dreamily, "I wish I had a cornucopia. I wish I could find it."

"Why not? Everybody has a right to their dreams. I'm curious, Lucy. Do you mind if I get a little nosy?"

"Not at all."

"Are you and Sidney Heep what they call an item?"

"Mother only introduced us a short while ago. I like him, but I really don't know him all that well. Did we look that intimate at the restaurant?"

Bogart shrugged. "There's intimate and there's intimate. Now I hate to hurry you on your way . . ."

"Of course. Your dinner date. I'll let you know about the service." She grasped the shopping bag and hurried out of the house. Bogart stood in the doorway watching her. Something bothered him. He couldn't put his finger on it, but something bothered him. As he shut the door, the phone rang. He went to the living room, sat in the chair next to the phone and picked up the receiver. "Hello?" It was Mayo. "The house is in tip-top shape. How'd you guess I was here?"

"The clerk at the hotel told me. Are you staying in the house tonight?"

"If I'm in shape to get back."

"Meaning?"

"I'm having dinner with Lily and Dash at Musso's. I'm picking them up at the Allah."

"Why aren't you meeting them at Musso's?"

He looked at the ceiling in exasperation. "Because it's easier to round them up at the Allah. When I left them, they were drinking with a gang of professional drinkers and you know what that can lead to. I spent the day playing detective with Herb Villon. Lily and Dash joined us for a while but then left us when we had to go see Sam Goldwyn."

"What the hell does he have to do with the case?"

"I'll start at the beginning." He recapped the day's activity ending with the unpleasantness at Leo Bulgari's.

"Well," said Mayo, "all that and Theda Bara, too. Listen, my mother wants to tell you something. That's really why I'm calling."

"Aw. I thought it was because you missed me."

"Only when I take aim," she retorted.

He snapped his fingers. "I knew there was something wrong in this room."

"What do you mean?"

"I'm sitting here talking on the phone and nothing's gone whistling past my head."

"You big sap. Here's Mother."

Bogart heard some fumbling noises as the phone was passed from daughter to mother and then winced as her sharp voice sliced into his ear. "Hello Humphrey."

"Hello Evelyn. How are you?"

"Much better now that Mayo is here with me." Hypocrite, thought Bogart. I can still picture your sigh of relief complete with sound effects as you saw your daughter off to New York that landmark day so many years ago. "Humphrey . . ." The way she pronounced his name it was like having an ice pick plunged into him. "Mayo and I have been talking about the ransackings, of course. Frankly it's all we can think about. My apartment is still a bit of a mess though Mayo's been a dear helping me straighten out."

He heard Mayo say with irritation, "Oh for crying out loud, Mother, get on with it."

"Don't be so impatient, Mayo!" bristled Evelyn.

Bogart thought, throw something, Mayo. Hit her with a pillow.

"Now Humphrey," said Evelyn. "In all this horror and confusion I forgot something that might be helpful to the police."

"The Portland police or the L.A. police?"

"If it was the Portland police we wouldn't be phoning you, would we?"

"You've got a point there," he said, and thought, and hold on to it especially if it's very sharp.

"That large carton of my husband's in your basement."

"I know where it is. You don't have to worry about it. It wasn't broken into."

"Yes, Mayo told me. Humphrey, I think that's the carton with the false bottom."

He sat up. "You kidding me?"

"You know I never kid. I suppose it's safe to tell you now, he's been dead long enough."

Bogart refrained from telling her that some people are never dead long enough as he was afraid she'd take it personally.

"How shall I put it without making it sound too illegal? Oh well, in for a penny, in for a pound." Haven't heard that one in a long while, thought Bogart. "Jack kept an apartment in Shanghai. For his long stayovers." The devil, thought Bogart, grinning. "He would pack his belongings into that carton and of course have it delivered to his apartment."

Bogart asked, "And what did he pack into the false bottom?"

She said briskly, "He smuggled, to and fro. Don't ask me what kind of contraband he dealt in because what I have expressed is a suspicion, it's not a statement of fact." She paused for a moment. "He did bring me the occasional vial of perfume, frivolities like that."

"I think that was very thoughtful of him."

"Yes, I suppose it was. Anyway, Humphrey. It's worth a go. I don't know how it opens but if it's the right carton, then I suspect the cornucopia might be there."

Mayo pulled the phone from her mother's grip. "Bogie, you get right out of that house!"

"Why? I own it."

"The ransackers aren't stupid. It might occur to them the carton might have a false bottom."

"But they never touched it in the first place."

"Please, Bogie," she pleaded. He was touched by her concern.

"You might be right. There've been a lot of people in and out of here the past twenty-four hours. After the police left a crew came in from Warner's and set the place to rights. And oh yeah, when I got home tonight, I found Lucy Darrow in that spare room Hannah used to work in."

"What was she doing there?" asked Mayo with a soupçon of suspicion.

Bogart recognized the suspicion. It was a constant with Mayo. "She tried to rape me." Mayo shrieked. "Calm down, kiddo, calm down. I'm only kidding."

"I wouldn't put it past her, what with her record."

"What record?"

"I never told you before?"

"What the hell are you talking about?"

"She's been hospitalized." She paused. "Mental problems."

"You mean she's nuts?"

"Relax. She's been out a few years now."

"Now you listen to me, when they're nuts they're nuts and they stay nuts. Come to think of it, this morning she gave me Hannah's keys to the house."

Suspicion again. "When this morning? Where?"

"Come on, kid. You know she was coming to the Garden of Allah to pick up her mother's handbag. That's when I got back Hannah's keys. When I found her here she said the crew let her in on their way out. But she could have used Hannah's spare key."

"What spare key?"

"The one Hannah kept in their apartment in case of an emergency."

"What emergency?"

"I don't know. Make one up. Listen, I've got to track down Herb Villon. I'm hanging up."

"Wait!"

"What?"

"I love you." She slammed the phone down. He smiled. He searched in his pocket address book, found Villon's number and dialed it. Jim Mallory answered the phone.

Mallory said, "Detective Villon."

"Come off it, Jim, I know it's you."

"Bogie! I've been ringing you. Your line's been busy. And we're just on our way out."

"Hold your horses, I've got to talk to Herb. It's important. It's a lead."

Villon snapped his fingers and Mallory handed him the phone. "Bogie. We've got an emergency. You can meet us at Bulgari's."

"Why there, for Chrissakes!"

"Because, old buddy, he's been found in his apartment in back of the store with a stab wound in his chest."

"Is he dead?"

"Very."

"Well that's a relief. I'll be right over."

"Don't rush. Drive carefully. He's not going anywhere."

A few seconds later, Bogart was going through the house bolting windows and doors. In the kitchen, he locked the door leading to the basement and pocketed the key. He hurried to the front door, pulled it shut after him and double-locked it. In the street, twilight now descending, he looked for the blue coupe. There was no sign of it. He got into his car, and was soon on his way to the pawn shop at Santa Monica and La Brea.

Humfairy Bogart.

Bulgari, it serves you right.

Dash and Lily. Dinner. Damn. He saw a drugstore with phone booths and pulled over. He got through to the bar but there was a delay getting Hammett or Hellman. Bogart nervously jingled coins in his pocket. He could hear laughter and the sound of the cash register and then finally Lillian Hellman asked, "Hello?"

"It's Bogie, Lily. Listen, something important's come up. I can't make dinner."

"I didn't know you could cook." The slur in her voice was overpowering.

"My apologies to you and Dash."

"Why? Because you can't cook?"

"Lily," he shouted, "I won't be at Musso's."

"I don't blame you. The food's lousy."

"Good-bye, Lily!" He slammed the phone down and raced back to his car.

Lillian Hellman managed to make her way back to her group.

"Who was that?" asked Hammett.

"Some son of a bitch who can't make dinner because he can't cook. Well personally, I think he's having a nervous breakdown. Where's my drink?"

"In your hand," said Hammett.

"Oh."

Bogart was feeling a tingle. What Bogart had told Lucy Darrow earlier, a detective waits for a break, and now Bogart felt the break was at hand. His palms were sweating and his upper lip felt stiffer and of all times to be hungry. Ahead he saw the three brass balls. He also saw police cars and photographers and groups of people clustered on both sides of the streets. He decided it would be wiser to distance himself. He parked half a block away, locked his car, and walked to the scene of the crime. Villon or Mallory had apparently or-

dered the area in front of the store to be cleared as Bogart
saw policemen ordering onlookers and reporters and photographers to back away. Meanwhile, an ambulance pulled
up and two orderlies descended into the street. They went to
the rear of the vehicle, opened the door and pulled out a
bound stretcher. They carried this into the pawn shop little
realizing a movie star was following in their wake. Hazel
Dickson was using the shop's phone telling somebody somewhere that the pawnbroker to the stars had been redeemed at
last. Bogart pinched her cheek as he passed her and entered
the rear of the shop. He found himself in a pleasant, one-
room apartment complete with kitchen and bathroom and
barred windows that overlooked an alley. Leo Bulgari lay
face up, eyes half open in appraisal of nothing. The forensics
men were busy as always. Villon motioned to Bogart when
he saw him enter and pointed his face at a shelf laden with
cornucopias. Bogart whistled while Jim Mallory was cursing
the fate that brought about the circumstances keeping him
from the desired company of Zelda Sweet.

"The only good thing about being here," said Villon, "besides the beached whale on the floor is that I didn't need a
search warrant. There's more in the basement."

"So he's been collecting them," said Bogart.

"I would assume they've been amassed over the years.
There was a time when these things, filled with fruits, candies, cakes, or flowers were a popular decoration."

"What's the basement like?" asked Bogart.

"You wouldn't want to live there."

"I'm not apartment hunting. Any leads? I'm only asking
you that because I've spoken that line so many times in so
many pictures."

"Well I figure this is the scenario. He closes shop—you
might have noticed the sign in the door window apologizing
for being closed, please call again. He comes back here to do
the day's figures. You'll notice on the desk over there there's
a ledger open and a pile of receipts and a pen. I suspect he
was waiting for someone."

"Wouldn't the closed sign discourage them?"

"You forget, Bogie, all residences in tinsel town come with back roadways for garbage collection." He indicated a door in the back wall. "There's the back door. You notice it is equipped for a bolt but the bolt is resting against the wall and not in place where all good bolts should be because the killer left by the door he entered with and of course could not bolt the door behind him."

The coroner, who Bogart recognized as the same one who had examined Hannah Darrow and Joshua Trent grunted as he got to his feet, being slightly arthritic. Bogart asked Villon, "He your favorite coroner?"

"He my only coroner. I'm thinking of adopting him." He looked at Mallory. "Jim, a hangdog expression doesn't become you."

Bogart asked, "Who found the body?"

"Some extra walking his dog saw the door ajar and knowing there's a pawn shop here suspected the possibility of foul play, and since his dog was a savage French poodle he felt it safe to investigate. He saw fatso and the blood and called us and here we are. And there's little else we can do here."

The orderlies needed some policemen to help them lift Bulgari onto the stretcher and strap him in. Bogart clucked his tongue. "There goes an awful lot of halvah. He got a family?"

Villon pointed to some framed pictures on the desk. One was a chubby woman and the other was three chubby children, two boys and a girl. "We're tracking them down," Villon said. He bent down and picked Bulgari's fez from the floor. He offered it to Bogart. "Souvenir?"

"I'll pass," said Bogart.

"Now what's this about a lead?" asked Villon.

"Hell yes. I went back to my place to see if the Warner crew had cleaned it up, which they did. I found Lucy Darrow there."

"Alone?"

"Quiet as a mouse." Bogart recapped the incident and then continued with the phone call from Mayo and her mother. Mallory had joined them and was enjoying the small smile on Villon's face. It was always a small smile when he thought he was on to something promising. Never a broad grin or a whoop of joy, just the small smile in case he was in for a disappointment. Villon was always careful to cover himself.

"A secret compartment," echoed Villon. "Gee, I used to love them in spy movies. I always wanted to come up against a secret compartment, and my dream is about to be fulfilled." He thought for a moment and then asked Bogart, "You think there's anything significant in the fact that she's served time in looney bins?"

"I reserve opinion. Outside of the fact that he was undoubtedly a rat, who do you suppose had it in for Bulgari?"

"I can't give you names but I can give you types. But my guess is, he's tied in with the cornucopia. Bogie, I've been playing with this idea since we parted company earlier. I think Bulgari was part of a group pledged to find the bloody thing and if there was a treasure, they divide it. I figure with all his cornucopias they suspected he found the right one but hid the gems until the time was safe to convert them into cash. Now I'm not accusing anybody, but there was the strong possibility that the members of this cabal could have been in addition to Bulgari, Edgar Dickens and his little Nell, Sidney Heep, Joshua Trent, and Ned Aswan . . ."

Bogart's eyes widened. "That could explain the suicide attempt!"

"That's right," said Villon. "Not that he lost his beloved, but that had he been at home and not in Santa Barbara, he could have bought his passage to forever."

"What about the other ladies? Bara, Mrs. Harper, Karen Barrett."

"Red herrings. Bara's a rich lady with a rich husband. Angelica Harper knew of only one cornucopia and that's the one Bara borrowed and Barrett hocked. But there is a lady who I think might have been involved."

"Who?"

"Your housekeeper. Hannah Darrow."

SEVENTEEN

Bogart was scratching his chin. "Hannah Darrow. Talk about your least likely suspect even though she was a victim. Well, let's take it from the top." He walked to a kitchen table and took a seat. Villon and Mallory joined him. Hazel Dickson walked in and asked if they were holding a seance and why. Villon told her to sit down and not move her mouth unless there was gum in it. Hazel started to bristle but a wink from Bogart which was both friendly and wise caused her to settle down and listen. "I think it begins with my wife." Villon nodded agreement. "She and Hannah spend a lot of time together. Mayo's not working and lonely. So she gets chummy with Hannah who's a nice lady and also a smart one. They do a lot of jawing and learn a lot about each other. Hazel, when she finally feels comfortable about it, tells Mayo about her daughter, Lucy. Mayo tells her about her mother and what a famous news hen she is in Portland. Then she gets going on her father and he's a hell of a lot more colorful. Sea captain on the Orient run and that's pretty exotic. And about the most exotic thing that Hannah heard about in Hollywood is Grauman's Chinese. Mayo is a great one for icing on the cake so she tells Hannah about the cornucopia. Hannah loves it and tells her daughter Lucy who's the dreamy type with a faulty mechanism between her ears and she looks into cornucopias. She probably begins by looking it up in the dictionary."

"And then comes the Old Curiosity Shop," interjected Villon.

"Most likely. Mayo has brought Hannah there and that leads to Lucy's introduction to the place. And whether this is conjecture or not, Lucy and Sidney Heep hear harp music when they look at each other."

"I may weep," said Hazel.

"You may just shut up and listen," said Villon.

"Edgar Dickens has cornucopias but they're not the one they want. Dickens is chummy with Joshua Trent and Ned Aswan. They do a lot of buying, selling, and trading in addition to interior decorating. Trent and Aswan get all steamed up. They agree to join the hunt."

"Not knowing where to begin?"

"They begin with Mayo. Hannah knows she's got her father's carton there among other things. She offhandedly wonders if Mayo has the cornucopia and Mayo just as offhandedly tells her no she doesn't because Mayo doesn't know anything about it except what her mother told her. And Mayo doesn't give diddly piss for it because all Mayo wants is a job in a movie or a fistfight with her husband to prove she's as much of a man as he is."

Villon said, "All this is recent."

"It has to be. What sets it into motion is the arrival of la Contessa di Marcopolo. She and her gang . . ."

"There're only three of them," Jim Mallory reminded him.

"And not your usual crowd," said Bogart. "They ransack my mother-in-law's place and then hightail it here. Mayo's mother calls her and Hannah Darrow overhears. She tells the others. And one of them gets very greedy, and knowing that with la Contessa in the picture time is growing short, ransacks my place not knowing Hannah is still there, probably up in the workroom she used. Hannah hears the noises and investigates and catches a knife blade, probably from my own kitchen." He said to Hazel. "We have some very fine cutlery."

Hazel said while looking coldly at Villon, "I might borrow one."

"Then killing Hannah inspires the killer to fresh heights. Gets rid of what the killer thinks is excess baggage, such as Joshua and Ned. Joshua's available but Ned isn't, but so it shouldn't be a total loss when the opportunity presents itself, Joshua is wiped out. Ned can be taken care of later."

"But why ransack the place?" asked Villon.

"Look," said Bogart. "Joshua Trent once sold a cornucopia to Sam Goldwyn. Stands to reason he has been in possession of others. He might still have them."

Hazel said, "Then the people out at the Old Curiosity Shop and the countess and her playmates are marked people."

"But not easily disposed of," said Bogart. "Countess and friends are in a hotel suite and for the most part travel together."

Villon said, "On the other hand the killer knows they don't have the cornucopia. Why bother to kill them? At least not now. Wait until they get their hands on it if they'll ever get their hands on it. As to Edgar Dickens and his crowd of two, he doesn't have the treasure either. There's only one person left to kill."

"Who?" asked Hazel.

"Me," said Bogart.

"She could have done you when you found her in the house," said Villon. Hazel and Mallory were bemused. Found who in what house?

"It wouldn't work. The house has already been searched. Go through the motions again? Stupid."

"So where do we find the murder weapon?" Mallory asked.

"In my kitchen. All washed and dried and magnetized hilt in place on the wall above the work counter. That's really why she went back to the house. After she murdered Leo Bulgari who she knew was a nuisance and couldn't be trusted."

Hazel exploded. "Who the hell are you talking about?"

"Oh didn't you know?" asked Bogart. "Lucy Darrow, my housekeeper's daughter. A lady with a dream." He paused. "Poor bitch, she's better at creating nightmares." He said to Villon, "I locked up my place tighter then a drum, but I'd still like to get back there and examine that carton."

"What carton?" asked Hazel.

"One with a secret compartment," said Villon.

Very annoyed and perplexed, Hazel said, "You guys had better watch out. I'm going to scream."

Villon patiently told her about Mrs. Methot's phone call to Bogie and about the benighted Lucy Darrow.

"Well why in God's name don't you arrest her?" asked Hazel.

"On what charges?" asked Villon. "All we've got to work with is a supposition. And it's nice thinking, Bogie, really good." To Hazel he said, "But I haven't a shred of evidence against her. And another thing, she didn't work alone."

"I had an idea you had an idea," said Bogart.

"Those ransackings. No one person could have pulled them off."

"You think it was Sidney Heep?"

"The most likely, isn't he?"

"Because we saw them together once?"

Bogart smiled. "You're a cautious little devil, aren't you?"

Villon smiled in return. "I could get into a lot of trouble for false arrest. And to make accusations without a solid body of proof could lead to cases of libel and slander."

Hazel gasped.

Villon asked her, "Indigestion?"

Hazel said, "It suddenly dawned on me what you're saying! You're saying Lucy Darrow murdered her own mother! It's unthinkable!"

Bogart said with equanimity, "Many's the time I thought of slaughtering mine. She wasn't a very nice person and one of the meanest bitches crawling around on all fours. She was hell on my sisters and me, hadn't the vaguest idea what love and affection meant. My sister Pat ended up in an institution."

Villon asked, "I wonder if she ever ran into Lucy?"

Bogart laughed. "Opposite ends of the country."

Villon was on his feet. "Let's get going to your place, Bogie. I've been having one of my tingles and I don't want to give it a chance to decelerate. Cheer up, Jim, it's still early. You might still have time to catch up with Zelda Sweet."

"By the time I catch up with her she may not want to be

caught up with," replied Mallory dispiritedly.

Hazel patted Mallory's cheek. "Now Jim, my mother has two favorite expressions where getting involved with someone else is concerned. Her favorite is, 'There's a cover for every pot.' Her other one is, 'If you miss the bus, there'll be another one along in fifteen minutes.'"

Villon asked, "Hazel, have you ever thought of murdering your mother?"

Villon and Bogart walked to Bogart's car. Mallory's unmarked police car was parked outside the pawn shop and Hazel's was across the street in the hot dog stand's lot. All would rendezvous at Bogart's house. Hazel bought a hot dog and a soft drink to eat on the drive to Brentwood. Mallory, after a moment's thought, dashed back into the pawn shop and phoned Zelda Sweet at her home, fingers crossed that she'd be there. The gods were smiling at Mallory and Zelda was at home and promised she'd wait for Mallory to call back, probably within an hour. Zelda's mother scolded her daughter for making herself so available to a man, especially one she had just met today. It was at a time like this that Zelda entertained the notion of murdering her mother.

At Cedars of Lebanon hospital, Ned Aswan's private room resembled an arboretum. When he came out of his coma, he squealed with delight at the sight of the wreaths, vases filled with flowers, and lovely floral arrangements that filled the private room. The nurse told him he'd probably be able to go home within a day or two and the news did not please him. He knew why Joshua was murdered and that it could very well soon be his turn. Which one of those greedy bastards did it, he wondered. After the nurse left, a young police officer came into the room, took off his hat and hung it on a door hook, and sat on a chair facing Ned Aswan with a pleasant look on his face.

Ned asked, "If I'm under arrest, what for?"

"You're not under arrest. I've been assigned to protect you."

"From who? Or is it 'From whom'?"

"I can't help you there. But I can help you here. I don't

know who's after you because I don't think Herb Villon knows who's after you but I'm here for safety's sake. My name's Amos Colbert like in Claudette but no relation not even distant. Lots of pretty flowers. Smells like a funeral parlor. Oh. Sorry."

"You're right. It does smell like a funeral parlor. It's all those goddamn gardenias. Do you know how long I've been out of it?"

"Not long at all. Not as long as most botched suicides. Oh. Sorry."

"No need. I did botch it. I need Josh to count the correct amount of pills. You can't swallow too many and you can't swallow too few. How long have you been with the police?"

"A little over a year. I guess I'll be going into the army soon, however."

"And when you get out, back to the police?"

"If I survive, I suppose so."

"Have you ever thought of being an interior decorator?" He hoped he didn't sound coy or effeminate or on the make, which he did and he was. But Amos Colbert was something rare and unique to Hollywood. He was an innocent.

"You know, I'm glad you asked. I know who you are and I was too shy to ask, you just out of a coma and all that." As though one was given to going into and coming out of comas with alarming frequency. "Well, in school I was pretty fair in my art classes. My teachers told me I had a nice sense of style and color. Do you think I ought to set my sights on something more fulfilling then being a cop?"

"Amos," said Ned with what he hoped was a provocative smile framing his mouthful of capped teeth, "I think we were destined to meet."

In Bogart's car, Villon was telling him, "You've seen Lucy a couple of times."

"Three," corrected Bogart.

"She strike you as someone freshly derailed?"

"I can't make a judgment, Herb. I mean, I know a lot of nut cases in addition to my sister." He reeled off, "Jack Warner, Peter Lorre, my wife . . ."

"Hazel's aghast at the thought of Lucy having murdered her mother."

"Well Hazel's another one of the walking wounded who believes in the sanctity of motherhood. This morning I liked Lucy at the Garden of Allah. Although presumably in mourning, she was doing a good job, I thought, of facing up to it and getting on with the burial. She asked me to speak at the funeral."

"Well, you're proven box-office."

Bogart smiled. "At Canter's I began to wonder what she was doing with a creep like Sidney Heep. But I have to remind myself there's a hell of a lot of my fellow players sharing their beds with creeps and worse, so there's a lot of truth in that saying there's no accounting for tastes. Then when I found her in my house packing her mother's stuff, there was something very creepy about her. I'm wondering now if she's the murderer and if I had found her in the kitchen cleaning the knife, would I be here discussing her?"

"Well you wouldn't for a couple of good reasons. The first being you caught her with the knife and the second being she has no option but to kill you as you've caught her with the goods."

"Well I'm awfully glad I didn't catch her in the kitchen." He thought for a moment. "I wonder which knife it was if it was one of our cutlery. If it's the carving knife, there'll be no beef carved at our table ever again. How'd Jim Mallory beat us here?"

"He passed us a little while ago. You're not exactly a demon at the wheel." Bogart pulled up behind the unmarked car and a few seconds later, Hazel parked behind them and joined them on the sidewalk.

"Where's your handkerchief?" Villon asked her.

"What do you need with my handkerchief?"

"There's mustard on your chin."

"Thanks," she rasped, extracting a handkerchief from her handbag and wiping her chin.

"A little more to the left," said Villon.

Bogart was unlocking the front door. He entered and

turned on the foyer lights. Villon's voice prevented him from going any further.

"Hold it, Bogie. Let Jim and me proceed." Villon indicated for Mallory to do the upper floor. Hazel stood with Bogart as Villon went quickly from room to room. "Okay down here!" Villon shouted.

"Likewise up here," shouted Mallory. He descended rapidly and the three followed Bogart into the kitchen. He unlocked the basement door, switched on the light and led the way to the storage room. He opened the door and there was the carton as it had been left when they last saw it, bound with a strong cord.

"Well, gentleman, with any luck, do you suppose this is the end of the rainbow with the pot of gold?" asked Hazel.

Bogart said, "Hazel, I feel more like Pandora about to unleash the Furies. Anybody know how to open a secret compartment? I've never had to deal with one before."

Villon said, "Jim, you're the mechanical one. Have a go at it."

Hands on hips, Jim slowly circled the carton, examining the bottom with great care. He cut the rope binding the carton with his penknife.

"If we have to, we can slash the thing open," said Villon, always the pragmatist.

"Patience, Herb, patience. I see a smudge. The kind of smudge made by dirty fingers." He knelt and pressed the smudge. They heard the sound of a release of springs and a section at the bottom of the carton popped out slightly. Mallory helped it by prying with his fingers. There was an object wrapped in oilskin held together with masking tape. Mallory tightened his grip on the penknife.

Villon said, "It looks about right for a cornucopia. Cut it open, Jim."

Bogart said, "Such stuff as dreams are made on.' " And then added, "And also nightmares."

EIGHTEEN

For Bogart, there was something incomplete about this moment in the basement. It lacked the sweep and the majesty of a Max Steiner score, very exotic, very oriental, with a clash of cymbals to underline the moment of discovery.

"It looks like nothing special to me," rasped Hazel, shattering Bogart's fantasy. Jim Mallory picked up the package and carried it to the bar.

"Is it heavy?" asked Villon.

"It's heavy," Mallory told him.

Bogart and Villon exchanged looks. Hazel went around the bar for a better position for the unveiling. Mallory unwrapped the oil cloth and pushed it to one side. Under the oilcloth was brown wrapping paper. "It's an awful lot of wrapping," said Mallory.

"Captain Methot was a bit of a fussbudget," Bogart told him. "That's where Mayo gets it from."

With care, Mallory removed the wrapping paper. There was indeed a cornucopia. It had a very beautiful, very elaborate design that twisted from its tail to its broad mouth.

"It's a dragon," said Villon.

"In China, they're very big with dragons," said Bogart. "Is the mouth sealed with cement?"

Mallory tested it with a finger. "It's putty. Just plain old putty."

From the strange look on Hazel's face, Bogart could tell the basement had been invaded. He said to Villon, "I think we've got company. Hazel, we got company?"

"Why yes," said Hazel, "and he's absolutely gorgeous."

Marcelo Amati was pointing a revolver at them from the

bottom of the stairs. "Will the detectives put their weapons on the bar, please. Very slowly. Very gently. No sudden movements. I'm a crack shot and totally without mercy." Violetta came down the stairs behind Marcelo, and behind her, very regal, with the look of a panther about to pounce on its prey, came the Contessa di Marcopolo.

"How nice to see you again so soon," trilled Hazel as she clutched her handbag tightly. "I love your dress, Contessa."

La Contessa reacted without removing her greedy eyes from the cornucopia. "It's a Chanel."

"Very tasteful," said Hazel winsomely. Bogart was wondering if he was in the middle of a dangerous situation or at the closing night of a drawing room comedy that had been slaughtered by the critics.

"That is indeed my cornucopia," whispered the Contessa. "The dragon tells me. It is the true cornucopia, not the bargain basement garbage we saw in Venice." She looked at Bogart. "We were positive it was in your wife's possession. You are Mr. Bogart, aren't you?"

"I'd better be. Why didn't you find it last night?" asked Bogart.

"We weren't here last night," said Marcelo, sounding a bit offended. "Had we been here last night, the housekeeper would still be alive. We are adventurers, not murderers."

"Oh my precious cornucopia! You are mine at last!" cried la Contessa.

Villon was moving slowly and subtly to Hazel's side.

Violetta spoke up. "Let's take it and leave."

"What's the rush?" asked Bogart. "You won't get very far with it."

"Do not threaten us, Mr. Bogart. We are not secondary players in your grade B movies."

"Aw now don't be so insulting and condescending; some of them pictures were pretty damn good. It's not nice to be insulted when you're a guest in my house, especially an uninvited one. I suppose you used a skeleton key."

"Mr. Bogart, forgive me if I sound like an ungrateful guest, but the security in this country lacks a certain savoir faire, a je ne sais quoi. In my country, a child could pick your locks without so much as a by-your-leave."

"Okay, big mouth, drop the gun." The voice came from the staircase. "My gun's bigger then your gun and my trigger finger is itchier." She spoke over her shoulder, "Come on down, baby doll. I've got the drop on them." Nell Dickens was a vision in black leather from head to toe. Behind her, Lucy Darrow came slowly down the stairs, Rebecca in search of her Sunnybrook Farm.

"Anybody else?" asked Bogart.

"Just us chickens," said Nell. Lucy had walked slowly toward the cornucopia seemingly hypnotized.

"Where's Heep? Where's Daddy?"

Nell smiled. "Daddy? You mean Edgar? He's not my daddy. He's my husband. I married him when he was Nino Brocco years ago in Italy."

"Aha! I knew it!" cried la Contessa. "I thought he was familiar. Nino Brocco! Master thief! Criminal! Forger of works of art and masterpieces! And you," she pointed a finger at Nell, "you shall not rob me of my heritage. It is my cornucopia! My father's!" She pointed a shaky finger at Bogart. "His father-in-law stole it!"

"Now not so fast, Contessa," Bogart said swiftly, "I never held any brief for Jack Methot but in this country you're innocent until you're proven guilty."

"In my country you would get the firing squad!" countered the countess.

"I find that a little impetuous." From a corner of his eye, he could see Hazel Dickens very carefully opening her handbag. Villon was now at her side and Bogart repositioned himself so that they could not quite be seen by the others. "Are Heep and Daddy waiting in Lucy's blue coupe or do they have wheels of their own?"

"When last seen they were suffering smoke inhalation. The shop caught fire."

"What a shame," said Bogart, and he really meant it,

"there goes another of Hollywood's priceless landmarks." He looked at Lucy. "Lucy, I'm disappointed in you."

She was wide-eyed with amazement. That Bogart would be disappointed in her was unthinkable. She liked him. She respected him. And she told him as much. The innocence she managed to project was almost touching in its sincerity.

"But Lucy. Matricide!" exclaimed Bogart.

"What?" she asked, face screwed up with questioning.

"*Matricide.* A fancy word for murdering your mother."

"I didn't murder my mother. Why would I murder my mother? Nell murdered my mother. With your bread knife."

"Oh well that's a relief," said Bogart, with a quick look at Villon and Hazel. Villon had Hazel's gun but was in no rush to make his move. Here was the lucky break every detective prayed for. Mallory was closest to Lucy and he was prepared to use her as a shield should there be much cross fire. "Nell, that wasn't nice murdering Hannah."

"She did a damn fool thing. She was the one who grabbed the knife in the kitchen. She came at me. She didn't see Lucy. She didn't know Lucy was with me. That's right, isn't it, baby doll?"

"Yes. That's right. You tripped her. Then you jumped on her and got the knife from her and we took it with us to use on Joshua Trent and that smelly pawn broker and . . ."

"It was very nice of you to bring it back and clean it and place it where it belonged," said Bogart.

Lucy said with pride, "My mother taught me to clean up after using anything and put it back where it belongs."

"You're not mad at Nell for killing her?"

"I could never be mad at Nell. She was so good to me in the hospital. She helped me to survive. Nell loves me."

"That's for sure, baby doll. Now pick up that thing and let's get going. And don't come chasing after us, coppers, because you can't. We've slashed your tires."

"Mine, too?" asked an incredulous Bogart. "They're brand-new, damn it! I just bought them!"

"Mr. Bogart, this is neither the place nor the time for a temper tantrum. We'll just collect our spoils and be on our way."

"Miss Dickens," said Villon, "I think mine is a bit bigger then yours. And I don't give a damn who I kill."

Nell wheeled on him but Villon was too fast for her. He pulled his trigger and caught her in the shoulder. Mallory was fast and picked up Nell's weapon and Marcelo's. Marcelo made a move toward Mallory but Villon shouted a warning. Mallory spun on his heel and his right fist connected with Marcelo's fragile jaw. Villon sent Hazel to the phone to call the precinct while he reclaimed his and Mallory's revolver.

"I want my property!" bellowed la Contessa. "It is mine, it is rightfully mine!" Violetta went to her side to comfort her. Bogart helped Marcelo to his feet. La Contessa was at the bar stroking the cornucopia, tears in her eyes. "This is the only link left to my father. It is all I have. It's mine."

Lucy knelt beside Nell, cradling her in her arms.

"Oh my God! It's true! The Curiosity Shop's in flames!" cried Hazel.

Bogart said to Nell, "My God but you're an evil bitch. Are Dickens and Heep dead? Did you murder them?"

Nell said matter-of-factly, "We just tied them up. Edgar is indestructible. I'm sure he's been rescued." She yelled at Hazel. "Do you mind getting me an ambulance."

"Not at all," said Hazel, "and I'll tell them to bring along a box of straitjackets." She did as she promised.

Villon and Mallory herded the others together at the far side of the bar. Violetta held Marcelo's hand while la Contessa made unpleasant whimpering noises. Lucy helped Nell to her feet and then provided her with a chair. Bogart viewed the miscreants with a mixture of contempt and amusement. Then he turned to Villon. "Hey Herb, I'm rehearsing a scene similar to this tomorrow except the company I'll be with is a hell of a lot more appealing."

Hazel was finished with the phone for the moment. She'd soon be peddling her story to the highest bidder. She reclaimed her gun and plopped it into her handbag. "Good old Harriet, at last you served a purpose." Thanks to Villon she had a permit. She had no need of the gun until now. She couldn't hit an elephant if it was standing next to her.

Bogart picked up Mallory's penknife. He stared at the cornucopia. He said, "Herb, I claim the rights to do the honors. It's been taking up space in my basement all these years."

"It's mine! It's mine! It belongs to me!" blubbered la Contessa.

"Oh be quiet!" scolded Marcelo, anxious to see what the object contained.

"I'm cutting your allowance!" snarled la Contessa.

All eyes were on the cornucopia. Bogart dug into the putty slowly. He cut away small pieces. Behind him he heard heavy breathing. The air was so thick with tenseness it could have been cut with a machete. Tiny beads of perspiration were forming on Bogart's upper lip and forehead. In the distance they were alerted to the sound of approaching police sirens. Villon's and Mallory's eyes were on their captives. Villon honestly didn't give a damn what the cornucopia contained. He had his murderer, assuming Nell Dickens would confess to all, aided and abetted by Lucy Darrow.

Hazel Dickson watched Bogart pull a hand full of jewels from the cornucopia's gut as though he were eviscerating a chicken!

"Mine! They're mine!" screamed la Contessa.

Hazel dug around in her handbag and found a jeweler's loupe. She screwed it into her eye and picked up a jewel for a very close Dicksonian examination. She was her mother's daughter. She examined a second and then a third. She smiled at Bogart and then at Villon and then turned to la Contessa. "It's all junk, sweetie."

"No! No! It can't be!" La Contessa seemed on the verge of swooning, and if she did, Villon wondered who among them would be brave enough to risk a hernia by catching her.

"Paste," said Hazel. "You can buy better at the five-and-ten." They heard the police cars arriving followed by an ambulance. La Contessa sagged against the bar. Then by way of reassurance, picked up one of the fake jewels and held it up to the light. It looked like an emerald, it almost felt like an emerald, but as Hazel later told her mother, it belonged on a stripper's brassiere. Villon shouted up to the reinforcements who came tramping down into the basement. Hazel lost no time and phoned her scoop to the *L.A. Times.* Mallory was ready to commit a homicide by strangling Hazel for grabbing the phone before he could reach Zelda Sweet. Villon said to an officer, "This is Nell Dickens. Book her on suspicion of multiple murder, suspected arson, and endangering my life."

"Arson my eye!" shouted Nell. "Lucy set the fire, I didn't."

Lucy's eyes were aglow. She endearingly misquoted Edna St. Vincent Millay. " 'My candle burns at both ends . . . oh what a lovely glow.' "

Bogart said to Villon. "I suppose she'll plead insanity."

"Why not?" replied Villon, "she's cornered the market." Villon turned Marcelo, Violetta, and the contessa to the charge of two other officers. "Menacing with weapons, obstructing justice," and fixing the countess with a steely eye, "and a pain in the ass."

She said something to him in Italian, which though he did not speak the language, he got her message.

Hazel got off the phone and Mallory captured it. Bogart looked around the basement and said to Villon, "Looks like Warner's going to have to send me a fresh crew tomorrow to clean up this mess. You need the cornucopia as evidence."

Villon laughed. " 'Such stuff as dreams are made on!' The Boulevard of Broken Dreams! Look at Jim. He looks like a teenager who just got himself a prom date."

"Give him a break, Herb. Send him on his way." Bogart raised his voice. "Last one out turn off the lights! I'm going to get very very drunk." He spat an expletive. "But first I've got to phone Mayo and her mother." In the living room, he sat down next to the phone. He looked at the ceiling and said, "God give me strength and may *The Maltese Falcon* be the hit I have a feeling it's going to be. And then I suppose we might follow it with *The Chinese Cornucopia*." He dialed as he said, "God forbid."

Three days later, the day before the start of the actual shooting of *The Maltese Falcon*, Mayo returned from Portland with her mother in tow. The driver of the cab that brought them from Union Station brought in the bags. Then he brought in a small carton which Mayo asked him to put on the kitchen table. Evelyn Methot looked at the living room as she removed her gloves. "The place looks awfully good. You'd never know a brutal, bloody murder took place here." The cab driver returned from the kitchen, accepted his tip from Mayo with a bewildered expression on his face and wondered if this place had any connection to the murders that had made headlines recently, the ones involving Humphrey Bogart. As he left, Bogart drove up and parked. The cab driver recognized him at once and was delighted.

"Say, Mr. Bogart, is this your place?"

"Yeah."

"Where the murders took place?"

"Singular, son, just one murder here. I don't want to make a pig of myself."

"I guess I just brought home your missus and her mother."

"I'll never forgive you."

Bogart entered the house. He could hear Mayo and Evelyn upstairs in the guest room. He shouted, "Hey you two! Cut the chatter and let's get to the martinis." He threw his hat and his script on the couch as Mayo came hurrying down the stairs and into his arms. They kissed as Evelyn followed Mayo down the stairs. "Well Humphrey, you're looking well despite your recent ordeal."

"Hello Evelyn. Welcome," he lied and kissed her on the cheek. "Sorry about the cornucopia. You can have it back from the precinct anytime you want it. They don't need it."

She took his hand. "Come with me, Mr. Bogart." She led him to the kitchen. Evelyn followed them. She patted the carton box on the table. "We've got a little surprise for you."

Bogart stared at the box with suspicion. Mayo demagnetized a knife from the wall.

"That's a bread knife," said Bogart.

"As Gertrude Stein would say, Bogie, 'A knife is a knife is a knife.'" She cut the rope with which the carton was bound.

Evelyn said, "After you called us the other night, I suddenly remembered. When I was ransacked, I had some items out being cleaned and repaired. Well, dear boy, *this* was one of them."

Mayo had the carton open. She lifted out a beautiful cornucopia sealed at the mouth with putty. It too had an elaborate dragon design.

"It's sealed," Bogart said lamely.

"That's right. Jack refused to unseal it. He'd been warned against it."

"What do you mean 'warned against it?'"

"The dealer who sold it to him said it had a curse," Evelyn said with an icy smile. "He who dares to open it shall meet a horrible death."

Mayo held the bread knife out to Bogart, the other hand on her hip. "Go ahead, honey, I dare you."